A Corpse Among the Carolers

Books by Debra Sennefelder

Food Blogger Mysteries

The Uninvited Corpse
The Hidden Corpse
Three Widows and a Corpse
The Corpse Who Knew Too Much
The Corpse in the Gazebo
A Corpse at the Witching Hour
A Corpse Among the Carolers

Resale Boutique Mysteries

Murder Wears a Little Black Dress
Silenced in Sequins
How to Frame a Fashionista
Beauty and the Deceased
Sleuthing in Stilettos
What Not to Wear to a Graveyard

Cookie Shop Mysteries

How the Murder Crumbles

A Corpse Among the Carolers

Debra Sennefelder

A Corpse Among the Carolers
Debra Sennefelder

Cover design and illustration by Dar Albert, Wicked Smart Designs

Beyond the Page Books
are published by
Beyond the Page Publishing
www.beyondthepagepub.com

ISBN: 978-1-960511-92-8

Chapter One

The countdown to Christmas was on, and it came with a universal truth that set Hope Early's pulse skittering when she looked at her calendar earlier in the day. No matter how much you planned, this time of the year was crazy busy. Which was why the stop at the Snowflake Holiday Market was a must. Just like the two cups of extra-strong coffee she downed while she finished editing a new cooking video for her food blog, *Hope at Home.*

Now if she could find a parking space.

The Unity Grace Church's parking lot was packed, and not a single empty space came into view as she weaved her Explorer through the rows. That was, until she spotted a minivan backing out of a spot way on the other side of the church's grounds. She pressed down on the accelerator and made record time crossing the lot.

With her vehicle parked, she grabbed her tote and reusable shopping bag before getting out and closing the car door. A gust of brisk December air came up behind her, prompting her to raise the collar of her wool coat for extra warmth.

Joining a group of fellow shoppers who were also walking from their vehicles, Hope made her way to the entrance of the church hall. The path was lined with over-the-top holiday decorations, from giant candy canes to inflatable snowmen. Between the hall and the church building there was a Santa's village set up and a nativity scene in front of the church on view for all passersby.

Hope entered the hall and was greeted by two Nutcracker soldiers anchoring the entry into the market. The large space was used for various events throughout the year. In the spring, there was an Easter Bazaar, and in the fall there was a craft fair. Now, it seemed as if Christmas exploded from the ceiling, from a sky full of glittery paper snowflakes dangling over them, to the large black boot footprint decals on the floor leading to the mailbox for letters to Santa Claus.

A trio of energetic redheaded boys raced around a Nutcracker soldier and bumped into her, distracting her from admiring the decorations. Their mother rounded them up swiftly, offered a sincere apology, and then the family made a quick exit.

Hope continued forward, walking deeper into the holiday market. As she passed by the vendor booths, she made a mental note of the ones she wanted to return to after visiting her sister's booth. Good Day, Good Dog had a display of festive harnesses, and she wanted to get one for Bigelow's stocking. He enjoyed long walks, and it seemed she was always replacing his harness and leash. The refreshment area came into view and she made a quick stop for two cups of hot apple cider and continued looking for Claire's booth.

As she approached Staged with Style's booth, her pace slowed so she could admire the lovely display. The long table was draped with a red cloth, and on top, items perfect for gift giving were exhibited. There was an ample selection of vases, photo frames, crystal bowls and Em Bailey candles. Hope's gaze drifted over the seasonal fragrances, and she fought the temptation to lay down her credit card for a candle. Or two.

"You have enough candles," Claire said. She had a knack for reading her sister's mind.

Hope frowned. Her sister was right. She had more than enough candles and they were expensive.

"Besides, you never know what Santa will put in your stocking." Claire, in a festive green sweater and black pants, stood with her hands on her hips. Her nails were painted in a candy cane stripe, matching her dangling candy cane earrings. A splash of red lipstick finished off her holiday look.

Hope smiled. "Santa knows me so well."

"Yes, he does. Is one of those drinks for me?" Claire asked, reaching out for a cup. She pulled off the lid and took a sip of the hot apple cider. "This definitely hits the spot."

"Can you believe Christmas is only two weeks away?" The days between now and Christmas day would be jam-packed with work and holiday preparations. Like every year. But she'd never been so behind as she was this year. Then again, this was the first time she was planning a Christmas celebration with her boyfriend, Ethan Cahill, and his two daughters. Plus, there was the added stress of writing her first cookbook, which was due to her editor after the new year. "Wasn't it just Halloween?"

Claire sputtered on her apple cider. "Please, let's not bring that up. I'm hoping we can have a holiday without a murder."

Hope blinked. It wasn't as if she went looking for dead bodies. She just seemed to have a knack for stumbling upon them. And also for finding their killers.

"How's it going, ladies?" Lexi Hewitt arrived at the table with a big smile on her face. The church's secretary looked professional with her clipboard in hand. "I'm making my rounds and checking in on all the vendors. Is there anything you need, Claire?"

"I could use an assistant," Claire quipped between sips of cider.

"Then you should stop running them off," Hope said.

"Tough boss, are you?" Lexi asked.

A tinge of redness touched Claire's cheeks. She had not yet been able to keep an employee for more than three months. Her penchant for perfectionism had scared off all her recent hires.

"No worries. There are some members of the youth group who are volunteering. I'm sure one of them would be happy to help you," Lexi offered. She always seemed to have a solution for any problem. Hope liked that about the petite brunette.

"Sounds like a wonderful idea." Hope unbuttoned her wool coat and untied her scarf. "Don't you think so, Claire?"

Claire looked less than enthused. "I guess it wouldn't hurt."

"Perfect." Lexi made a notation on her clipboard and then looked up. "I'll get one of them right over here."

"Lexi, that's a lovely pendant," Hope said as she noticed the gold-tone initial charm around Lexi's neck. Maybe she'd get one for Claire's daughter. Hannah loved wearing necklaces. "What does—"

"Thank you," Lexi cut Hope off as her head swiveled, her wide eyes taking an appraising glance over the hall. "I better get going. Lots of vendors to check on, and I have to get Claire a volunteer. Enjoy the market." She sprinted away with a wave.

"She's a ball of energy, isn't she?" Claire asked. "Kind of reminds me of you."

"Lexi is very organized," Hope agreed.

"And just remember, sis, I'm not the only one who can't keep an employee. You've had two assistants so far." Claire set her cup down.

"It's not exactly the same thing." And it wasn't, but Hope didn't want to revisit the past. There was so much good happening now. So instead, she took another drink of her cider.

"Perhaps." Claire shrugged. Her resigned look brightened, prompting Hope to look over her shoulder. "Brody also got a booth for his shop."

Brody Fitzgerald, a fellow Main Street business owner at the Antique Alcove, approached, sipping a drink. His stride was relaxed as he reached Claire's table.

"Hey there, Hope," he said with a nod before turning his attention to Claire. "How's it going? It's been a busy day over at my booth. I finally got a break to get a drink."

"Is Alena with you?" Hope had noticed that Brody's stepsister had been spending more time in the shop since his dad, Mitty, retired a few months ago.

"No." Brody gave a small shake of his head and blew out a breath. "She's back at the shop. There wasn't anyone else to leave there."

"I'm sure she's doing a fine job," Claire said.

Brody looked doubtful as he took another sip of his beverage. "Hope, have you been to my mom's booth yet? She's been making the rounds at craft fairs since fall with her handmade ornaments and she got lucky at the last minute to get a booth here."

"She's been selling them at your shop for years. That's wonderful news that she's branched out. I'll make sure to stop by and check out her merchandise." Every year, Hope added one of Ruth Fitzgerald's ornaments to her tree. Maybe this year she'd get one for each of Ethan's daughters. And when they decorated the tree, they could hang them. "How's your dad doing? Is he enjoying retirement?"

"He really hasn't slowed down much. He still goes out every weekend looking for antiques up and down New England. In fact, he's coming by in a little while with some more inventory for my booth," Brody said. "Thankfully, it's busy and my mom's stall is way on the other side."

Hope cocked her head sideways. "Why is that?"

Claire cleared her throat and shot Hope a pointed look that said "don't ask."

"Their divorce wasn't amicable, and nothing has improved between them. Especially since he married Nora. I'd better get back to my booth." Brody hurried away, eventually disappearing into the crowd.

He was quickly replaced by two eager shoppers, both pointing to different items on Claire's table. Seeing that her sister had customers, Hope said a quick goodbye and set off to do her shopping. She leisurely walked along the aisle, checking out each booth and stopping at a select few for Christmas presents. By the time she reached Ruth Fitzgerald's table, her shopping bag was more than half filled with stocking stuffers.

Beside Ruth's table was a five-foot tree decked out with her beautiful ornaments, all hand-painted and topped with delicate green and red ribbons. Along the tabletop were dozens of ornaments and a sign saying that custom orders could be made and would be delivered in time for Christmas Eve.

Ruth was seated on a folding chair behind the table with her head down and her fingers aggressively tapping on her cell phone. It appeared she was in the middle of an angry text.

Hope was hesitant to interrupt, but after a quick look around, she realized Ruth's booth was the only one that was not swarmed with customers. And it was probably because of Ruth's antisocial behavior.

"What a lovely tree," Hope said, drawing the woman's attention from her phone.

"Good to see you, Hope." Ruth quickly replaced her scowl with a small smile as she straightened and set her phone on the table. She wore a red dress cinched in at the waist by a wide black belt. Her auburn hair was swept up into a bun with loose wisps framing her heart-shaped face. "I see you've been shopping."

"I have." Hope moved closer to the table and in a low voice she asked, "Is everything okay? You looked a little . . ." She searched for the right word. "Intense. Is something wrong?"

Ruth waved away Hope's concern with a flick of her hand and stretched out her smile to show she was fine. "It's nothing really. Just some unfinished business with Mitty. Silly me for thinking all the loose ends of the divorce were all tied up."

"I can certainly understand how frustrating it can be." Hope had gone through her own series of loose ends when she went through her divorce. There had come a point when she thought the process would never end. Luckily, she'd been wrong. "It's not easy, is it?"

"Honestly, it would be a whole lot easier if he were dead," Ruth snapped.

Shocked by the statement, Hope drew back. And it must have shown on her face because Ruth quickly said, "Pay no mind to what I'm saying. The holiday season is crazy. I've been running on too little sleep lately preparing for this market."

"The stress of the holidays can get the better of us."

"Exactly. But I don't think you stopped by to help me reduce my stress level." Ruth stood and inched closer to the table. "Are you interested in purchasing some ornaments?"

"Indeed I am. I'm looking for something for Ethan's daughters, Molly and Becca. It's going to be our first Christmas together." Hope spotted a collection of white and pink ornaments displayed in a wicker basket. She lifted one and admired Ruth's fine workmanship. The poly-foam ball was covered with lace and a cameo centered within a cluster of pink rhinestones. The ornament was topped with a pear-shaped clear stone and a pink satin bow. "This is exquisite. I'll take this one."

"Marvelous choice," Ruth said as she took the ornament and wrapped it in tissue paper.

Hope selected another ornament; this one had a large pink stone set in among clear rhinestones instead of a cameo. "This one also."

It only took a few minutes to complete the transaction, and Hope then put the securely wrapped ornaments into her bag. "The girls are going to love these. Oh, before I go, don't forget about the Cookie Social tomorrow. We'll need to be at the community center an hour before the Jingle Bell Stroll begins. There's a lot to set up."

"I'm looking forward to it. Caroling and cookies. What could be a better way to spend the night? See you then, Hope." Ruth picked up her cell phone from the table. It appeared she was going back to texting.

As Hope walked away from the booth, she also couldn't think of a better way to spend an evening. She enjoyed caroling every year with her sister and her family. This year she'd be bringing Ethan and his daughters. Excitement bubbled in her as she strolled along the aisles admiring all the beautiful offerings, until she remembered who she enlisted to play Santa Claus to lead the group of carolers along Main Street.

Mitty Fitzgerald. Ruth's ex-husband.

Would the divorced couple be able to behave civilly toward one another in public, or would they devolve into a hot mess of an argument?

No. She wouldn't spend her time at the Snowflake Market worrying about what could go wrong. If an issue came up, she'd deal with it then.

By the time she was ready to leave, her bag was filled to the brim. She might have overdone the Christmas shopping, but wasn't that what the holidays were all about, a little overindulgence?

She rounded a corner and bumped into Drew Adams, her best friend and a reporter for the *Gazette*, a weekly newspaper for the northwest corner of Connecticut where Jefferson was tucked into.

Several inches taller than Hope, he wore a deep brown suede bomber jacket over a green Henley top and dark jeans. Draped around his neck was a camera fitted with an impressive lens, and in his hand was a notepad and pen.

"I didn't know you'd be here today," he said, stepping aside to let another shopper pass by. He then peered down at her bag. "And how much shopping have you done?"

Hope shrugged. "I didn't know I'd be here today but I'm running out of shopping days. As for my purchases, they're some small gifts . . . wait . . . I don't have to justify my shopping to you."

Drew's lips stretched out into a grin. "Just messing with you. Is there anything in there for me?"

"Guess you'll have to wait until Christmas to find out."

"You're mean." He pouted.

"Correction, I'm exhausted, and I still have a full day's work ahead of me when I get home. Walk me out?" Hope asked as she pivoted to the exit. "So, you're covering the market for the *Gazette*?"

Drew fell into step beside Hope. "Yes. I'm pretty much done. I just want to talk to Lexi and maybe another vendor. Any suggestions?"

"How about Ruth Fitzgerald? I just picked up two of her handmade ornaments for Molly and Becca. They're beautiful. She does amazing work, and I'm sure she could use the exposure in the newspaper."

"Thanks for the suggestion." Drew hurried ahead of Hope and pushed open the door that led out to the back parking lot used by the vendors.

"How's Trixie?" Hope asked. Right after Halloween, Drew worked on a story for a local animal rescue group, and there he met a girl who stole his heart. Her name was Trixie, and she was a four-month-old Jack Russell terrier. So, he thought it was a good idea to double down on the chaos of his life, which included renovating his new home, by adopting a puppy. Since she'd pretty much done the same thing, she couldn't judge her best friend.

"She's in her absolute terror phase. And those sharp little teeth are brutal. But when she's asleep, she's adorbs."

Hope chuckled. She'd warned him, but he'd heard none of it. Though, she was confident he would survive Trixie's puppyhood.

They stepped out of the church hall, their breath visible in the chilly winter air. She tucked a stray lock of dark hair behind her ear, her gaze wandering across the parking lot and stopping abruptly on a heated argument playing out just a few feet away.

Ralph Lang's face was flushed with anger as he pointed a trembling finger at Mitty Fitzgerald. "You think you can get away with cheating me? Let me tell you, you've got another thing coming!"

Mitty Fitzgerald, his usual calm manner slightly rattled, replied, "Look, I didn't cheat you. You don't know what you're talking about."

Hope watched with fascination as her curiosity was piqued. What had driven these two mild-mannered men into such a heated confrontation? Then she remembered. She'd heard that Ralph believed that Mitty had sold him a fake antique six months earlier. A tall, lanky man with a perpetual smile and a reputation for being the town's easiest-going and most honest handyman, Ralph hadn't missed an opportunity to gripe about Mitty and the lamp he purchased.

"This isn't good," Drew whispered to Hope. "We should break it up."

Hope nodded, and together they stepped forward. But they were too late.

Before her eyes, Ralph's frustration reached its boiling point, and he shoved Mitty hard enough to send him stumbling back into the side of his pickup truck. The impact echoed through the quiet parking lot, and Hope gasped in shock, her heart pounding.

"Whoa!" Drew's eyes bugged out and, in a split second, he took off in a sprint. He put himself between the two arguing men. "You both need to cool off."

Meanwhile, Hope hurried to Mitty, who peeled himself away from the side of his truck and signaled to Hope that he didn't need any help.

Ralph's chest heaved as he shot an accusing glance at Mitty. "This man is a swindler, Drew! He ripped me off, and I won't stand for it. In fact, you should write an article in the *Gazette* about his shop and warn the public."

Mitty, still shaken from the shove, shook his head. "It's not true. I have never sold fake antiques. I have sold reproductions, but I've always made it clear what they were."

Ralph huffed in frustration, then turned and stormed away. Before disappearing, he cast one last warning glance at Mitty. "You'll regret this, Mitty!"

Hope couldn't help but be astonished. Ralph was the last person she'd expect to lose his temper like that, and Mitty's calm response was a stark contrast to the accusations. Something didn't add up.

Chapter Two

Hope settled into a corner booth at the Village Diner, a cozy haven in the heart of Jefferson's Main Street. She sipped her latte while she waited for Ethan to return to the table. When he was Jefferson's police chief, having a lunch date was nearly impossible. But now that he worked as an investigator for their mutual friend, defense attorney Matt Roydon, Ethan had more flexibility in his schedule. And since he was working on a case that kept him close to Jefferson, he was able to meet her for lunch.

She hadn't heard Ethan return to the table. Her attention had been on the view outside the large window of the diner. Snowflakes started falling when she'd arrived at the restaurant, and even though the forecast was for little if any accumulation, it still looked magical. It seemed that in a blink of an eye between Thanksgiving and now, Jefferson had turned into a winter wonderland with holly, fresh wreaths and garlands draped everywhere imaginable. There was no question about it, Christmas was in the air.

"Sorry about that," Ethan said as he reclaimed his seat. "Have you decided what you want to order?"

"Huh?" Hope dragged her gaze from Main Street to Ethan. How lucky was she that her high school crush had come back into her life after it imploded following a series of disasters? She joked that that period of life had been the trifecta of calamities—loser on a baking competition TV show, unemployed and divorced. Then again, if all that hadn't happened, she wouldn't have returned to her hometown and reconnected with Ethan. "Sorry. I guess I was lost in my thoughts. What did you say?"

"What are you ordering?" He gestured to her discarded menu.

Hope set her cup down and lifted the menu from the table. "Probably a BLT. What about you?"

"Burger deluxe. Before Matt called, you were telling me about the Snowflake Market. How was Claire's booth?"

"Absolutely beautiful. She did a great job with the display, and Lexi Hewitt arranged for one of the teenagers from the volunteer group to help Claire. Then I picked up two ornaments from Ruth Fitzgerald's booth that I think Becca and Molly will love." Before Hope could describe the ornaments, their server came over and took their orders. Once they were alone again, Hope gave Ethan a rundown of all the gifts she bought and what was left to buy.

Their meals were served and, as they ate, Ethan shared the limited details of the case he was working on. He'd been working for Matt for less than a month. It was after Halloween when he gave Maretta Kingston, Jefferson's mayor, his notice and spent the following weeks assisting in the transition of the department's leadership. Currently, there was an acting chief of police in place while Maretta and the town council conducted their search for a permanent chief.

"That's all you can tell me? Talk about vague. Now I'm more curious than I was before," Hope joked as she wiped her mouth with her napkin. "You told me more about the cases you were working on when you were a cop."

As Ethan chewed his bite of burger, he nodded and the lines around his dark eyes crinkled. After he swallowed, he set his burger down and reached for his soda glass.

"Sorry, babe. Now I'm dealing with the whole client confidentiality thing."

"I know and I understand." Hope reached for her water and took a sip. "I almost forgot to tell you about what happened when I was leaving the Market. I ran into Drew—"

"How's the new puppy dad doing?"

She laughed. "Exhausted and up to his eyeballs in puppy antics. But Trixie sure is adorable. Anyway, we left through the back of the building and came out into the smaller parking lot for the vendors. To our surprise, we found Mitty Fitzgerald and Ralph Lang in a heated argument that ended with Ralph shoving Mitty. Drew got right in between them and broke it up."

Ethan's easygoing attitude morphed into concern. "Was Mitty hurt?"

"No, he wasn't. Ralph accused Mitty of selling him a fake Higganum lamp."

"Is it valuable?"

"That depends on if it's authentic. In the early twentieth century, Wilson Higganum, an acclaimed artist, designed a series of exquisite lamps that became highly sought after due to their intricate stained-glass designs. Unfortunately, his premature death only fueled the lamps' allure, resulting in extraordinary prices among fans. I'll admit, I don't know Mitty very well, but I find it hard to believe any of the antique dealers in town would engage in such activity."

"You'd be surprised by the shady side of the antique business. You know that old saying, buyer beware? Well, it's advised you practice that when buying any antique from any dealer."

"Of course. I do my homework when I make a purchase, and I buy only from trusted sources," Hope said.

"Have you ever bought from Mitty?"

She shook her head. "No. I've been in the shop a few times but I never found anything that caught my eye. Do you think Ralph is right about the lamp being a fake?"

Ethan shrugged. "Don't know. He did come to us and told us about the alleged crime but he never pursued pressing charges."

"Did you investigate?"

"Nope. Without Ralph filing a report, there wasn't anything we could do."

"I'd hate to think our Santa is a crook." Hope lifted what remained of her sandwich and took a bite. After swallowing she said, "Speaking of which, I'm excited that we're taking the girls caroling tomorrow night. And I have tomorrow all planned out. After lunch at their aunt's house, we'll go to Maple Hill to get our tree." Every year Hope visited the farm's tree lot to get not one but two trees for her home. She placed a towering Fraser fir in the family room and a smaller one in the living room of her farmhouse.

Ethan patted his mouth with his napkin and then shifted in his seat. "About the tree farm."

Instantly, Hope's shoulders slouched, and her excitement dwindled. "Don't tell me. Heather?"

"Sorry, babe." He reached for her hand and entwined their fingers. "She wants to keep the girls all night."

"But—"

"I know it's not her night. But here's the deal. Her sister is getting her tree tomorrow, and Heather wants all of them to decorate the tree." He squeezed Hope's hand and gave a sympathetic smile. "It's important to her."

Hope pulled back her hand and pressed her lips together. She wanted to ask why Heather couldn't rearrange *her* plans. Then she remembered a piece of advice her mother gave once—pick your battles. And this was one battle she shouldn't take on. Instead, she'd make the best of the situation.

"Maybe it's for the best," she said. "With just you and me picking out the tree, it'll be faster. But I really want the girls to go caroling with us. I know they'll love the Jingle Bell Stroll. How about you pick them up just before the caroling starts, and I'll meet the three of you at the community center? That way they'll be with Heather and their cousins to decorate the tree. In fact, if their cousins want to go, bring them too."

"That sounds like a good compromise. But I can tell you right now Heather isn't going to be happy."

Now there's a shocker.

• • •

With her plans changed for tomorrow, Hope realized she didn't have to wait to go to the tree lot. In fact, she could go anytime, especially since Ethan found out as they were leaving the diner that he had to drive up to Massachusetts tomorrow for work. So, either she waited to get a tree or she went today. After saying goodbye to Ethan, Hope decided to head to Maple Tree Farm. The drive to the Langs' family farm took twenty minutes, and when she pulled into the lot, a pang of unexpected disappointment hit her.

The parking area was filled with dozens of families tailgating before they headed onto the farm to cut down their trees. This was a tradition the Langs started decades ago, and Hope had a snack planned for the girls, a thermos for hot cocoa and a flannel plaid throw folded in the cargo area ready to spread out on the ground. She shook off the thought as she stepped out of her Explorer. She reminded herself that even without them buying a tree together, they were going to have a wonderful holiday.

Hope pulled out a knit cap from her tote and covered her head. Even though she'd decided not to cut down the trees herself, she'd be walking around for a bit of time, and the wind was whipping hard on the open field.

She walked toward the entrance of the tree lot. Even though the chill of the winter afternoon set in, she couldn't help but feel the warm embrace of the holiday spirit as she stepped onto the idyllic scene laid out before her. A sign highlighting all the activities available greeted her. Out of the corner of her eye, she glimpsed families bundled up in scarves and mittens eagerly lined up for the hayride on a vintage horse-drawn wagon adorned with festive decorations.

A few yards ahead, another sign caught her attention. This one was for a selfie station. A lit-up pole nestled next to a Norway spruce tree had three hand-painted boards attached, each featuring a social media platform with a reminder to tag the farm and share. Being a blogger, she couldn't resist. Hope pulled out her phone and snapped a selfie in front of the festive sign. She started typing a short caption but realized she didn't have a signal.

"That's odd," she murmured. "Guess I'll post later." She dropped the phone into her coat pocket.

Her nose wrinkled at the heavenly aroma of roasting chestnuts in the air, and she was torn between dashing over to the snack bar, where delicious hot cocoa and freshly backed gingerbread cookies were offered or staying on task and searching out her perfect Christmas trees.

"Hope! Good to see you," Albert Lang called out as he passed by with a three-foot evergreen balanced effortlessly on his sturdy shoulder and a young family trailing in his wake. With his towering stature and broad shoulders, he resembled a modern-day lumberjack cloaked in layers of vibrant plaid and his head crowned by a snug trapper hat. "Give me a minute and I'll be back to help you."

Albert and the family disappeared, but Julia Lang quickly appeared carrying a basket of pine boughs. "I thought you were coming tomorrow with Ethan and his daughters."

"That was the plan." Hope sighed. "We had to rearrange a few things, so here I am to pick out our trees."

"It's a hectic time of year. But I don't know why we get so worked up. It's not like we don't know Christmas is the twenty-fifth of December every year." Julia chuckled. Her rosy cheeks puffed out, and her hazel eyes shined.

"Point taken. Are you off to make swags?" Hope pointed to the basket of cuttings.

Julia nodded. "I need something to calm me down. We just got off the phone with Ralph. Oh, boy, was he seething. He told me he had a run-in with Mitty Fitzgerald."

"Yes, he did. I saw their encounter. Ralph shoved Mitty," Hope said.

"What? Are you serious?" Julia's cheeks blanched, and deep lines furrowed between her brows. "My brother-in-law is usually so mellow. You know he wouldn't hurt a fly."

"It appears that issue with the lamp has gotten out of hand," Hope said.

"I agree. Unfortunately, I don't know much about antiques. I wish I did because I could probably settle the matter," Julia said. "But my area of expertise is baking. Which reminds me, I need to get back to the snack bar. We're short-staffed today. Be sure to stop by for a cookie. It's on the house."

Hope thanked Julia for the offer and then set off to browse. She wandered through the fragrant rows of trees. The aroma of pine and cedar filled the crisp winter air, stirring memories of Christmases past. The deeper she got into the maze of majestic evergreens, the more the magic of the season wrapped around her like a cozy blanket.

She arrived at the generous selection of Fraser firs. This tree had always been her favorite. She loved the coloring of the blue-green needles with silvery undersides. She appreciated the stiff branches that held up well to ornaments. And its needle retention was a big plus.

Hope spotted the one. About seven feet tall, it was full and healthy-looking. The closer she got, the more certain she was that the tree would soon be in her family room. She pulled out her phone and snapped a photo of the fir tree to send to Ethan later when she got a cell signal.

Now, she needed to get Albert to help her load the tree on top of her Explorer.

"I thought you said the old man finally retiring would give you the reins to the shop," a man's voice said, grabbing Hope's interest.

Hope scanned her surroundings, but there was no one in sight.

"It seems like he's still got his hands in the day-to-day operations," a female voice answered.

Suddenly, Hope realized the voice was coming from the other side of the lush evergreen wall. Although she knew she shouldn't pry, the conversation was too intriguing to ignore.

"Brody's desperate for his dad's approval. But don't worry, I think Mitty will be out of the picture soon," the female voice, which sounded familiar, asserted.

Just as Hope was about to ponder the meaning behind those words, Albert's voice interrupted her thoughts.

"Hey, Hope, have you picked out a tree?" he asked, pulling her away from eavesdropping.

Hope's head snapped around, and she found herself facing Albert. Though she remained silent for a moment, her mind raced to process what she'd overheard. The man's voice remained a mystery, but Hope was able to place the woman's voice—it was Alena Smedley, Mitty's stepdaughter and Brody's coworker at the antique shop.

Hope glanced back at her tree and pondered Alena's mysterious remark about Mitty's uncertain future.

Chapter Three

On Sunday night, Hope arrived at the community center to prepare for the Cookie Social, the grand finale of the Jingle Bell Stroll. With a determined stride, she navigated the single-story building, leaving her jacket and tote in the coat room and stealing a quick glance at her watch. Two hours remained before she was to meet with Ethan and his daughters for caroling. It was time to roll up her sleeves and dive into work. Her legion of volunteers would soon join her.

First on her agenda was to assess the placement of buffet tables that had been arranged by a team from Unity Grace Church. They were one of many of Jefferson's organizations that had contributed to the evening's festivities. She nodded in approval at the perfectly aligned tables along the left side of the room, each topped with neatly folded red cloths. Once the tables were dressed, an abundance of cookies, baked by dedicated volunteers, would grace their surfaces. Hope, like the others, had delivered her trays earlier, contributing sugar cookies, rugelach, and cranberry-nut delights.

The clank of the heavy side door interrupted her thoughts. Five ladies entered, offering greetings before hurrying to the coat room. Among them was Ruth Fitzgerald, prompting Hope to silently pray for a smooth night. After all, not only was her ex-husband playing Santa, but his current wife had volunteered at the last minute to assist with the Cookie Social setup.

Shrugging off her reservations, Hope refocused on her task—covering the buffet tables. As she started unfolding the first cloth, Meg Griffin arrived and quickly joined her. Meg, responsible for decorations, reassured Hope that everything was under control, especially since she had enlisted three new volunteers at the last minute. She then launched into her vision for the table decorations and, after a deep breath, praised the gift donation boxes.

All attendees were encouraged to donate unwrapped toys or gifts suitable for the elderly. Large boxes, wrapped in Christmas paper, were arranged alongside an inflatable Santa in a sleigh, serving as designated spots for those gifts.

Ethan had coordinated the collection and would oversee deliveries to the town's participating nonprofit organizations.

"I've got things under control here. Why don't you head into the kitchen and start preparing refreshments?" Meg suggested as she smoothed out a tablecloth.

"Good idea." Hope pivoted toward the kitchen just as another group of volunteers arrived. Among them, Nora Fitzgerald, Mitty's new wife, dressed in an eye-catching faux fur coat and matching hat, started a conversation with a fellow volunteer.

Hope's stomach tightened into a nervous knot as a flurry of chaotic possibilities raced through her mind. With bated breath, she silently pleaded for the evening to unfold without any explosive confrontations between Ruth and Nora, hoping against hope that peace would prevail for everyone involved.

"Hope!" a strained voice called from the kitchen. "There's a coffee urn missing!"

"That can't be possible," Hope replied. With over a hundred people expected in just a few hours, she didn't need any glitches, big or small. "I'll go find the coffee urn while you start on the tables." She broke away from Meg and dashed into the kitchen.

The coffee urn was quickly located in the kitchen after a search. Hope and her team then diligently tackled each task, steadily checking items off her list. Time was of the essence; caroling was set to begin in under thirty minutes.

Exiting the kitchen, Hope surveyed the hall. The buffet tables were draped with red cloths, laden with an assortment of cookies and accompanied by lush evergreens. In the room's heart, twenty round tables stood, cloaked in pristine white, awaiting their playful centerpieces. Meg's creative vision featured glass cylinders brimming with candies and oversized lollipops for an enchanting touch.

The enchanting mood vanished when Hope noticed Ruth and Nora locked in a dispute at the buffet table.

Meg, sneaking up behind her, nudged Hope and commented, "They're even worse than us," nodding toward the ongoing clash between Ruth and Nora. "They've been at it since Nora arrived. I tried to intervene, but it was a lost cause."

Hope agreed with a nod. She and Meg had a complicated history dating back to grade school, but they always managed to put their differences aside for the greater good, resolving their disputes privately. Ruth and Nora, on the other hand, were anything but discreet.

Nora, her faux fur now discarded, revealed a snug red knit dress adorned with a statement necklace in vibrant jewel-toned stones as she smoothed the tablecloth and adjusted her tray of cookies, pushing aside a tray of snickerdoodles.

Ruth, arranging evergreens along the table's length, made slight adjustments to three platters, two of which were shaped like Christmas trees. She remarked, "I'm sure Mitty does. Although nothing can compare to his grandma's original chocolate crinkles, no matter how many different chocolates you put in them."

Nora raised an eyebrow, propping a hand on her hip. "It's called variety. The same *old* thing gets *boring*."

Nora's challenge was clear in her tone and Hope winced. Ruth's irritation with the current Mrs. Mitty Fitzgerald was evident.

"Now that was a low blow. You'd better intervene before we have a disaster on our hands," Meg muttered, walking away.

Hope sighed, and since there was no other option, she decided to take action. She marched over to the two feuding women with the intention of defusing the situation as delicately as possible. "Everything looks beautiful. We all did a great job setting up and now we can head out for the Jingle Bell Stroll."

The stare-down between Ruth and Nora intensified. *Oh, boy.* "Nora, if I recall correctly, this will be your first Jingle Bell Stroll."

Nora blinked as a smile slipped onto her lips. "You are correct. How could I pass it up with Mitty playing Santa?"

"It's only been a beloved town event for decades," Ruth said, glancing again at the cookie displays. "I go every year."

Nora propped a hand on her jutted-out hip. "Well, aren't you—"

"The more the merrier," Hope said quickly before Nora could finish her thought. "And this year it's going to be one to remember. How about we get our coats and head out?"

Nora's face brightened. "Yes, let's do that. I want to find my husband and take a photo of us together. I'll sit on his lap and whisper into his ear what I want for Christmas." She spun on her high heels and dashed across the hall, disappearing into the coat closet.

Hope grimaced at the vision now floating around in her mind and worried that Ruth's head would explode with a similar image. Hers would be far worse than the one Hope was envisioning. After all, Nora's husband was Ruth's ex.

"Coming, Ruth?" Hope asked.

"No. No. You go on ahead. There are just a few tweaks I want to make."

Hope's shoulders slumped. She didn't want to leave Ruth like this. "Are you all right?"

"Of course. This wasn't my first run-in with Nora. I'll catch up with you in a bit. Go on," Ruth insisted.

"Don't keep us waiting too long," Hope said with a smile, her voice tinged with a mix of concern and excitement. Caroling was one of her favorite activities of the season. "Promise you'll find me and Ethan, okay?"

Hope received a subtle nod from Ruth, and with a determined stride, she made her way toward the coat closet. Just before turning the doorknob, she stole a glance back at Ruth. The change in her friend's demeanor was palpable. Where there had been anger yesterday, today an air of melancholy enveloped Ruth. The complexities of divorce weighed heavily on her, and Hope empathized deeply.

Despite these somber thoughts, tonight was about something different. It was about caroling with Ethan and the girls, coming together as a family to spread joy. The thought of being *a family*, those two little words, kindled a warm, reassuring fire within her heart.

• • •

The Jingle Bell Stroll began on time and was led by four costumed carolers. The gentlemen donned tails and top hats, exuding a touch of timeless elegance, while the ladies were draped in velvet capes and plaid skirts that swirled like a vision of yuletide magic.

Hope, with the warmth of Becca and Molly's hands nestled in her own, followed closely behind her neighbors, Gilbert and Mitzi Madison. In their wake trailed Hope's sister, Claire, who had somehow lost track of her two spirited teenagers amid the merriment. The noticeable absence in this wintery tapestry was Ethan, who'd dropped off the girls before going back to his office to finish some paperwork that couldn't wait until morning. He'd promised to join the festivities as soon as he could.

The procession arrived at the doorstep of a narrow Federal-style home belonging to Agnes Witherly and her aunt. These two hearty souls stood bundled in heavy coats, braving the cold, their faces wreathed in smiles as they listened to the joyous strains of "Jingle Bells" reverberating through the night. It was a heartwarming moment, a scene that seemed to have stepped right out of a classic holiday tale.

While Suzy Meadows, the lead singer, had provided song books for carols, Hope knew each song planned by heart and it appeared Molly and Becca did too. They belted out "Jingle Bells" like a couple of pros, and they seemed to be enjoying themselves. Too bad Ethan was missing the moment. As the song came to an end, the Witherlys thanked the singers and waved goodbye as the carolers moved along Main Street.

Santa Claus, aka Mitty Fitzgerald, rang his golden bell and offered a hearty ho-ho-ho as the group passed the Witherly home.

It was his job as Santa to signal the group when it was time to move on once the set of songs was done. Hope was pleased at how well Mitty had stepped into the role, and based on his performance, she guessed he was enjoying the experience.

As they moved along, Hope double-checked Molly and Becca's hats and coats. The December night was colder than forecast. She glanced up at the night sky, and it was cloudless with a clear view of the half-moon. Approaching the Merrifield Inn, a striking Victorian home built by one of Jefferson's founding families, Hope hung back from the group so she could speak with Mitty. As she made her way to him, she spotted Nora in the group nestled between her fellow volunteers from the Cookie Social.

"I hope you're enjoying yourself. You're doing a great job," Hope said.

Mitty, with his midsection padded to give him a big, rounded belly and a fake white beard covering his normally clean-shaven face, looked like the real deal in the iconic red suit.

"I am. Thank you for twisting my arm to play Santa," Mitty said.

"Play Santa?" Becca's eyes widened with confusion as she looked between Hope and Mitty.

"Don't be a baby, he's not Santa," Molly said to her younger sister with a shake of her head.

Becca's lips trembled and she appeared to be on the brink of a meltdown.

Uh-oh.

"Oh, boy, I'm sorry, Hope," Mitty said.

"Becca, your sister is correct. This is"—Hope gestured to Mitty—"one of Santa's helpers. He's been dispatched from the North Pole to help us celebrate the season. You know the real Santa is busy getting ready to deliver all the toys and gifts."

Becca studied Hope for a long moment and then smiled. "Makes sense."

Hope exhaled a relieved breath. "Okay, let's join the others. Look, Sally and Jane have come out of the inn for the next carol."

The girls let go of Hope's hands and darted off toward Claire.

"That was a close one," Mitty said, resting his gloved hands on his padded belly. "Guess I need to be more careful of what I say. Little ears pick up everything."

"Yes, they do."

"I'm going to take a seat." Mitty nodded in the direction of the wrought iron bench anchored by two potted dwarf evergreens. "This old knee has been acting up."

"I'm sorry to hear that. The cold weather doesn't help, I'm sure. Luckily, we're almost finished." Hope patted Mitty on the arm and then returned to the carolers. She sidled up to Claire and the girls, joining in on "We Wish You a Merry Christmas." When the song ended, the Merrifields and their inn guests burst into enthusiastic applause.

Claire couldn't conceal her relief. She turned toward the beckoning glow of the community center and sighed, "I'm so grateful it's over now and we can head inside to warm up. A cup of tea sounds heavenly."

Hope, her agreement mirrored in the chill that had settled deep into her bones despite the layers beneath her sweater and jeans, nodded in agreement. The frigid air seemed to have penetrated every layer of warmth, and the promise of a cozy drink was irresistible.

As the carolers drifted away from the Merrifield Inn, a voice pierced the night. Drew Adams, camera in hand, jogged across the street towards Hope, his face lit with excitement. "What a night!" he called out.

Claire asked, "Did you capture some amazing shots?"

"I sure did. How about I get a photo of you two with Becca and Molly?" Drew asked, raising his camera.

"Wait a minute. Santa hasn't given us the sign yet." Hope glanced over her shoulder. "He must have dozed off, though I can't imagine how with all this singing." Determined to rouse him, she made her way to the bench where Santa sat, calling out his name.

Her suspicion was confirmed as she neared him. Santa's head drooped low, his eyes closed in peaceful slumber. The evening's festivities had clearly sapped his energy, but a last hearty "ho-ho-ho" was still on the agenda.

With a careful touch, Hope attempted to awaken him, her concern for his aching knee evident in her gentle prodding. Yet there was no response. Suddenly, her attention was diverted to the trees and shrubbery behind the bench for a nanosecond, but Hope returned her attention to Mitty. With a growing sense of urgency, she shook him a bit harder, and to her surprise, Santa's body tumbled forward, revealing a shocking sight—a crimson stain and a grievous wound etched into his back.

Chapter Four

"Here, have a sip. It's decaf." Claire handed Hope a piping hot cup of coffee, and her comforting touch soothed the chill in the room. "I can't believe Mitty is dead. Or that you found another body."

Hope took a sip of the coffee, noticing it was a tad light on the cream on top of it being decaf. Her eyes scanned the community center, once adorned for a joyous gathering but now draped in a somber atmosphere. It resembled a tacky funeral reception more than anything else.

All the carolers had been gathered there and instructed to keep mum about the grim discovery. Hope knew that gossip flowed through the town's veins, but, surprisingly, it seemed that everyone was respecting the command. They meekly poured coffee, stirred tea, and half-heartedly nibbled on cookies. The children, including Becca and Molly, were situated at the Letters to Santa table under the watchful eye of Sally Merrifield. The retired librarian, known for her discretion, happily volunteered to keep the children occupied until the adults were cleared to leave by the police. She had them not only writing letters but also drawing festive pictures. Meanwhile, her sister-in-law, Jane Merrifield, a retired mystery author, had been sequestered at their inn with all their guests for interviews with the police.

As Hope observed the crime scene, before being removed to the community center, she couldn't help but wonder if anyone had noticed anything unusual during the caroling. The more she thought about it, the more she doubted it. Like her, everyone had been caught up in the festive tunes. The thought of Mitty meeting his tragic end while they all sang "We Wish You a Merry Christmas" sent shivers skittering down her spine.

Hope took another drink of her coffee and wondered who would have stabbed Mitty Fitzgerald. And why? One name quickly popped into her mind—Ralph Lang. But she'd known him for years and couldn't imagine him killing anyone, even if he believed he'd been wronged by the victim. She shook the image of Ralph out of her mind, and it was quickly replaced by Nora, who'd been devastated when Hope made the discovery. Overwhelmed with grief and shock, Nora was driven home by a police officer.

"Did you see Ruth in the crowd?" Hope asked after taking another sip of her coffee.

Claire shrugged, her eyes flickering with a hint of indifference. "I hadn't noticed. Then again, I lost track of Hannah and Logan. Wait . . . you don't think Ruth stabbed Mitty. Do you?"

Hope tilted her head to the side, her mind piecing swiftly piecing together fragments of the evening. "Ruth was angry with him, and then she and Nora had a *thing* while setting out the cookies. She could have snuck up behind Mitty and plunged the knife into his back."

The air crackled with uncertainty, the words hanging between them like a suspenseful cliffhanger in a gripping novel.

"Well, that's a chilling thought." Claire sipped her coffee. "Did you share it with the police?"

"No. I didn't mention it to the responding officer. I'm waiting for the detective to show up." Hope's stomach constricted at the thought of Detective Reid entering the community center. So far, he'd been the detective on duty for all the murder cases she'd been involved in. And she doubted her luck would change anytime soon.

"We're not supposed to be discussing the case." Claire folded her arms and gave her sister a firm look. "Don't you always follow the rules?"

"I'm just thinking out loud."

"Nice spin," Claire said with a grin. "Anyway, Ruth isn't a killer, and she definitely wouldn't do that with children nearby."

Drew weaved his way through the tables, passing the somber carolers, and finally reached Hope's side. His suede jacket hung open, revealing a festive red sweater decorated with a humorous reindeer. "Well, this isn't exactly how I pictured the evening going."

Hope sank into a chair. "I couldn't agree more. Did you manage to dig up any tidbits that might be of interest to the police?"

Drew settled in beside her, his eyes reflecting a mixture of intrigue and concern. "The folks I talked to claim they didn't see a thing," he admitted with a sigh. "I just wrote a piece for the *Gazette*'s website, and I plan to keep it updated as the night unfolds. Looks like I've stumbled upon a real scoop."

Claire chimed in before heading off. "You most certainly have. Though, I wish it were about anything other than Mitty's murder. He was a good guy. And he was one of our best advocates for small businesses in this town. I'm going to check on the kiddos." With that, she disappeared into the crowd.

"She's right about him being a champion for our small businesses," Drew said. "He was always at the chamber of commerce meetings."

The main door swung open with a sharp, echoing clang, drawing Hope's attention. Her heart leaped in relief as her gaze fixed upon Ethan entering the room. Yet, that initial relief was swiftly replaced with anxiety when she noticed Detective Reid trailing just behind him.

"Excuse me," she murmured to Drew, rising from her seat. She crossed the room, meeting Ethan halfway. As he enveloped her in a comforting embrace, an immediate sense of safety washed over her. "I'm so happy you're here," she confessed, her voice tinged with gratitude.

Ethan released her from his warm hold, but his gaze remained locked onto hers with a hint of concern. "Are you alright?"

She nodded resolutely. "Any leads on who might have done this to Mitty?"

Ethan's expression grew solemn. "I don't have access to that kind of information anymore. I'll take the girls back to your place while you speak with Sam. Are you up for driving home?"

"Of course," she replied with a heavy sigh. "I'm so sorry. This was meant to be a joyful evening for all of us, and now it's . . ." Her voice trailed off as Detective Reid stepped closer.

"A murder," Reid declared bluntly. He wasted no time in getting to the point. The seasoned detective stood tall and confident in his dark blue overcoat, methodically removing his leather gloves and tucking them into his coat's pockets.

Hope returned to her seat, and Reid settled across from her, poised with his notepad and pen. She couldn't help but sigh inwardly; this routine was becoming as predictable as her uncanny knack for finding dead bodies. He'd ask questions, she'd answer them, and inevitably the cautionary lecture about her involvement in the case would rear its head. It was a dance she knew all too well, a dance she'd grown weary of.

Despite Hope's apprehension, Drew seized the chance to address Reid directly, his eyes gleaming with anticipation. "Detective Reid, have you uncovered any leads on the identity of the attacker?"

Reid maintained a poker face, his response measured. "The Jefferson Police Department doesn't have any comment at this point," he said, a neutral mask over his features. "If you don't mind, I'd like to talk to Hope alone."

"Can't blame a reporter for trying." Drew stood, squeezed Hope's shoulder and walked away from the table.

"I can sense the gears turning in your head, Hope," Reid murmured, his voice a subtle blend of resignation and understanding. "And I've come to accept that advising you to keep your distance from this investigation would be like telling a cat to avoid curiosity."

Hope's eyes widened. Had she heard him correctly? "You have?"

He nodded solemnly, the lines on his face reflecting the weight of their shared predicament. "So, what can you tell me about Mr. Fitzgerald?"

"Probably nothing more than what you already know. He owned the Antique Alcove until recently, when he retired and turned its ownership over to his son, Brody. Oh, poor Brody. They were very close."

Reid nodded.

"He lived in Jefferson for over twenty years. He was always friendly, but he never really socialized. The only place he was active besides his shop was the chamber of commerce. He was always involved in some event or campaign to drive business to Main Street. You know, I was shocked when he said yes to being Santa this year."

"Why did you ask him if you believed he'd say no?" Reid asked.

"I was desperate. Oliver Tully usually does it, but he got pneumonia. Mitty was suggested by someone on the committee. I didn't think he'd say yes but he did. And now he's . . . dead."

"Is there anything else you can tell me about him or about when you discovered that he was dead?"

"Yes, there is." She recounted the chilling encounter between him and Ralph Lang yesterday at the Snowflake Holiday Market. She nibbled on her lower lip, debating whether to reveal Ruth's unsettling statement from the day before: *It would be a whole lot easier if he were dead.*

Reid glanced up from his notepad, his manner softening. He cocked his head slightly and his eyes were no longer steely but now curious. "What's troubling you, Hope?"

Hope leaned back as she weighed the delicate balance between idle anger and dangerous action that Ruth had straddled. She understood the complexities all too well. However, there lingered a slim possibility that Ruth had acted on her heated words—a possibility Reid needed to explore for the sake of his investigation.

"Ruth Fitzgerald, Mitty's ex-wife, uttered something yesterday that you should know," Hope confessed, the weight of the words heavy. She recounted their conversation to Reid, his pen racing across the paper. "Although, I doubt she meant it in a literal sense."

"Anything else?"

Hope's thoughts drifted back to the scene where she had stumbled upon Mitty, seemingly asleep. A fragment of memory pushed its way to the forefront of her mind.

"What I do remember is that when I approached him, I thought he was asleep. I called his name, but there was no response . . . though . . ." Her words trailed off as a chilling vision resurfaced, a phantom figure in the shadows and the ominous sound of a branch breaking. "That's why I looked up from Mitty and looked at the shrubbery behind the bench."

Reid leaned forward and asked, "What caused you to look behind Mr. Fitzgerald? What are you recalling, Hope?"

"I heard what sounded like the snap of a branch not too far away," she said. "And then, I saw someone."

Reid leaned in further, eager for every detail. "Who was it?"

Hope's eyes darted around as if she could still catch a glimpse of that elusive figure in the shadows. "I can't say for sure. It was more like a shadowy silhouette. They were lurking not far from the bench where Mitty sat, but just distant enough that their face remained hidden. I can't believe I forgot about this until now."

"Given the shock of discovering Mitty's body, it's perfectly understandable. Memories can be a tricky thing. I'm not going to press any further. You should go home and get some sleep. If anything else comes to mind or you remember more about the shadowy figure, don't hesitate to reach out at any time."

"I will," Hope replied, rising from her seat. Though she wasn't sure she'd get much sleep. She bid Reid good night and scanned the room for Claire, who emerged from the coat closet with their jackets in hand. "Perfect timing. My conversation with Reid is over."

Claire handed Hope her jacket and slipped into her own. "Logan and Hannah are waiting in my car. What about the cleanup?" She tossed a look over her shoulder.

"Meg is going to handle it. She's encouraging everyone to take home as many cookies as they want to ensure there's no leftover food. We'll deal with the rest in the morning." Linking arms with her sister, Hope led the way out of the community center, right into a swarm of reporters who had caught wind of the murder.

Maretta Kingston, the town's mayor, stood surrounded by the reporters, giving an impromptu press conference. Questions were hurled at her like daggers. Unfortunately, public relations wasn't her strong suit, so her voice was tight and her answers clipped.

Hope couldn't help but imagine the sensational headlines that would soon be printed in newspapers and on websites: "Santa Stabbed at Jingle Bell Caroling Event." And from the icy glare Maretta directed her way, it was evident she wasn't the only one envisioning those scandalous headlines.

Claire squeezed Hope's arm, pulling her away from the throng of reporters and the building. "Don't pay any attention to her."

Hope sighed, her thoughts drifting to a more pressing concern. "I'm not worried about Maretta. I expect her to blame me since I'm the one who got Mitty to play Santa. It's Heather. Once she finds out her daughters witnessed a murder, she's going to make our lives miserable."

Chapter Five

As the sun struggled to pierce through the frosty haze, Hope savored the crisp air on her walk from the chicken coop back to her house. With each step, the crunch of the snow beneath her boots echoed her anticipation, mingled with a hint of apprehension about the somber occasion ahead on that Monday morning.

She stepped back into the warmth of her kitchen, greeted by the aroma of the bubbling casserole cooking in her oven. She poured a cup of coffee and sipped it while checking her latest video for Graham Flour, one of her blog's sponsors. The comments were favorable, and there were dozens of shares. Just what the sponsor wanted. Hope stole a quick glance at her watch. She needed to get moving if she was going to pick Claire up on time. Luckily, the oven timer dinged, signaling the casserole was done. After setting it on the trivet, she dashed upstairs.

A hot shower, her skin-care routine and a blowout gave Hope a reprieve from the heaviness that had settled over her since finding Mitty's body last night. In her closet, selecting her outfit for the visit to his widow, the weight of sadness and regret pressed down heavy on her. Why had someone killed Mitty? Why had she asked him to play Santa? She gave herself a mental shake. What happened wasn't her fault. The only person responsible was the killer. With a newfound resolve, albeit a little shaky, she reached for a burgundy sweater dress and a pair of black boots with a low heel so she could navigate icy sidewalks. Minutes later, she was dressed and putting the final touches on her updo. After adding gold stud earrings and a simple necklace, she left her bedroom.

Back downstairs, with the casserole carefully cradled in her arms, Hope ventured outside, the frigid air nipping at her cheeks. Her breath formed wispy tendrils in the wintry landscape as she made her way to her Explorer. Behind the wheel, her thoughts drifted to the impending condolence visit, a delicate dance between offering support and navigating the uncharted waters of grief.

• • •

As Hope idled in front of her sister's house, she drummed her fingers impatiently on the steering wheel. Her gaze flicked back and forth between the dashboard clock and the imposing front door, willing her sister to hurry up. Finally, after what felt like an eternity, Claire emerged from the house, swaddled in a luxurious cashmere coat and carrying her beloved satchel.

Claire walked as if she were tiptoeing through a minefield rather than along a brick path. Then again, she was wearing high-heeled pumps instead of sensible boots. When she reached the car, she opened the door and slipped into the passenger seat. Her designer purse found its perch on her lap like a prized possession.

As Claire secured her seat belt, she cast a concerned glance at Hope. A gray turtleneck peeked out from beneath her coat. "Have you heard from Heather?"

"Me? No. But Ethan got an earful last night, and it started again this morning," Hope said as she eased her car out of the driveway. "Becca had nightmares last night," she continued. "I know Heather. She's going to use this situation to try to get full custody of them."

Last spring, Heather had checked herself into rehab, desperate to conquer her crippling pill addiction. Ethan had been awarded full custody of their daughters and still had it despite Heather's release a few months ago.

"Let's give her some time to calm down. No one could have possibly predicted what happened last night. It's almost inconceivable that Mitty met his end during our caroling event."

After a series of turns, Hope arrived at the Fitzgerald house. She maneuvered her Explorer into the long driveway.

The house, a stately two-story Colonial, had been decorated for Christmas. Wreaths hung on the front windows and the three attic dormers, with a grand one hanging proudly on the vibrant red front door. Lush evergreen garlands encircled the portico's stately pillars.

With her casserole in hand, she approached the front door with Claire beside her. The front door swung open, and Alena Smedley appeared before them looking less than mournful in a vibrant pink sweater and white jeans. Her tanned face was made up fully, while her long auburn hair was pulled back with a velvet headband.

Maybe there was a reason why Alena looked anything but grieving.

And maybe it had something to do with the cryptic conversation Hope overheard at the tree lot between Alena and an unidentified man. Alena's words echoed in Hope's mind: *Brody's desperate for his dad's approval. But don't worry, I think Mitty will be out of the picture soon*. She also couldn't forget that she had failed to share that information with Reid last night following Mitty's murder.

While the exchange between Alena and the unidentified man had initially stirred Hope's curiosity, she now found herself even more intrigued by Alena's prediction. What had the young woman known just two days ago?

"It's lovely that you've come to visit my mom." With a polite smile, Alena extended an invitation to enter. "FYI, Mom is tired. She didn't sleep much last night."

"Of course," Hope replied. "We won't overstay our welcome. I've made a portobello penne casserole. It just needs to be reheated."

"How . . . how very thoughtful of you." Alena accepted the dish. "I'm sure it's delicious. I'll put it in the refrigerator. My mother is in the living room." She turned and walked down the hallway, disappearing into the kitchen.

"I hate these visits," Claire whispered. "Even the house feels sad."

Hope nodded in agreement and continued into the living room with her sister beside her. There they found Nora seated on the plush sofa, her gaze fixed on the dancing flames within the fireplace. When her eyes finally met Hope's, a profound weariness settled across her face. Nora's impeccably styled hair now hung listlessly to her shoulders, her once-bright brown eyes were heavy with fatigue, and her attire was somber black from head to toe, a stark contrast to her daughter's outfit.

"I must look an absolute mess," Nora said and sighed, running her perfectly manicured fingers through her disheveled hair. "I really believed I'd wake up this morning and last night would have just been a dreadful nightmare."

"We're very sorry for your loss." Claire entered the room and took a seat across from the widow. "Is there anything we can do for you? Hope made a casserole, and Alena is putting it in the refrigerator."

Nora's voice, barely more than a whisper, quivered as she

responded, "A glass of water, if you please."

Claire glanced at Hope, who nodded and silently left the room. She made her way down the hallway, following the path Alena had taken to the kitchen. When she arrived at the doorway, she paused for a moment. Alena was in the middle of texting. When Hope cleared her throat, it drew the young woman's attention toward her.

"Your mom asked for a glass of water," Hope said, entering the room. She squashed the urge to ask Alena about the conversation she overhead at the tree lot. Instead, she decided to gauge Alena's feelings about Mitty and the antique shop by engaging in conversation. It was possible that what Hope had heard was out of context since she hadn't heard the beginning or end of the conversation.

"Sure." Alena set her phone on the island and moved to an upper cabinet. She retrieved a glass and filled it with water. "Would you and Claire like anything to drink? I could put on the teakettle."

"No, thank you. We won't be staying that long." Hope crossed the tile floor and stopped at the narrow island. "I can't imagine how hard this must be for you. After all, Mitty was your stepfather. And mentor."

A flicker of confusion crossed Alena's face as her head tilted questioningly to one side.

"He brought you into the antique shop. I'm sure he was showing you the ropes of the business."

"Yes. Yes, he did. He wanted me to be a part of the family business."

"I'm sure there was so much to learn. And now it'll be Brody's and yours."

"Probably. But Brody really takes care of the day-to-day business of the shop. Like all the paperwork. He'll probably handle the life insurance policy, too."

"Life insurance policy? Mitty's?" Hope asked.

Alena nodded. "He often joked he was worth more dead than alive." She swallowed hard. "Anyway, I haven't given much thought to the shop or the insurance money. I'm sure you can understand."

"There's a lot to think about at a time like this. It's hard to imagine that Mitty hadn't planned for the shop in the event of his death. Then again, he just retired, and Brody has been running the shop since then.

Now with Mitty out of the picture . . ."

Alena's posture stiffened. Hope suspected it was from hearing her own phrase repeated back to her. "I know you think you're some kind of detective, but we'd appreciate it if you don't interfere in the police investigation. My family has great confidence that the Jefferson Police Department will find the killer and we, as a family, can start healing. Now, I'm going to take my mother her water." She brushed by Hope and with a determined stride she left the kitchen.

Hope set off to follow but the ringing of Alena's phone on the island caught her attention. She snuck a glance at the caller ID.

Stan Baby.

Reluctantly tearing her gaze from the phone, Hope rejoined her sister and Nora in the living room. As she entered, Alena passed by heading out of the room, muttering about taking care of something. As Hope sank into the chair next to her sister, her eyes were drawn to the Christmas tree standing proudly between the windows. But the festive cheer that once filled the Fitzgerald household seemed like a distant echo now. Hope then noticed how much more relaxed and alert Nora looked after taking a drink of water and placing the glass on the end table.

"I had a chat with Alena." Hope leaned back in the plush chair and crossed her legs. "She told me Mitty had taken her under his wings at the shop."

Nora clasped her hands together, her expression full of gratitude. "I consider myself lucky to have found such a generous and loving soul. Mitty really wanted Alena to be a part of the family business."

"Learning about antiques isn't an easy thing to do. It must have taken up so much of Alena's time," Hope said. "It probably doesn't leave her any time for a boyfriend."

Claire gave Hope a curious look.

Ignoring it, Hope couldn't shake off the feeling that Stan Baby might be Alena's boyfriend and the man she was with at the tree lot.

"There isn't anyone special in Alena's life right now. She's much too busy with the shop. Though, I think Brody could turn over more responsibilities to her. But that conversation can wait for another day." Nora reached for her glass again, took a sip and returned it to the table with a thud. "Maretta called me first thing this morning and told me to take as much time off as I need." She worked in the Economic and Community Development office since she'd moved to town.

"That's very thoughtful of her," Claire said.

Hope agreed. Deep down, beneath the older woman's perpetual scowl, was a heart after all.

"Hope, there's something I need to discuss with you." Nora inched to the edge of her seat cushion. "I can't help but worry about the police investigation. Ever since Ethan stepped down as chief, with this interim chief in charge . . ."

"Don't worry, Nora," Hope reassured her, leaning forward. "Ethan always had faith in his team, and their interim chief is more than capable of handling the investigation. Detective Reid is even assigned to Mitty's case."

"That's what's troubling me," Nora said, taking a deep breath. "I've heard that it was *you* who solved the murder of Birdie Donovan last spring, and that you played a significant role in other murder cases."

"It wasn't just her," Claire chimed in, surprising Hope. Before Birdie's murder, Claire had scolded Hope for getting involved in the investigations. But now, Claire seemed eager for recognition, having joined forces with Jane and Drew to solve the murder that occurred on Halloween night.

"I don't care how it happened," Nora interrupted, directing her attention back to Hope. "I need your help. I want to ensure the police conduct a thorough investigation and find Mitty's killer, no matter what."

Nora's request was the opposite of Alena's insistence that Hope stay out of the case only moments ago in the kitchen. It made Hope wonder why Alena wanted to make it crystal-clear right from the beginning that Hope stayed out of the investigation. She was about to respond to Nora when Lexi Hewitt suddenly appeared, clutching a foil pan in her hands. She froze in her tracks, her eyes locked on the towering Christmas tree. It was clear that the sight of the exquisitely decorated tree hit her just as hard as it had Hope, given the reason they had gathered there that day.

"Nora, I'm so sorry for your loss," Lexi offered sympathetically. "I'm still in shock over what happened. Who could have committed such a heinous act?"

"I can't believe someone would hate Mitty enough to kill him," Nora said.

"I heard that Mitty had a heated argument with Ralph Lang at the Snowflake Holiday Market. It was a good thing Hope and Drew intervened. I wonder if the police are considering him a suspect?" Lexi asked.

"This is the first I'm hearing of that." Nora shot a concerned glance at Hope. "What happened? Was it about that ridiculous lamp?"

"Mitty didn't tell you?" Hope asked. Great. She hadn't wanted to bring up the incident knowing it would upset Nora. "It was about the lamp. Drew and I witnessed Ralph push Mitty."

Nora gasped in shock.

"I've already informed Detective Reid about the altercation," Hope assured them. "He'll definitely want to have a word with Ralph."

"He'd better," Nora interjected, her voice tinged with anger. "Ralph's behavior is completely out of line. First, he spread unfounded rumors about Mitty and his shop, and then he resorted to violence the day before my husband was murdered?" Her hands clenched into tight fists. "Mitty should have just taken the lamp back and given Ralph a refund. He was so stubborn."

"Um, I'll just go put this tuna casserole in the fridge," Lexi said quickly, darting out of the room.

Nora sighed, fatigue coloring her expression. "Looks like it's going to be one of those days. I'm sorry, I don't mean to sound ungrateful."

Claire and Hope exchanged glances. "We understand. That's why we're going to take our leave," Claire declared, rising from her seat and signaling for Hope to do the same.

Hope and Claire said their goodbyes and left the house. In unison, they walked toward Hope's Explorer, a heavy silence weighing them down.

Claire finally broke the silence, her voice tinged with anticipation. "Looks like we've got a job."

Hope's reply was firm, dismissing the idea. "No. We're not hired because we're not detectives."

"That hasn't stopped you before." A mischievous smile played on Claire's lips. "What if we started our own PI agency?"

"In our spare time?" Hope's head shook with determination, her mind already swirling with the tasks ahead. "I have to get back into my kitchen and continue working on my cookbook. I still have nine more casseroles to whip up."

The portobello penne casserole she just delivered to Nora was the first of the ten planned for her cookbook. After meticulously refining it through two previous iterations, she had finally perfected the recipe. But now, with nine more creations on her agenda, the real work lay ahead. The journey of recipe development was a grueling one, leaving her kitchen filled with the remnants of countless trials and errors to be cleaned up.

"Oh, puh-leese, you know you're going to butt into Reid's case. But I'm not going to push. You'll call me when you're ready."

Hope's stride hesitated, her grip tightening on her sister's arm as she glanced discreetly across the street. A nondescript sedan, worn and weather-beaten, sat motionless just as it had when they first arrived. "Look over there . . . wait, don't look," she murmured urgently.

"Which is it?" Claire quipped.

"Look but act natural. Keep heading to my Explorer," Hope instructed, her tone tinged with caution. "Take a peek at the car parked across the street."

Claire stole a furtive glance at the vehicle as she veered toward the passenger side of Hope's car and swung open the door.

Inside the SUV, they fastened their seat belts.

"That car was here when we pulled up," Hope stated, firing up the engine.

"Probably just a reporter," Claire mused, reapplying her lipstick in the visor mirror. "Given the crime and the circumstances, I'm surprised there aren't reporters swarming Nora's house."

Hope's gaze flickered back to the parked car, skepticism lingering. The driver's head was tilted downward, and she couldn't get a good look at his face. "Then why hasn't he made a move toward the house or us?"

"Us? Why would he bother?" Claire tilted the mirror back up, settling into the warmth of the seat.

"Most reporters would leap at the chance for an exclusive quote from friends or family," Hope countered, her concern deepening with each passing moment. "No. I don't think he's a reporter."

• • •

Hope pushed open the weighty door of the Coffee Clique on Main Street, stepping into the bustling haven of caffeinated delights. The air was thick with the rich scent of freshly brewed coffee, while an array of tempting pastries sat enticingly on the counter. After dropping Claire off back at her house, Hope continued into town to run an errand and pick up a coffee.

As she approached the line, she saw Drew ahead of her waiting to place his order with the barista.

"Good morning," she said, coming up behind him. "What are you getting?"

Drew glanced over his shoulder, and he looked exhausted. His usually vibrant blue eyes seemed dull, and his disheveled blond hair added to his overall disarrayed appearance. So it wasn't a surprise when he declared, "I'm in desperate need of a double shot with extra foam and a bear claw." He gestured toward the enticing pastries in the display case.

"You look like you could use three shots," Hope quipped before she stepped forward as the line moved.

"Hey, not nice," Drew countered, weariness in his voice. He stifled a yawn with his hand. "I barely got any sleep last night, and thanks to Trixie, I was up at the crack of dawn. I don't know how you do it."

Hope patted his arm. "She'll grow out of this phase. I promise."

"I hope so. Anyway, I was at the police department first thing this morning praying for an update on the murder." He stepped forward to the counter and placed his order, swapping out the bear claw for an egg and cheese on a roll.

Hope moved up and was helped by the other barista. After placing her order for a large hazelnut with cream, she turned back to Drew.

"Was there an update?"

"Nope." Drew sighed, his fatigue clear. "I'm waiting to hear from my source at the coroner's office."

Hope raised an eyebrow. "What for? It was clear how Mitty met his end." She couldn't help but shudder at the memories of the gruesome scene, the blood-stained stab wound forever imprinted in her mind.

"Of course." Drew nodded. "I'm hoping for details, specifics about the type of knife used, stuff like that. If you're not in a hurry to get home, want to walk with me to the office?" The *Gazette* was located at the edge of Main Street.

Smiling at the offer, Hope replied, "Sure, why not? It's a beautiful day, and I could use the fresh air. Plus, I have a recipe waiting to be tested, and the extra steps won't hurt. I'll be waiting for you outside." Breaking away from the line, she exited with her coffee, ready for a stroll. She'd circle back to get her car to drive home.

The crispness that had filled the air earlier now had a frigid bite, carrying with it the promise of snow. Hope couldn't suppress her grin as she envisioned another dusting of snow blanketing Jefferson. With every sip of her coffee, she indulged in thoughts of the snowy adventures she could share with Molly and Becca, her excitement mounting. That is, until a stranger caught her attention up ahead. Dressed in a dark brown leather bomber jacket, perfectly matched with dark jeans, the man stood outside the Antique Alcove.

There was a familiarity about him she couldn't place until he turned to face her, and the pieces clicked into place.

In an instant, her mind raced back to the previous night when she tore her eyes away from Mitty's lifeless body and noticed movement in the shrubs nearby. It seemed to have all moved so fast. So fast that she hadn't fully registered that because of the faint glow of a nearby light pole, she had gotten a brief look at someone's face. And now, the same man was looking directly at her!

Panic gripped her, and without hesitation, she knew she had to call the police. Her trembling fingers fumbled in her purse, her heart pounding as she desperately searched for her phone. The tap on her shoulder jolted her like a bolt of lightning.

"Whoa," Drew exclaimed, scrutinizing his suede jacket for any traces of spilled coffee. "What's got you so on edge? Stumble upon another body?"

Hope's gaze darted toward the Antique Alcove, and with a hushed urgency she pointed in its direction. "No," she replied, her voice trembling. "But I believe I've stumbled upon a killer."

Chapter Six

"Looks like I'm not the only one running on empty," Drew exclaimed, rubbing his tired eyes. "Maybe you should have gotten an extra large like I did."

"I'm not sleep-deprived or hallucinating. Last night, after finding Mitty dead, I saw someone lurking around," Hope revealed anxiously as she launched forward. "Are you coming?" she called out over her shoulder.

"Wait. What?" Drew exclaimed as he followed. "You saw the killer? Why didn't you tell me this earlier?"

"It all happened so quickly. Mitty's body crumpling to the ground before my eyes," Hope recounted, her words tumbling out rapidly, "and in that fleeting moment, I caught a glimpse of a shadowy figure in motion. I saw his face. It didn't register then, but now . . . now I know I was inches away from him a second ago."

Rushing forward, Hope reached the Antique Alcove, her gaze darting to the store's window. She scanned the interior, her pulse quickening with each passing second. But the stranger was nowhere to be seen.

"Where'd he go?" she muttered, frustrated with the man's disappearing act.

"The police haven't disclosed this information yet. Do you know what this means? I've got the scoop of a lifetime!" Drew's excitement spilled over. He juggled his coffee cup and pastry bag to pull out his cell phone from his back pocket.

Hope bit her lip. She doubted that Detective Reid wanted Drew or any other reporter to reveal that there's a witness who might be able to identify the killer. "Drew, please promise me you won't write about this just yet. There's a chance I'm mistaken. Maybe the person I saw has nothing to do with Mitty's murder. Maybe he was at the wrong place at the wrong time."

"There's also the chance the person *you* saw was the killer." Drew's phone buzzed, distracting him. He tapped on its screen and read the text message. "I have to get going. Another crisis at the office."

"Drew, promise me you won't write anything about me possibly seeing the murder. Please," Hope pleaded.

"Fine. For now, I'll keep this quiet. But remember, I want the exclusive rights to this story. Call me later," Drew said, hastily turning on his heels and rushing down Main Street.

The word *exclusive* in Drew's vocabulary could mean only one thing—an interview with her. Until now, she had skillfully evaded inquiries about the murders she had become entangled in. However, it seemed that her luck had finally run out. She clung to a glimmer of hope that Drew might forget or that she could gracefully back out of it. But for now, her focus shifted back to the stranger who had slipped away. Scouring the length of Main Street, she sought any trace of the man, but it proved futile.

However, during her search, she spotted the very same car she had seen earlier outside the Fitzgerald residence.

With caution, she approached the vehicle. After a quick look around for the driver, she leaned in closer, her breath fogging the window as she peered into the driver's seat. The worn leather bore the imprint of countless journeys. The passenger seat, a chaotic collage of newspapers and crumpled take-out bags, hinted at a lot of time sitting in the vehicle. Just like the driver had been doing earlier outside the Fitzgerald house. Her gaze drifted to the backseat, where a black overnight bag had been tossed.

Suddenly, a tap on her shoulder sent her heart racing, and she spun around, startled. Relief flooded her as she met the familiar gaze of Detective Reid.

"Oh, it's you," she exhaled, her tension evaporating like mist in the late-morning sun. "Why is everyone sneaking up on me?"

Reid raised an eyebrow at her rather icy welcome. "Nice to see you too, Hope."

"Sorry," she murmured as she composed herself. "I'm under-caffeinated for the kind of morning I'm having so far."

"It's been a busy one, has it?" Reid slid his hands into his coat's pockets. "How about we start with an explanation for why you're snooping around someone's car?"

"I saw this car parked across the street from the Fitzgerald house when Claire and I went to pay our condolences to Nora. The driver was inside, but I couldn't get a good look at him."

"Why are you looking inside the car now?" Reid asked.

Hope hesitated for a moment. "When I left the Coffee Clique, I spotted a man standing in front of the Antique Alcove. I believe he's the same person I mentioned seeing last night, the one behind the bench near the shrubs. At first, I didn't think I'd seen his face clearly, but now I'm certain I did. You were right when you said that memories are tricky. All of a sudden I remembered seeing the man's face lift up just enough so I could get a look at him. The memory hit me like a ton of bricks."

Reid moved toward the vehicle and gave it a thorough once-over just like Hope had done. "You think this car belongs to the man you just saw last night by Mitty's body?"

"Yes. Maybe?"

He looked less than enthusiastic about her vague response. But he did cast a quick glance up and down Main Street. "Where did he disappear to?"

Hope shook her head helplessly. "I don't know. Drew came out of the coffee shop, and I took my eyes off the guy for just a second, and then poof, he was gone. I looked inside the Antique Alcove, he wasn't there. It's like he vanished without a trace. But he'll have to return to his car eventually, won't he?"

Reid nodded in agreement. "That's a reasonable assumption. Can you come to the police department and give a description of the man?"

Hope glanced at her watch. "Could I go there now? I've got some time. Or you could come over to my house if now isn't good. I'll be recipe testing."

Reid's cell phone buzzed, interrupting the conversation. With an apologetic smile, he stepped away from Hope to answer the call. After a brief exchange, he redirected his attention back to her. "Something's come up. I'll swing by your place in about an hour." He walked away, returning to his call.

Hope gave a final look at the sedan before pivoting. It was time to go home. As she walked, she made a determined effort to etch every detail of the stranger's face into her memory. She focused on his sagging jowls, thinning black hair, and those bushy brows. How could she have forgotten seeing that face?

And his intense, dark eyes.

Those eyes had locked onto her, raising the haunting question: had he seen her last night?

The notion pierced through her like a lightning bolt, sending tremors to her very core. Even more reason to find him.

She retraced her steps back to the Coffee Clique, passing by the Antique Alcove. She was just past the shop's door when she backtracked. She realized that an hour wouldn't be enough time to start a recipe, only to have to stop when Reid arrived. Instead, she'd take a few minutes and pay her respects to Brody.

As she stepped inside the Antique Alcove, raised voices echoed from the back—Brody's and Alena's. She was surprised that Alena hadn't stayed home with her mother during this difficult time. Surely there were arrangements being made for Mitty's funeral that Alena could have helped with.

Hope navigated through the maze of the well-stocked shop toward the sales counter. The scent of history mingled with a tinge of mustiness, and a layer of dust covered the surfaces. The shop's eclectic inventory was a magnetic force that kept patrons returning, dust and all.

Just as she arrived at the counter, both Brody and Alena emerged from the back room, still arguing. Looking startled at the sight of Hope, they quieted down immediately.

"Hope, we didn't hear you come in," Alena remarked, hurriedly masking her surprise with a polite smile.

"It sounded like the two of you were in the middle of a spirited conversation," Hope said. She caught a flicker of annoyance passing over Alena's face while her stepbrother looked embarrassed by the situation. "I wanted to extend my condolences to you, Brody."

"We're open because it's what Mitty would have wanted." Alena adjusted her purse's strap on her shoulder. "I'm going to get us some coffee. I'll be right back." With that, she marched out of the shop.

"Brody, I am very sorry for your loss. How are you doing?" Hope placed her tote bag on the countertop. "How's your mom doing?"

A somber mood clung to him as he approached the counter, fingertips drumming a nervous rhythm. His usual uniform of graphic tees and ripped jeans had been shed for a more formal attire—a crisp black collared shirt straining against his broad frame, paired with sharp dress pants. The vibrancy that normally danced in his brown eyes was replaced by a hollowness.

"It's hard to say," Brody admitted. "I don't think it has fully sunk in yet for either of us. I just can't fathom someone taking my dad's life."

"Do you think it's possible that it was Ralph Lang? He seemed pretty upset with your dad at the Snowflake Market."

"Sure, he'd been badmouthing my dad, but that's all it was. Ralph has been a little off since his wife's death."

"Brody, he shoved your dad," Hope said. "Mitty didn't tell you?"

Brody shook his head, clearly caught off guard. "He actually pushed my dad?"

"I'm sorry to be the one telling you about it. Drew and I witnessed the whole altercation," Hope said. "I told Detective Reid about it."

"Good. Then they'll investigate it. I didn't think Ralph would put his hands on my dad. I know he's been angry since he bought the Higganum lamp. They're very collectible, and my dad got lucky and found it in someone's attic."

"So, it's authentic?"

"Absolutely. Or we wouldn't have sold it as a real one. Now, we do have a few reproductions . . . like that table over there," he said, pointing. "It's not a real Chippendale and we've indicated that on the tag."

Hope looked over her shoulder at the rectangular table in pristine condition. At a quick glance, it could pass for an authentic Chippendale piece. "Do you have any idea why Ralph believes your dad sold him a fake Higganum?"

Brody shrugged, a tinge of guilt evident in his eyes.

"I didn't want to get dragged into their dispute. My dad assured me he could handle it. But now, looking back, maybe I should've been more involved in his life. It's been tough with all the changes—the divorce, his remarriage, and his sudden retirement."

"Don't be too hard on yourself. There's been a lot of change," Hope said. "Though, your stepmother may need some help. I saw her a little while ago. She's very distraught, which is understandable."

Brody's response carried a hint of resignation. "No need to worry about her. My dad had a substantial life insurance policy, and Nora has a knack for looking out for herself. Just like Alena."

Hope's next question for Brody was abruptly silenced by the creak of the shop's door swinging open. In strode Leila Manchester and Dorie Baxter, two of Hope's nosiest neighbors. Despite their love for gossip, Hope adored them because they were genuinely kindhearted people.

"Brody, we are deeply sorry for your loss," Dorie said, striding over to the counter. Her silver hair was crowned with a purple fedora, and she wore a stylish coat that matched perfectly. "Aren't we, Leila?"

Leila, standing beside Dorie, peeled off her purple mittens. Her brown hair, cut short with a fringe of bangs, was topped with a matching headband that Hope suspected she had knitted herself. "Terribly sorry," Leila chimed in, affirming their shared sentiment.

Brody murmured his gratitude, and Hope took the opportunity to excuse herself.

Surprisingly, it was easier than she expected to escape. Then again, Dorie and Leila seemed completely focused on Brody.

As she stepped out of the shop, Hope glanced at her watch once more. There was just enough time to make a quick detour to the Merrifield Inn and check on Sally and Jane. She hadn't spoken to them since the murder.

Walking along Main Street, the inn soon came into view, along with the infamous bench. Last night, crime scene tape had surrounded it, but today, it was gone. At first glance, nothing seemed amiss, but a closer look at the passersby revealed the truth. Their eyes flitted from the bench to the inn, suggesting an unsettling connection between the two. The inn had unwittingly become a victim of its proximity to the murder.

Hope entered the grand Victorian house, crossing the threshold into its inviting lobby, where open doorways revealed a dining room on one side and a parlor opposite. A Christmas tree dominated the spot by the ornate staircase. Stretching to a height of nine feet, the tree was decked out with ornaments collected by generations of Merrifields.

Swift on her feet, she gracefully stepped aside just in the nick of time to avoid a collision with a young couple engrossed in their cell phones and blissfully unaware of her presence.

"Sorry about that, Hope. They've been like that since they checked in." Sally Merrifield finished straightening a stack of brochures and came out from behind the registration desk. "Good to see you this morning. What an awful night it was."

"I couldn't agree more." Hope dropped her tote on one of the chairs beside the desk and unzipped her jacket. "How are you and Jane doing? How are your guests handling the incident?"

"Like everyone, we're still in shock. Though, I'm glad that hideous crime scene tape is now gone. The police finished up out there a few hours ago. We had a couple check out last night after they spoke to the police." Sally leaned against the desk and folded her arms. "I couldn't blame them. They came to Jefferson to experience a good old-fashioned Christmas, not a murder."

"I'm sorry to hear that."

"How on earth did such a thing happen during the Jingle Bell Stroll?" Sally asked. "You know, I'd feel a lot more confident the perpetrator would be caught if Ethan was still the police chief."

Sally's sentiment was nothing new. Many folks had been lamenting Ethan's departure from the police department. But the department still had qualified and competent officers in its rank. Maretta Kingston had appointed the captain as the acting police chief until a permanent replacement was found. Still, the town's appreciation for Ethan's dedicated service was heartening.

"Captain Ackman is the acting chief," Hope said. "Maretta has full confidence in him."

Sally scoffed. "I've known him since he was a boy, and let me tell you, he loves to hear himself talk, which means he doesn't listen very well."

"Who doesn't listen very well?" Jane Merrifield breezed into the lobby, adding a sprinkle of holiday spirit with her festive apron and a tray of freshly baked sugar cookies. Her appearance was reminiscent of Mrs. Claus, complete with her wispy white hair and warm, welcoming smile.

Sally wasted no time filling her sister-in-law in on who they were talking about, to which Jane remarked, "You're absolutely right. He's a bit like Gilbert Madison. Although Gilbert does listen, and he doesn't always think he's right."

"Exactly," Sally said with a nod.

With a warm smile, Jane placed the tray of cookies on the desk, and then turned her attention to Hope. "It's good to see you this morning. I assume you're here because of the . . . murder."

The way Jane whispered the word *murder* made Hope suppress a chuckle. The gravity of the situation was not lost on her, but Jane Merrifield was incorrigible. Even after she stopped writing mysteries, Jane had never stopped seeking out a good puzzle.

"I came to check on both of you." Hope scooted closer to the desk, unable to resist the allure of a freshly baked cookie. She reached for one, and before indulging, she savored the delectable buttery vanilla scent that wafted from it. After swallowing her bite, her mind shifted to her own long to-do list, one that included baking. Christmas Eve was just a little more than a week away, and she would be hosting dinner at her home.

"That's very thoughtful of you, dear. Why don't you come into the parlor and have tea with us?" Jane gestured toward the open doorway, leading the way.

Glancing at her watch, Hope decided she had time for a quick cup of tea. "That sounds delightful, although I do have a meeting scheduled with Detective Reid at my house shortly."

Jane settled herself onto one of the plush sofas in the parlor. "What's the meeting with Detective Reid about? Perhaps an update on the investigation?"

Hope settled on the sofa opposite Jane. The crackling fire cast a warm glow, while the patio doors framed a charming view of the snow-covered patio. Family heirlooms were scattered throughout the room, lending a feel of history and coziness.

Before Hope could answer, Sally entered the room accompanied by her niece, Eliza Merrifield. The young woman towered over her aunt even in ballet flats. Her glossy black hair cascaded beyond her shoulders in loose waves, and the white lace collar of her gray dress brushed her elongated neck.

"Nice to see you, Hope." Eliza set the tray she carried down and poured tea from an exquisite blue and white teapot. "I selected Earl Grey for them. It has a delightful citrusy twist. Did you know it's named after Earl Charles Grey, the former prime minister of England from 1830 to 1834?"

Jane, clearly proud of her niece's expertise, said, "Eliza is quite the connoisseur in this field."

Hope raised an eyebrow, impressed. "English history?"

Eliza, with a hint of modesty, clarified, "In tea. It's always been a passion of mine, and I've had the privilege of working in a few tea rooms since graduating college."

"Since she's staying with us for the holidays, we're putting her expertise to good use. Our remaining guests are enjoying a proper afternoon tea, curated by none other than a tea sommelier." Jane took a sip from her steaming cup.

"Aunt Jane, I'm not certified yet," Eliza politely corrected her aunt. "There are a few things I need to finish up in the kitchen. It was wonderful seeing you again, Hope." With that, she swiftly exited the room.

"It's wonderful to have Eliza here for Christmas, but it's such a tragedy that she had to be here during that dreadful murder," Sally lamented as she sat next to her sister-in-law on the sofa.

Jane nodded in agreement, her gaze turning to the window, as if recalling the unnerving night. "I must confess, I felt some unease last night. Falling asleep was difficult. We've never had any type of crime so close to the inn." She took another sip of her tea. "I can only imagine Maretta is in quite a frenzy . . . once again."

Sally leaned back with a contemplative expression. "When is her term as mayor coming to an end? It might be a welcome change to have someone more experienced and capable take the reins."

"Politics can wait for another day," Jane said.

"That it can," Sally agreed. "Our thoughts should be with Mitty's family. They've suffered a loss. I can't help but wonder how Ruth is coping with it all. Jane, we must pay her a visit and offer our heartfelt condolences."

Jane nodded. "You're right. We should go this very afternoon. Despite their divorce, they were married for many years, and he's the father of her son. Ruth will undoubtedly need all the support she can get."

"When I spoke to her at the Snowflake Holiday Market, she was angry with Mitty," Hope revealed. With her tea now drained, she pondered a refill, but knowing she'd be leaving shortly, she set her cup and saucer down on the tray.

"I can only imagine the bitterness of their divorce. But you know, she might be wrestling with guilt now," Jane confided.

"Guilt? Why's that?" Hope asked, her need to know was now through the roof.

Jane leaned forward and said, "Well, she told me she was terrified that she might be the one who was going to die."

Chapter Seven

"For heaven's sake, Jane, this isn't one of your mystery novels," Sally said as she rose and made her way to the fireplace, adjusting the display of ceramic angels with a thoughtful touch.

"She was fighting for her life," Jane insisted.

"Indeed." Sally stepped back from the mantel and appraised the decorations. With a final tweak, she appeared content enough to return to the sofa. "Cancer, if I remember correctly."

"Yes, she confided in me that she had been terrified about many things back then," Jane shared. "Dying, naturally. But there was more. Medical bills were piling up, and she wasn't working at the time. Even though Mitty owned the shop, they didn't have sufficient insurance to cover their debts. She even mentioned they came close to losing the house."

Curious about the outcome, Hope inquired, "Did they lose it?" She'd been living in New York City at the time.

"No, somehow they managed to keep it, and Ruth later told me that all the medical bills had been paid," Jane said. "To say she was relieved would have been an understatement."

"Mitty was a good man. A good provider for his family. Perhaps that's why Nora latched on to him so quickly," Sally reflected. "She said her first husband, Alena's father, was a cruel man. Sounds like she did the wise thing by leaving him."

"At that time, Nora had a friend who lived here," Jane said. "She liked the town and moved here, eventually getting a job at Town Hall. You know, Nora is quite close to Maretta."

"I've heard Nora was not thrilled about Mitty's retirement," Sally stated. "I was actually surprised by his decision. He always seemed like the sort who liked to keep busy."

Hope checked the grandfather clock and saw it was time to leave. Detective Reid would be showing up at her house soon. After bidding her farewells, she left the inn and headed for her car. As she walked, she pondered how Mitty had managed to pay off the hefty medical bills. If his family's home had been at risk, she imagined the debt would have been significant. Perhaps his antique shop thrived more than she realized. Though, considering the current inventory, she doubted that theory. She supposed it was possible he could have acquired and sold some high-ticket items to cover those unexpected expenses.

Hope arrived back at the Coffee Clique and hurried along the busy driveway that wound its way to the communal parking lot in the rear. When she reached it, her eyes locked on Ralph Lang standing beside his Jeep, a shopping bag in hand. With a friendly wave, she called out, "Ralph! Getting some Christmas shopping done?"

He glanced at the bag and then back at Hope. "I should be, but I'm a notorious last-minute shopper. I'm guessing you're well-prepared," he remarked with a chuckle.

"You've got me there. Everything's wrapped and ready for Santa on Christmas Eve," she replied, coming to a stop beside Ralph's vehicle. "I'm sure you heard about what happened last night while caroling."

"Who hasn't?" Ralph unlocked the cargo door. "And before you ask, I was home last night. I think I'm coming down with a cold, so I decided to stay in and miss the Jingle Bell Stroll."

"Have the police interviewed you yet?" Hope inquired.

"Whether they have or haven't is not your concern, Hope." Ralph stowed his bag in the cargo area and closed the door. "You only need to know two things."

"And what might those be?"

Ralph raised one finger. "I didn't kill Mitty." He raised a second finger. "He probably got what he deserved."

Hope gasped. "That's a terrible thing to say. Don't you think your feud has gone too far?"

"He was nothing more than a scammer!"

Surprised by Ralph's outburst, Hope drew back from him.

"Sorry. I shouldn't have raised my voice like that." Ralph took a moment and calmed himself. "The provenance he provided for the Higganum lamp was a fake, and he refused to refund my money. I don't doubt for one minute that I wasn't the only person he swindled.

How he's stayed in business all these years boggles my mind."

Then a realization struck Hope like a bolt of lightning. Had Mitty turned to selling counterfeits to cover mounting debts? Maybe it had started as a desperate move to save his home and pay for Ruth's medical bills, but he couldn't or wouldn't stop. Maybe, just maybe, Ralph was onto something, and there were others who had fallen prey to Mitty's deceit, with one of them seeking the ultimate revenge.

"It's not like I have a lot of money to squander on fake antiques. I can't believe I trusted a guy like Mitty. We're all fools." He spun around and marched to the driver's side and got into the Jeep.

"What evidence do you have that the lamp is a fake?" Her words fell on deaf ears as Ralph sped out of the parking lot, leaving her in the dust. "I just want to help."

• • •

Hope had barely set foot in her kitchen when Bigelow greeted her, eager for a treat. Meanwhile, Princess, her regal diva of a cat, lazily lounged on her luxurious perch atop the cat tree and barely opened her eyes to acknowledge Hope's return. As she picked up the canister where she kept homemade treats for her dog, her cell phone buzzed. The caller ID gave her a heads-up that it was Detective Reid calling. Much to Bigelow's dismay, she tapped on the phone, putting it on speaker before she reached into the jar for a mini pumpkin donut.

"I just walked through the door," she informed him. Racing against the clock because of her detours while in town, she wasn't going to have much time before he arrived. "Are you on your way over now?"

Reid's voice crackled through the speaker, as if he was driving and getting a low signal. "No. Something has come up. We have to reschedule."

"Something related to the case? A break?" She slid the canister back on the counter, then moved to the granite island. The kitchen renovation she embarked on after buying the hundred-year-old farmhouse had been an ambitious project, involving tearing down walls and replacing worn-out flooring with stunning antique pumpkin pine boards she'd discovered while exploring Vermont antique shops with Drew. Now, instead of separate rooms, she enjoyed a spacious haven for cooking, dining, and relaxation, complete with a breathtaking view of her three-acre property from the large bank of nine-over-nine windows now trimmed with an evergreen garland. "Has someone confessed?"

"I'm not at liberty to discuss the ongoing investigation. I'll call you later to reschedule. Goodbye, Hope."

The line went silent. Hope's sigh of frustration filled the air, mirrored by a woof of sympathy from Bigelow.

Contemplating her next move, she gave Bigelow another donut. She had a recipe to test and blog comments to read and reply to, but she couldn't help but think about having another conversation with Ralph.

He'd taken off so abruptly that she hadn't processed his cryptic remark about knowing better than to trust a guy like Mitty. What did he mean by that?

A guy like Mitty?

Pondering the question, she absentmindedly tapped her fingertips on the cool granite countertop. Bigelow joined her at the island, his deep brown eyes reflecting her own uncertainty.

"Why shouldn't Ralph have trusted Mitty?" she mused aloud, addressing Bigelow as if he held the key to unraveling the meaning of the comment. "Or was Ralph just ranting and had nothing to back up the statement? And how did Ralph discover the lamp's provenance was fake? Did he have it appraised? By whom?"

Bigelow tilted his head, seemingly as puzzled as she was.

"Ralph may not be forthcoming, especially after shutting me down earlier," she acknowledged. "But it's worth a shot." Decision made, she resolved to pay Ralph a visit. But first, she needed to whip up a batch of treats. After all, she couldn't arrive at his doorstep empty-handed.

Bigelow let out an enthusiastic woof, as if wholeheartedly endorsing her plan. She rewarded him with a pat on the head and one last donut before swiftly grabbing her apron, ready to dive into action.

She knew just what to bring. It was one of her most downloaded recipes on her blog this time of year. Before she gathered the ingredients for her eggnog scones, she left a voicemail for Drew, urging him to delve deeper into Mitty and his business. She was convinced that if Ralph's claims were true, there would be some chatter or information out there. Either among other antique shop owners or online. While leveling a cup of flour, her phone buzzed with a text from Drew, indicating he was already on it for his upcoming article.

Not too long after making her decision to visit Ralph, the aroma of freshly baked scones, just out of the oven, filled the air as Hope took off her apron. With the scones now cooled and snugly nestled in a pastry box, she slipped into her jacket and stepped out into the crisp winter air and hurried to her Explorer.

As she drove toward Ralph's house on Grover Lane, snowflakes began to swirl. Turning onto the picturesque road, she found herself enchanted by the scene before her. Each house along the street was a masterpiece of holiday cheer, adorned with elaborate decorations and twinkling lights that danced in the falling snow. The sight left her wondering if a friendly competition brewed among the neighbors, each vying to outshine the other with their festive displays.

As she drew nearer to Ralph's two-story gambrel-roof home, set back from the road on a deep front lawn, her attention wavered between the decorations and the presence of JPD cruisers parked in the driveway alongside a familiar sedan.

Detective Reid was there.

Suddenly, the rescheduling of their meeting made perfect sense. Once the initial shock subsided, she grabbed her tote and exited her Explorer. The flurry of activity surrounding Ralph's home struck a nerve of unease in her gut. This wasn't a mere interview. Detectives investigating a homicide didn't assemble a small army of uniformed officers without cause.

No. This was bad.

She'd barely shut her car door when Reid appeared, and he looked none too happy to see her there. With every purposeful step he took toward her, his displeasure echoed through the air.

"What are you doing here, Hope?" His voice held an air of authority, devoid of any frivolities.

Hope retrieved the pastry box from her tote. "I came to visit Ralph. I baked eggnog scones with dried cranberries."

Reid scrutinized the box with the hint of a smile.

"Why are there so many officers here?" She couldn't help asking questions even though she anticipated the elusive *it's a police matter* reply. "What's going on?"

Reid cast a brief glance at the house before returning his gaze to Hope. With a subtle nod, he divulged, "We're conducting a thorough search of the property, and in the garage we found what we believe might be the murder weapon. That's not to be repeated, understand?"

Hope's mind spiraled in disbelief. She had never expected such candor from him, nor could she fathom the idea that Ralph could be capable of ending a life. It just didn't seem possible. She couldn't help but voice her thoughts, desperate for clarity in the chaos.

"Everyone knows Ralph never locks his garage door," she interjected, her voice tinged with skepticism. "His late wife used to complain about it incessantly. Ralph insisted on easy access to his tools and workbench. Why on earth would he leave the alleged murder weapon lying around in his own garage? Wouldn't he have disposed of it?"

Reid remained stubbornly doubtful, but Hope was determined to prove him wrong.

"What about the man I saw last night? The one who ran off right after Mitty was murdered?" she persisted. "It wasn't Ralph."

"We're looking into the man you said you saw, but at the moment, I have the murder weapon, a motive, and no alibi. I can't overlook all of that, Hope," Reid explained firmly.

"Of course he doesn't have an alibi. He was home by himself because he wasn't feeling good."

"How do you know?"

"He told me so earlier. I ran into him in the parking lot behind the Coffee Clique, and we talked." Hope was hesitant to reveal their conversation. But since there was no such thing as food blogger–friend confidentiality, she had no choice but to tell the detective. Besides, what she'd heard wasn't any more shocking than what had unfolded at the holiday market.

Before she could relay the conversation, the activity around her halted, and a moment later Ralph emerged from the house, accompanied by an officer. Despair was deeply carved into Ralph's face, making him look a decade older.

"You're arresting him?" Hope blurted, her dismay evident.

"I'm innocent, Hope," Ralph, handcuffed, murmured quietly as he passed them. Moments later, he was placed in a police cruiser and then it drove off.

She looked at Reid, ready to say something, but he shook his head, signaling for her to let it go.

"Go home, Hope. There's nothing more you can do here." His words struck a chord within her.

He was right. With the murder weapon, Ralph's public quarrel with Mitty, and his lack of an alibi, Hope lacked conclusive evidence to clear him.

She handed Reid the pastry box. "Someone might as well enjoy these." Without waiting for a thank-you, she walked back to her car. Before slipping into the driver's seat, she sent a text to Drew.

Leaving Ralph's house. The police are here. They found a weapon. They arrested him.

• • •

Tuesday morning rolled around faster than Hope had expected. After returning from her trip to Ralph's house the day before, she got caught up in a conference call with her editor and agent, followed by dinner with Ethan and the girls. She whipped up a quick dinner of sloppy joes and onion rings so they could spend the evening decorating the Christmas tree. Glancing over the top of her laptop computer on the dining table, she smiled at the decked-out evergreen. From the angel on top to the quilted tree skirt she'd made years ago, it was a magnificent sight.

Her smile faded as she remembered where she had to go that afternoon. At two o'clock, there was the funeral service for Mitty. Pulling her gaze from the tree, she exited out of the *Gazette*'s website. As she ate a leftover eggnog scone and drank her coffee, she read Drew's article about Ralph's arrest yesterday. While the newspaper went to print weekly, the website kept up-to-date on any breaking news. She closed the laptop and drained the last of her coffee. Swiping up the mug and plate, she headed into the kitchen. On her way, she caught a glimpse of Poppy, her Rhode Island Red hen, perched on the patio wall. She tended to stay close to the house while the rest of the chickens free-ranged all day.

Hope reached the sink and loaded her plate into the dishwasher, but she kept her mug out because she was contemplating another cup of coffee. It seemed that morning required copious amounts of caffeine.

"Hey, any coffee left?" Ethan asked as he entered the kitchen through the mudroom. He'd called after dropping the girls off at school and said he'd swing by on his way to the office. "It was a late one last night."

"Did the girls have trouble falling asleep again?" Hope took out a travel mug from an upper cabinet and poured the remaining coffee into it.

A wry chuckle escaped his lips. "Molly did," he confirmed, brushing a kiss on Hope's cheek. "And then Becca woke up too." Reaching into the pocket of his worn suede field jacket, layered over a thick fisherman's sweater, he retrieved his phone. A quick scroll through messages brought a grimace to his face. "Looks like it's shaping up to be one of those mornings already."

Hope handed him the travel mug and then rinsed out the coffeepot. "I'm so sorry. If I hadn't insisted on them going caroling . . ."

"Babe, this isn't your fault." Ethan set the mug on the counter, pocketed his phone and reached out for Hope, pulling her close to his chest. "No one knew that there was going to be a murder. The girls will be fine. They just need a little time."

"What about Heather? How much time will she need?"

Hope's hand rose instinctively, her fingers brushing against his hair. The rich brown, the color of a strong espresso, had grown out since his police days. She liked the change, the way it softened the sharp lines of his face and spoke of a life less regimented.

He shrugged. "Never can tell with her. Look, don't worry about Heather. I'll handle her."

Hope's heart squeezed. Ethan always managed to smooth things over with his ex-wife.

She attributed it to all the training he'd gotten in negotiations as a police officer.

"I just read Drew's article about Ralph's arrest," she said. "I wonder if he's still in custody or has been released."

"He's being arraigned this morning," Ethan said.

"You've spoken with Reid?"

Ethan shook his head. "I talked to Matt."

"He's representing Ralph? That's wonderful." She knew firsthand what a top-notch attorney he was. She'd first met him when Claire had been suspected of murdering fellow real estate agent Peaches McCoy. After that case was resolved by Hope figuring out who the killer really was, Matt decided to buy a weekend house in Jefferson. Which was a good thing, considering Hope needed his representation when her neighbor had been murdered last spring. "So, are you working the case?"

"Remember the talk we had about my job? Everything is confidential," Ethan said. "There's no sharing of information. Sorry, babe." His cell phone buzzed. "I have to take this call." He reached for the travel mug, kissed her goodbye and left.

Hope folded her arms. Luckily, she didn't need his information. She had her own sources and methods.

Chapter Eight

Hope navigated the bumper-to-bumper parking lot of Maple Hill Farm and finally snagged a spot near the entrance. Adjusting the straps of her trusty tote bag and nestling deeper into her cozy plaid scarf, she braced herself against the crisp morning air. Today's mission: Christmas wreath supplies, including one for Drew. This holiday season marked his inaugural celebration in Fenn House, the treasured family home recently acquired from his aunt. Between the ongoing remodel, training a puppy and now working 24/7 covering Mitty's murder for the newspaper, she doubted he'd had any time to buy or make decorations for his home. At least now he would have a wreath for his front door.

As she entered the bustling farm, she found herself among clusters of eager shoppers and the atmosphere alive with laughter and excitement. They moved across the grounds in pursuit of perfect gifts, towering Christmas trees, and warming cups of cocoa. But there was one topic on everyone's lips that united them all—the sensational news of Ralph's arrest. It was a stark reminder that gossip had a way of spreading like wildfire in their close-knit community, especially when it involved handcuffs and neighbors as witnesses.

Hope overheard snippets of hushed conversations as she navigated the throng of shoppers.

"They found it, the murder weapon," a voice declared, sending shivers down her spine.

Another voice chimed in, "He wasn't the same after his wife's death. That lamp thing pushed him over the edge."

Suddenly, Hope found herself face-to-face with Amy Phelan, the town's resident true-crime podcaster, clutching a steaming cup of cocoa and a half-eaten cookie.

"Well, hello, stranger," Amy drawled. "It's been ages . . . well, a couple weeks at least."

"Hi, Amy. I didn't expect to see you here," Hope said.

Amy rolled her eyes in a playful way. "I'm not playing hooky. I promise. I took the day off from the real estate office since I worked last weekend. Today I'm running errands and working on my podcast." When not at Jefferson Town Realty, where she worked as a secretary, she produced and hosted the true-crime podcast *Search for the Missing*. Drawing closer to Hope, she leaned in and asked, "I heard you were there when they arrested Ralph. Is that true?"

Hope nodded in confirmation.

"Did he say anything to you?" Amy pressed.

"He maintained his innocence. And I believe him."

"Everyone's innocent until proven guilty," Amy remarked. "But if there ever was an unlikely suspect . . . though he was certainly riled up with Mitty. Now, Mitty seemed like a nice guy, although I didn't chat with him much. As for Brody, well, he's easy on the eyes." Amy winked playfully. "But Alena, she's something else, just like her mom. Two peas in a pod."

"Why do you say that?"

"Alena acts like she's too good for Jefferson, just like Nora. And don't get me started on Nora and Mitty."

Hope knew she wouldn't have to say another word. All she had to do was stand there and be quiet.

"You know when you see a couple and they just click, like you and Ethan?" Amy observed, teasing. "Anyway, that wasn't Mitty and Nora. Something felt off, and I think it was her, not him. Maybe it's just my gut feeling. Perhaps I'm a bit more suspicious now because of the podcast. Oh, speaking of which, I've got to run. I should have been on my way back home by now. Bye."

Hope lingered for a moment, her gaze following her friend's departure before shifting toward the busy shop ahead. She made her way toward the modest structure and peered inside. Her gaze swept over the checkout area, and there it was: a queue that seemed to stretch on forever, like a silent congregation waiting with bated breath. The hushed tones of the customers were no coincidence; it was Julia at the cash register. But Hope saw beyond the masks of politeness. She could practically read the unspoken words circulating among the patrons. The evidence was in Julia's strained yet well-practiced smile. Beneath the veneer of festive cheer, it was plain to see that her mind was consumed with worry for her brother-in-law, battling to maintain the illusion of holiday joy even as anxiety clawed at her heart.

Hope carried on with her mission and gathered an overflowing cart of vibrant greens for her wreaths. When she had more than enough for Drew's wreath plus a few others, she headed to the checkout. As she approached, Julia's face instantly brightened with relief, as though she had been eagerly anticipating Hope's arrival.

Julia let out a sigh, her weariness evident in her slumped shoulders. As the transaction was processed, she beckoned one of her employees to take her place at the register. Then, leaning in closer to Hope, she asked, "Do you have a moment to spare?"

Hope's response was swift and reassuring. "Of course I do."

Julia came out from behind the counter and pulled Hope along to a spot away from prying ears.

"I'm at a loss for what to do," Julia confided, her voice quivering with despair. "Albert is in absolute shambles about Ralph's arrest. The very moment Ralph called him, he stormed off to the police station, demanding to see his brother. He feels utterly powerless. But he did manage to secure a lawyer for Ralph."

"Matt Roydon," Hope interjected. "Ralph couldn't be in better hands."

Julia's head tilted ever so slightly, a spark of recognition lighting up her warm brown eyes. "He's the attorney Ethan's with now, isn't he?" she inquired, her voice carrying a glimmer of hope.

Hope nodded.

"I'm so glad to hear that," Julia murmured, her hand pressed against her chest. "Having Ethan on his side gives me hope—"

"Julia," Hope interjected gently, "I don't know if Ethan will be directly involved in the case. He keeps his work confidential. But maybe that's for the best."

"Best for whom?" Julia retorted, her frustration bubbling over. "Ralph needs every bit of help he can get. It's crystal-clear he's been set up. Anyone with a shred of common sense can see that." She let out an exasperated breath before sharing a personal detail. "He bought that outrageously expensive lamp for Denise."

"His late wife," Hope said.

"She loved them but she never purchased one because she knew how hard Ralph worked for their money. After she passed away so suddenly, he lost his way. He stumbled upon that lamp in Mitty's store while doing repairs, and he bought it for her."

"That's both sweet and heartbreaking."

Julia's gaze turned earnest as she made a heartfelt plea. "Hope, would you consider helping Ralph? It seems like you possess a unique talent for unraveling this sort of thing."

Hope hesitated. Even though her curiosity was working overtime, she wasn't sure if inserting herself into another murder investigation was a good decision. Especially if the stranger she'd seen earlier on Main Street was indeed the killer, because if she saw him on the night of the murder, he had to have seen her. "I'm not—"

"Please, Hope," Julia implored, her voice filled with desperation. "We could really use a miracle now."

Hope pressed her lips together and considered her choices. One was to sit on the sidelines and do nothing, while the other would be to help someone she didn't believe was capable of murder. It was settled.

"I'm not sure I can promise a miracle, but I will do what I can to help."

• • •

Later that day, at half past three, Hope trailed behind Claire, her steps heavy. The mourners ahead, returning from Mitty's burial to the Grace Unity Church, seemed like a blurred mass. Her eyes caught on Alena, whose hurried steps and hushed conversation with an unknown man was a stark contrast to the somber mood. The two were doing their best not to be seen. A prickle of unease joined the weight of grief in Hope's chest.

"Hope, are you coming?" Claire asked, giving her sister a *get moving* look just as Ethan hurried to catch up with Hope.

"Why did they choose to host the reception here instead of at Mitty and Nora's house?" he asked, sliding an arm around her waist.

They all entered the Fellowship Parlor, which was discreetly tucked away from the church's main hall. The spacious room was filled with plush seating, a well-stocked buffet table, and colorful stained-glass windows.

Lexi Hewitt, her clipboard clutched firmly in hand, appeared from behind and scooted around Hope, Ethan, and Claire. "The Fitzgerald home is all dressed up for the holidays, so Nora felt it wouldn't be quite appropriate for the funeral reception," she explained. "This parlor has seen its fair share of functions, and it's the perfect setting for such occasions."

"Lexi, you've outdone yourself with this stunning buffet," Claire praised as she slipped out of her wool coat. "Reverend Comstock is truly fortunate to have found you."

Lexi dipped her head, her cheeks flushed from the praise. "I think it's the other way around," she replied with a heartfelt smile.

As Sally approached the group, holding a small plate of delectable appetizers, she reflected, "Funerals are never easy, but those during the holidays seem to tug at our hearts even more." Her gaze was pensive. "At least we can find some solace in the fact that Mitty's passing wasn't the result of some random tragedy."

Eliza, elegant in her maxi-length black velour dress and hair gracefully tied back with a coordinating bow, joined the conversation. "I must admit, I do feel safer now," she shared.

Jane, following her niece with a teacup in hand, approached Hope's side. "Let's not jump to conclusions just yet," she cautioned. "Ralph hasn't confessed. In fact, he's maintained his innocence."

"Confessing would be the right thing to do," Sally added before nibbling on a mini-quiche.

"I trust that Sam will conduct a thorough inquiry and reach the right conclusion," Ethan said confidently.

"I have to side with Jane on this," Claire added. "Detective Reid hasn't always been spot-on in the past . . . Hope and I can attest to that. Besides, Ralph has never demonstrated any violent tendencies before. Stabbing someone is a truly violent act."

"It most certainly is." Jane nodded in solidarity with Claire.

Just as uncertainty tinged the conversation, Lexi interjected, "But the knife was found in his garage—" A scream pierced the air, cutting Lexi off and drawing everyone's attention across the room.

"What on earth?" Hope's gaze traveled over Lexi's shoulder and she saw Nora and Ruth face-to-face. "This isn't good."

"I knew you being here would be a mistake!" Nora pointed at Ruth as she closed the gap between them. "You were ungrateful right up to his dying day. He paid all your medical bills and helped you get better. And what did he get in return? You left him."

"I'm sure you're grateful for Mitty's hefty life insurance policy," Ruth retorted.

Fury engulfed Nora, and she raised her hand, poised for a harsh slap against Ruth. But before she could strike, Brody lunged forward, snatching her arm in midair, abruptly halting her intended action.

"Let go of me!" Nora demanded, her voice filled with outrage.

Ethan swiftly maneuvered through the crowd, pushing past Hope, finding his way to the center of the commotion. "Everybody, let's take a moment to cool down," he calmly suggested, stepping between Brody and Nora. "Brody, why don't you take your mom outside to get some fresh air?"

In a venomous tone, Nora spat out, "You both should leave. Neither of you are welcome here any longer."

With a piercing glare, Brody warned his stepmother, "You're making a grave mistake, Nora." He then guided his mother out of the parlor, leaving behind a chilling atmosphere.

The scene of the widow and ex-wife almost coming to blows had sent shock waves through the room, leaving all present speechless. Hope couldn't help but believe it would be the hot topic of conversation all over town the next day. It wasn't much longer after the unsettling scene that Nora departed with Alena, leaving a void in the room. It was at that point Lexi started the task of cleaning up and Hope offered to help. She packaged what was left of the appetizers while Eliza removed the coffee urn and whisked it away to the kitchen.

With the last of the mourners filing out of the parlor, Lexi did a final sweep of the room, gathering abandoned glasses and cups.

Maretta Kingston, her brown coat buttoned up, briskly passed Hope as she grumbled, "One would expect more decorum from Ruth. Her behavior was simply mortifying. I mean, Nora just buried her husband."

Pausing in her cleanup duties, Hope offered a thoughtful response. "Emotions tend to run high during such times. Let's not forget, Ruth was married to Mitty as well, and he was the father of her son. She's grappling with her own grief."

Maretta couldn't help but harrumph in disagreement.

Changing the subject, Hope tried to steer the conversation to a topic she was certain Maretta would be thrilled with. "I imagine you're relieved to hear that an arrest has been made."

"Absolutely," Maretta replied with conviction. "Swift justice is essential, particularly during this time of the year. If people don't feel safe, our town's businesses will suffer. We rely on tourists, after all. That's something you should have had in mind when you asked Mitty Fitzgerald to play Santa. If you chose someone else, we wouldn't be dealing with this mess."

"I'm not responsible for someone killing him. That's the fault of the killer," Hope said.

"But it appears you gave the killer an ideal opportunity to commit a grisly murder at the Jingle Bell Stroll. Now it's my responsibility as mayor to restore the Stroll's image." Maretta glanced at her watch. "I'd love to stay and chat, but I must get back to Town Hall." With determined steps, she hurriedly made her exit.

Hope resumed her cleanup duties after Maretta disappeared. The audacity! To pin the blame on her for what happened at the caroling event?

A shadow fell over Hope as Ethan materialized beside her. "Can you catch a ride with Claire . . ." His words faltered as he took in her expression. Concern creased his forehead, his gaze darting around the room. "What happened? Are you okay?"

Hope let out a weary sigh. "Maretta," she muttered, leaving the rest unsaid.

His hand moved instinctively, landing a comforting pat on her back. "She's still blaming you for what happened?"

Hope offered a tight nod, forcing a small smile. "Yeah, well, I'm used to it by now. So, about that ride . . ."

"I'm sorry about the timing but Matt just summoned me to the office."

She was about to ask if his sudden departure had something to do with Ralph's case, but she knew better than to ask. Ethan had made it clear he didn't want to discuss it with her.

"Later, I'll pick up the girls and bring them over to your place for dinner, if that's okay with you," he offered.

"It's more than okay. We can make wreaths tonight. The girls will have so much fun. Wait . . . does this mean Heather's not mad about the Jingle Bell Stroll anymore?"

Ethan sighed. "No, she's still mad, but her sister managed to calm her down. We had no way of predicting what would happen." He dotted a tender kiss on her cheek. "I have to run. See you later." With that, he turned and headed off.

"Maybe Heather's sister should talk to Maretta," Hope murmured as she gathered a stack of plates.

• • •

With the Fellowship Parlor all tidied up, Hope said goodbye to Lexi and strode down the carpeted hallway, heading for the exit. Claire had kindly offered a ride and said she'd pull up to the curb. The cold afternoon air outside nipped at Hope's cheeks, a stark contrast to the comforting warmth she'd just left behind.

Strolling along the sidewalk, Hope passed the colossal holiday decorations that had graced the church grounds since Black Friday. From enormous candy canes to towering inflatable snowmen and gingerbread figures, the display elicited awe and wonder from spectators of all ages.

Hope halted briefly, scanning for Claire's Mercedes. She caught sight of it as it meandered through the maze of parked cars. Along with the holiday market, the church was hosting a Christmas concert, which explained the crowded lot.

As she moved forward, planning to walk a little farther to meet Claire's car, Hope's heart raced. Mere feet from her stood the stranger she had seen on Main Street the day before. The same man who had been lurking near Mitty's lifeless body.

"You!" Hope exclaimed, her gloved hand pointing accusingly at the stranger. "Who are you?"

"Me?" he retorted, pointing an indignant finger at himself as he stepped forward. "Who wants to know?"

"Don't come any closer!" she continued, her voice trembling.

Despite her warning, he kept advancing.

She desperately grasped at the nearest defense, an oversized candy cane decoration, and swung it at the stranger. Startled, he threw up his arms to protect himself.

"Stay back!"

"Whoa, lady! Are you out of your mind?" he protested, shielding his face with raised arms. "I don't want to get anywhere near you! You're crazy!"

"I saw you near Mitty's body! Stay away from me!" Hope shouted, fear coursing through her.

"Like I would willingly approach someone as unhinged as you? You're nuts!" the man fired back, irritation creasing his face.

The piercing sound of a car horn suddenly shattered their confrontation. Hope's gaze snapped toward the source, finding relief in Claire's arrival.

"Claire! Call the police! This man killed Mitty!" Hope shouted. When she turned back to the stranger, he had vanished. "Where did he go?"

"He went that way!" Claire pointed. "Come on, get in."

Hope abandoned the candy cane and hurried into the car, and then Claire hit the accelerator, peeling away from the curb.

"We can't lose him, but you can't speed either," Hope cautioned.

"I know," Claire replied, making the turn into the smaller parking lot. "There are too many people around the lot."

As Claire navigated her vehicle along a row of parked cars, Hope noticed the beat-up old car she had seen around town speeding by them. Its driver, the stranger who had just confronted Hope, wasn't concerned about the safety of others. In the blink of an eye, the old car was out of the church's lot and out of sight.

Her frustration boiled over, and she slapped the dashboard. "Darn it! He's gotten away!"

Chapter Nine

Hope texted Detective Reid during the drive home, downplaying the candy cane incident but detailing her encounter with the stranger. She wished they'd been able to follow him, find out where he was staying. But he was speeding too fast and following him could have put not just herself but her sister in harm's way. Backing off was the right thing to do considering the circumstances.

When Claire turned her car onto Fieldstone Road, Hope checked her phone for a reply from Reid. So far, nothing. She wasn't sure what to make of that. Either he was wrapped up in something and hadn't read his messages, or he was planning on paying a visit in person to remind her to stay out of his investigation.

Regardless, Hope knew she wouldn't be home if Reid decided to pay her a visit. She had an errand to run—a task he likely wouldn't approve of. Then again, there wasn't much she did that he approved of.

When Claire pulled up to the driveway, Hope wasted no time exiting the car. Claire's hurried departure back to her shop suited Hope just fine. What didn't sit well was the stern warning to be careful her sister gave. And to also keep the doors locked. Because if Hope was right, there was a killer on the loose.

Hope didn't need the reminder. She was all too aware of the possibility she'd not only confronted a killer but pretty much told him she knew he did it. Admittedly, it wasn't the smartest thing to do, but she'd gotten caught up in the moment.

Entering her home, Hope quickly traded her somber funeral attire for comfortable jeans and a chunky sweater, and her stilettos were replaced with moto boots. After replenishing her tote bag with essentials from her clutch, she breezed through the kitchen, taking a moment to carefully package the remaining eggnog scones she had baked the day before, With the pastry box in hand, she left her house.

• • •

Hope glided into the driveway of an adorable yet weathered Cape Cod house nestled between two larger homes. She parked her Explorer and clutched the pastry box in her hands. As she walked along the brick walkway leading to the entrance, she noticed the home needed some tender loving care. Its pale green paint had seen better days, the concrete steps were webbed with cracks, and the railing had surrendered to rust. The constant upkeep of an old house was a never-ending, wallet-draining task. She ascended the worn steps, her fingers finding the doorbell, and then patiently waited.

The door opened and Ruth appeared. While her hair was still gathered in a bun, she had changed from her formal black attire to a more casual ensemble of jogger pants and a sweatshirt. Her pearl stud earrings remained from earlier, and her smudged eye makeup hinted at recent tears.

"Hope, what brings you by?" Ruth maintained her grip on the door, her expression hinting at weariness—both physical and emotional—from the day's events.

"I didn't have the chance to say goodbye earlier, and I also wanted to check on you." That was true and in normal circumstances Hope doubted Detective Reid would have cared about the visit. But considering Ruth was a person of interest in her ex-husband's murder, he probably would have preferred Hope to stay away. And definitely not visit Ruth alone.

"That's very thoughtful of you," Ruth said.

Hope lifted the pastry box with a warm smile. "I baked eggnog cranberry scones."

Ruth's eyes flickered to the box, and a small, appreciative smile tugged at her lips. "Well, come on in. I love your recipes. Never had one fail on me. How about I put the kettle on for us?"

Hope followed Ruth down the narrow hallway, briefly glimpsing the living room entering the kitchen. The absence of holiday decorations struck her. Except for the charming crafts in progress on the corner hutch, there wasn't any holiday cheer to be seen. Setting the box on the table, Hope removed her jacket and then sat on a chair while Ruth busied herself preparing the tea.

While they waited for the kettle to whistle, they chatted about the weather. They both agreed that this year it seemed winter came early and had settled in for a long stay. After the kettle whistled, Ruth filled two mugs with steaming water and set them on the table. She then retrieved a milk carton from the fridge and a box of tea bags from an upper cabinet. "It's been a draining day," she confessed, sinking onto a chair and adding a smidge of milk to her tea.

Hope followed suit, stirring milk into her tea and taking a comforting sip. "Emotions ran high at the funeral for everyone," she empathized, "and the murder has us all on edge."

"Especially those of us who are considered persons of interest by the police." Ruth took a drink of her tea. Peering over the rim of her mug, she continued, "I know you shared with the detective what I said about things being easier if Mitty were dead."

Hope's heart skipped a beat. Had Reid shared it was she who made that statement? It seemed unlikely. More plausible was that Ruth had deduced it herself if she hadn't divulged that sentiment to anyone else. She opted for the latter explanation.

"I had no choice but to share everything I knew," Hope replied evenly. "It was the only way to help solve this mystery."

Ruth raised an eyebrow, curious. "So, you see yourself as some kind of modern-day Nancy Drew, or perhaps the detective in Jane's mystery series?"

Hope chuckled, grateful for the brief moment of levity that lightened the seriousness of the situation. She took it as a sign that Ruth wasn't that angry with her.

"What was the character's name? I can never remember," Ruth said.

"Barbara Neal." Hope had read all five books featuring the college co-ed who had an uncanny talent for solving mysteries. After the last book in the series, Jane traded her typewriter for full-time motherhood. "But let's get back to our real-life investigation. The police need all the facts to solve Mitty's murder. Isn't that what we all want?"

"Unless . . . unless I'm the one they believe killed him?"

Hope, undeterred, responded, "I don't believe you are. But in solving a case like this, every small detail could make a difference. It might just be the missing puzzle piece that sets things right." She sipped her tea, her gaze locked on Ruth, waiting for the coldness in her eyes to thaw before broaching the next question. "If you don't mind sharing, I'm curious about why you and Mitty decided to divorce?"

A hint of irritation flashed across Ruth's face as she huffed and shifted uncomfortably in her chair. "You're diving right into the personal matters, aren't you?" She paused, collecting her thoughts. "Fine. I'll tell you. We met and fell head over heels in love. At the time, he was doing odd jobs, and I managed a furniture store. But after we got married, he had this sudden dream of leaving the city and opening an antique shop. He'd visited Jefferson before and decided this was where he wanted us to live. His grandfather had a passion for antiques and was an avid collector."

Hope nodded, connecting the dots. "Seems like Brody inherited that gene too."

"He did." Ruth took a sip of her tea. "Once my battle with cancer was finally over, I realized that life was meant for more than the confines of a small town. I wanted to travel. See some of the world. At a minimum, at least see some of this country. You know, I'd never been to the West Coast before. But Mitty was a homebody, firmly rooted in his familiar surroundings. We argued too much. First about traveling and then about everything else. I admit, I started feeling resentful." She paused, her breath a silent testament to the weight of her decision. "I am forever grateful that he was by my side when I was sick, but I couldn't live the rest of my life feeling that I'd miss out on something. So, I made the tough decision and filed for divorce."

"Deciding to end a marriage is never easy."

"It shattered me, but in the end, it was the only path that made sense for both of us. I never forgot the kindness or love Mitty showed me, despite what others may think." She leaned back. "After the divorce, I traveled for a year. It was invigorating, but I admit, I missed Jefferson. I foolishly had a glimmer of hope that we could reconnect if I came back. You know, start fresh." Her gaze dropped, revealing the vulnerability hidden beneath her strength. "But he'd moved on. He was engaged to Nora."

"That must have been difficult to accept."

Ruth nodded, her hand gently tapping the table, signaling a desire to steer the conversation away from the past. "When I returned from the church earlier, I went down to the basement. I stashed an old chest down there when I first moved into this house. It'd been in storage since Mitty and I split. I dumped so many things in that thing when I moved out of my old house."

Ruth rose from her seat and moved to the hutch. She pulled open a drawer and grasped a folder. Returning to the table, she pulled out the contents and spread out the collection of newspaper clippings.

"These aren't mine. I've never seen them before," Ruth explained with a puzzled expression. "Mitty must have put the folder in the trunk."

Hope's eyes darted across the newspaper clippings spread out before her. The headlines chronicled a daring jewelry store heist in West Hartford, where a staggering sum of precious gems had vanished one night. "Why would he hold on to these? Did he ever work there?"

"Not that I know of," Ruth responded, her gaze drifting toward the window above the sink. "When I first met Mitty, he stood at a crossroads, torn between two very different paths. He'd fallen in with the wrong crowd. He started with car thefts in high school and graduated to burglaries after that. Got himself caught once, and that's when he had to make a life-altering decision. It's also when our paths crossed."

Hope was at a loss for words. She never envisioned Mitty as a criminal. "It seems like he made the right decision. Do you think he kept these clippings because he knew the people responsible for the robbery?"

"I think it's more than that."

The comment puzzled Hope until she noticed the date of the heist in one of the articles. "Was this during the time you were battling cancer?"

Ruth nodded. "We had so many bills at that time and the shop wasn't bringing in enough money to cover all the debt. It kills me to say this, but I think he was part of the crew. He took that risk to keep our bills paid. I'm sure of it."

"That would have indeed been a risk. A big one. He could have ended up in prison."

"He gambled his freedom for me." Tears welled in Ruth's eyes, and her emotions overwhelmed her. "I'm sorry . . . I can't continue with this." She abruptly rose from her chair and fled the kitchen.

Resisting the impulse to follow, Hope realized that Ruth needed solitude to process her feelings, which seemed to range from grief to guilt. She returned her focus to the newspaper clippings. A swift scan confirmed that at the time of the heist, there had been no leads other than witnesses reporting that there were three perpetrators. However, a week after the robbery, a man named Denny Beyer had been arrested. Retrieving her phone, she swiftly snapped photos of the clippings. While Detective Reid must have discovered Mitty's criminal history, she wondered if it had turned up during Drew's research. He hadn't mentioned it yet. With her phone back in her tote, she tidied the table and returned the file folder with all its content back to the hutch. Quietly, she slipped out of the house, mindful not to disturb Ruth's solitude.

• • •

Later that night at home, a festive playlist of Christmas tunes filled the air and a flickering fire cast a warm glow across the family room, creating the perfect ambiance for a delightful wreath-making session. On Hope's dining table, the remnants of a delicious dinner were replaced with an array of evergreens, floral wire, sparkling ornaments, and colorful spools of wide plaid ribbon, waiting to be assembled into magnificent decorations.

From her regal perch on the cat tree in the heart of the family room, Princess kept an eye on everyone. Not far away, Bigelow, with his contented full belly, slumbered on his bed by the crackling fire.

Molly and Becca were huddled at the table, their hands busily working on a wreath for their mom while Hope meticulously added the finishing touches to a special wreath for Drew. With all the remodeling chaos, she knew that holiday decorations would be scarce. And she was determined to bring some holiday magic to his doorstep. She had more than just a wreath up her sleeve. Her surprise delivery would include a fragrant loaf of cranberry-apple bread, a token of warmth and holiday spirit.

"Will Bigelow and Princess have Christmas stockings?" Becca asked as she helped her sister cut a length of ribbon for the wreath.

Hope smiled as she answered, her hands deftly maneuvering the boughs into place. "Absolutely, Becca! Christmas just wouldn't be complete without stockings for every member of the family."

Hope's head swiveled as she heard the distinct creak of the back door opening and closing. It could only mean one thing—Ethan was finally back. He had called earlier, giving her a heads-up that he was on his way. Following his dropoff of the girls before dinner, he'd dashed back to the office, citing an important matter to discuss with Matt that couldn't be done over the phone. It seemed her hope for more quality time with him since he left his demanding job of police chief was not materializing. Now, it seemed, instead of leisurely evenings spent in each other's company, Ethan was working more than ever.

He entered the kitchen, welcomed by a chorus of "Daddy's back" from his daughters, and after he leaned in to kiss Hope on the cheek, he headed to the refrigerator, where he pulled out a beer. With the bottle cap removed, he returned to the table, only to find Bigelow waiting expectantly beside an empty chair, his soulful eyes craving attention.

"Hey there, little buddy." Ethan patted the pup's head and then Bigelow lowered himself beside the table, resting his head on outstretched paws. Ethan sat down and surveyed the wreaths in progress, then turned his attention back to the girls, kissing them both on the head. "How many are you making? I noticed the one by the fireplace."

With a soft chuckle, Hope replied, "Probably too many." She layered a red bow on top of a burlap bow and then attached a sprig of faux holly and a jingle bell to the wreath.

"You've certainly had a full day." He took a swig of his beer. "By the way, I spoke with Sam about the . . . incident after the funeral reception."

Hope tensed slightly as she nibbled on her lower lip. "He didn't sound pleased when I spoke with him earlier to brief him on the . . . situation." They both understood the importance of treading carefully around the kids, for anything overheard would inevitably be shared with Heather. The woman had a knack for prying information out of her children after they spent time with Hope and Ethan. Especially Hope.

Ethan nodded in agreement, his eyes reflecting his concerns. "I think the car chase part was where you and Claire may have pushed things a bit too far."

Hope leaned in, her voice soft and earnest. "It wasn't really a chase, we stopped when we realized . . ." Her voice trailed off when she noticed the girls were staring at her.

"I wish you hadn't engaged with him at all since we have no idea who he is or what his intentions were." Ethan set his beer bottle down and passed a spool of ribbon to Becca. "Here, honey." And with that move, his daughters returned their attention back to the project at hand.

"I didn't have a choice. I came out of the hall and there he was. Too bad I didn't find out who he was. Or what he's up to." Hope studied the final touch on the wreath. Perfect, she decided.

Ethan's chair scraped softly against the floor as he rose from his seat, and then he circled the table to join Hope. He leaned in close, whispering, "Perhaps we should save this discussion for later."

Hope couldn't resist shooting him a sidelong glance, suppressing the urge to remind him that he was the one who had started the conversation. "Sure, we can table this for now. That way I can tell you what I discovered while visiting Ruth earlier," she added, a mischievous smile playing at the corners of her lips as he pulled back. "It's rather shocking."

The incredulous expression that crossed Ethan's face only served to further amuse Hope, prompting her to burst into laughter.

"What's so funny?" Molly chimed in, reaching for more ribbon.

"Grown-ups are just silly," Becca said with a knowing grin.

Ethan, now the target of his daughters' teasing, pointed at his chest in mock protest. "We're silly?" He swooped down and playfully tickled Molly's belly, igniting a cascade of giggles. Bigelow jumped up and joined in the fun. The sound of his little toenails tapping on the pumpkin pine floorboards filled the air, while Princess expressed her displeasure by leaping from her perch and prancing out of the room. Meanwhile, Hope leaned back in her chair, taking in the heartwarming scene unfolding before her eyes.

• • •

The next morning, frenzied activity replaced the quiet wake-up Hope craved. She had her daily chores for the chickens, blog comments to review, a shower, and dressing for a meeting all before she could even dream of coffee. Liam, her general contractor overseeing the barn renovation, arrived on time and waited by his truck in her driveway. Her once small kitchen-office had blossomed into a spacious work area in the barn. It was surreal to think *Hope at Home*, born as a mere hobby in her New York City apartment just a few years ago, had come so far.

Liam wasted no time in presenting three change orders requiring approval before the remodeling continued. While the new workspace represented a sound investment, approving these changes meant dipping deeper into her budget, which was a tough decision. Joining the meeting was Drew's dad, architect Grey Adams, who reassured Hope she was making the right choices.

After signing the papers, she and Grey walked the interior of the barn and reviewed the changes and discussed the choices she had for the countertops and backsplash. The options were dizzying but she promised to have answers to him by the end of the month.

With the meeting ended and her cup of coffee poured, Hope spent a few minutes reviewing her to-do list for the rest of the day. Recipe development for her cookbook took priority, but a wreath and loaf of bread needed delivery. Checking the time, she decided to visit Drew's house before diving into the recipes.

Despite planning to visit Drew first thing after finishing her coffee, she got sidetracked by a phone call with her agent. Now, glancing at her watch, she saw she was running late. She hated being behind schedule. Hastily securing the festive wreath and cranberry apple bread in the SUV's cargo hold, she slid behind the wheel. Drew's house was conveniently near Maple Hill Farm, where she might need to grab more greens for one last wreath.

Upon reaching Fenn House, a picturesque Cape Cod residence with its fresh coat of pristine white paint and the shutters boasting an almost black-green shade, her eyes were drawn to the recently installed front door and the two elegant wall lantern sconces adorning the entrance. The house was taking shape beautifully.

She parked her vehicle beside a familiar sedan and another that she didn't recognize. She was happy that she'd have a few minutes to visit with Sally and wondered who Drew's other visitor was.

Balancing the wreath on one arm and clutching the loaf pan with the other, Hope made her way to the front door. As she approached, she noticed it was slightly ajar. Pushing it open wider, she stepped into the modest foyer, only to be met with a sudden uproar that sent her dropping the wreath to the floor and setting the loaf pan on the staircase. Without hesitation, she raced through the house, swiftly passing from the dining room to the under-construction family room.

There, she found Drew and his cousin, Susan Porter, in a state of frenzy. Susan wrestled with Trixie, who squirmed and yelped against her grip. Susan's gaze darted between the frantic puppy and the towering Christmas tree in the corner. Meanwhile, Drew's head swiveled in rapid motion, scanning the room.

At the doorway, Hope caught Drew's attention. He shot toward her, arms flailing.

"Get out of here! Now!"

"Drew, what's going on?" Hope asked, grabbing his arm.

He gestured toward the tree with a single, urgent gesture. "That."

Hope craned her neck, trying to get a clearer view. Then the tree shook.

"Oh, no," she breathed. "A squirrel?"

Drew sheepishly nodded. "It's been causing havoc ever since we brought the tree in."

"How on earth did it get in here?" Once she asked the question, the answer hit her. "Don't tell me you cut down this tree yourself?"

Drew nodded again. "I know. Rookie mistake."

"Drew!" Susan interjected, her voice tinged with exasperation as she struggled to contain Trixie, who was growing increasingly restless.

"I thought it would be cool," Drew said, enthusiasm in his voice.

Just then, the tree shuddered once more, prompting him to instinctively grasp Hope's arm, his grip surprisingly tight.

"Ow!" Hope cried, startled by the sudden squeeze.

Trixie let out another yelp, her bark echoing with a mixture of high-pitched urgency and whining distress.

"What are we going to do?" Susan inquired, her eyes wide with worry. "We can't let it run loose in the house. Should we call the police?"

"No need for them." Sally Merrifield intervened, breaking through Hope and Drew's embrace as she confidently strode into the room, clutching a blanket. "Here's the plan."

"Hey, that's my blanket," Drew protested.

"It's the only one I could find," Sally retorted. "You can wash it."

Drew shot Hope a horrified glance. "I'll just buy a new one."

"We need to coax him off the tree," Sally continued, undeterred. "Once he's on the ground, I'll toss the blanket over him, scoop him up, and take him outside." She ventured farther into the room. "Remember, he's probably more frightened than we are. Hope, take the dog. You have more experience with pups. Susan, you can open the back door ahead of me, so I can get this little guy out quickly."

"Me?" Susan appeared shocked.

"For heaven's sake, folks, it's just a squirrel," Sally said with a touch of exasperation.

"Who could bite and might have rabies," Drew retorted.

"They have treatments for rabies," Sally replied dryly. "Hope, it's great that you dropped by, but it's best if you stay back and keep Trixie under control."

"No problem," Hope concurred. After taking Trixie from Susan, she retreated a few steps to remain out of the fray. She held Trixie close to her chest and stroked the puppy's head, hoping to calm her.

The chaos escalated as Sally expertly maneuvered to corner the rogue squirrel. Drew and Susan squeaked nervously from the sidelines. It came as no surprise to Hope that Sally remained calm and composed; she was a true New Englander who did whatever it took to get the job done—whether it meant removing a squirrel from a house or anything else that came her way.

Carrying the bundled blanket with outstretched arms, Sally rushed through the family room with Susan jogging ahead of her.

"I will never ever cut down a tree again," Drew declared with a relieved breath after they watched Sally's daring squirrel rescue. "In fact, I'm going to order an artificial one now, so I'll be well-prepared for next year."

"Good idea," Hope chimed in as she handed off Trixie to him. "But look on the bright side, you've got your very first hilarious story about your first Christmas in Fenn House that you can tell year after year."

He shot her an incredulous glance.

"Too soon?"

Drew nodded. He kissed Trixie on the top of her head and made cooing sounds to help soothe her.

"How about a slice of homemade cranberry apple bread? It's out in the foyer along with a wreath I made for your front door," she said.

"Bless you," Drew said. "I need something to eat."

When Sally returned from releasing the squirrel outside, she announced she had to get back to the inn but was looking forward to a loaf of the delicious-smelling bread soon. Subtlety was never her strong suit. Susan also made her exit. She'd only come by to drop off two poinsettias for Drew and had to get back home.

"Looks like it's just the two of us," Drew said as he led Hope into the kitchen. "Let me settle this one in her crate. She needs a nap."

"That was a lot of excitement." Hope dashed out to the foyer and snatched the loaf of bread from the bottom step of the staircase. She returned to the kitchen and set the bread on the counter. As she pulled a serrated knife from the wooden block on the counter, Drew returned to the kitchen.

"While I make the coffee and you slice that delicious-looking bread, I'll tell you what I uncovered about Mitty." Drew filled the coffee maker's carafe with water.

"About his criminal past?" Hope asked.

"Oh, yeah." Drew nodded. "And the ties he had with a guy who died in prison."

Chapter Ten

Hope's knife slicing through the loaf of bread came to a sudden halt as her eyes widened with disbelief. She found herself at a loss for words once again, her heart racing as Drew dropped the bombshell.

"Are you talking about Denny Beyer? He's dead?" she asked.

Drew's eyebrows shot up in surprise as he poured water into the single-serve coffee maker. "Wait. How do you know?"

Gathering her thoughts, Hope hurried to explain, her movements quick as she retrieved her cell phone from her tote. "I went to see Ruth, and she showed me a folder she found with newspaper clippings," she said, tapping on her phone screen to access the photos. "I took pictures."

Joining her in the middle of the kitchen, Drew listened intently as Hope swiped through the images. "Mitty kept clippings about a robbery," she explained, her voice urgent as she relayed what she had discovered. "He had been in trouble with the law before he met Ruth." She pointed out the date of the jewelry store robbery, her mind racing with connections. "And look, it coincides with the time period when Mitty and Ruth were struggling with debt. Then suddenly, all the bills were paid off, according to Ruth."

"Interesting. Denny also had a few run-ins with the law before he got caught for the robbery. He was the only one ever caught and convicted for the jewelry store heist," Drew declared as he returned to the coffee maker.

Hope dropped her phone back into her tote. "What else did you learn?"

"Not a lot." Drew eyed the loaf with the desperation of a castaway spotting land. "Mind finishing slicing the bread? Starving here. I cut down a tree, you know."

Hope rolled her eyes and then returned to slicing the bread. As she placed two thick slices on a plate, she couldn't help but ask, "How did Denny Beyer die?"

Drew prepared the coffee and carried the two mugs to the table.

Seated, he grabbed a slice of bread, his expression darkening as he spoke. "He was killed in a fight just weeks before his release."

Seated across from Drew, Hope curled her fingers around her steaming mug of coffee. "How horrible. I wonder if Mitty ever visited him."

Drew shrugged, his gaze fixed on his mug. "It's hard to imagine that Mitty was one of the three robbers."

Hope set her mug down, her eyes narrowing with suspicion. "What I wonder is why Denny never turned on Mitty. He probably was offered some kind of deal in exchange for the name of his accomplices."

"Looks like Denny Beyer wasn't a rat," Drew mused as he took a sip of his coffee. "I wonder who the third person was."

One person immediately sprang to Hope's mind. "Do you think it's the guy I've been seeing around town? The one who showed up after Mitty's funeral?"

"Anything is possible. Why do you think he would show up now?"

"To kill Mitty?"

Drew raised an eyebrow. "Yeah, but why? And why now?"

Hope contemplated the possibilities. "Maybe there's something robber number three is looking for, and that's why he's in Jefferson."

"First, we don't know for sure if this stranger is robber number three," Drew cautioned. "And you said you think Mitty used the money to pay off all the bills, including the house payment. What do you think the third robber would be looking for?"

"Maybe Mitty didn't spend all the money. Maybe he has some jewelry that they didn't fence. Maybe the third robber is tying up loose ends."

Drew's eyes widened, a revelation dawning on him. "Another possibility is that Mitty could have been planning to confess his crime."

"And robber number three found out about Mitty's plan," Hope added. "If Mitty confessed, then he probably would have revealed who the third person was."

"So, he came to town to make sure Mitty didn't talk to the police."

"Of course. That makes sense," Hope said.

After swallowing his bite of bread, Drew jumped up to refill his coffee. As the coffee brewed, he turned back to Hope with determination in his eyes. "How are we going to prove this theory?"

With the coffee maker's soft gurgling in the background, Hope leaned back, sipping her coffee. "I'll figure something out."

• • •

Hope's mind was flooded with unanswered questions as she walked out of her garage after parking her Explorer. Had Mitty been involved with the jewelry store robbery? Had he stashed away stolen goods to save for another rainy day? Had he been considering confessing? Ruth seemed clueless, and Hope believed her. Maybe Brody or Nora knew something. It made sense for him to confide in those closest to him, those whose lives would have been impacted by the revelation of his criminal activity. Brody had just taken over the family business, where reputation meant everything, while Nora would have faced the public scrutiny of being married to a criminal. Now a new question lingered: How far would either of them have gone to keep Mitty's past hidden?

Hope knew that before diving headfirst into finding answers, she needed a solid plan. But first, she had work to do. Bills for the barn renovation kept pouring in and demanding her attention. There was also the cookbook, a longtime dream that was becoming a reality. She reassured herself that this busy phase would pass once she completed the recipe development.

As she entered her home, she took off her jacket and set down her tote, then made her way to the family room. There, she was greeted by the sight of her Christmas tree. Its towering presence filled the room, decorated with twinkling lights and cherished ornaments. It was a reminder that she had everything she'd ever wanted and that even in the darkness of murder, there was still Christmas magic. She just had to believe.

Bigelow's low woof pulled Hope's gaze from the tree. "Sorry, boy," she murmured, padding across the room to the kitchen. She grabbed a homemade pumpkin mini-donut, one of his favorites thanks to its dog-friendly peanut butter and pumpkin puree, and offered it to him. Tail wagging, Bigelow devoured the treat and settled contentedly by the fireplace as Hope retrieved her laptop and sat at the dining table.

She was determined to finish editing an upcoming blog post, complete a couple administrative tasks, and review the video she had shot the previous week. She set a timer, diving into her work with unwavering concentration. In between her focused twenty-minute work sessions, she took brief breaks to let Bigelow out and back in, engaged in playtime with Princess, who loved pouncing on her catnip mouse, and refilled her water bottle.

During one break, she couldn't resist checking her social media—a decision she instantly regretted.

Quite a swing food blogger Hope Early has.

The comment left her bewildered. Until she scrolled down to the photo.

The photo captured her with a giant candy cane in mid-swing at the stranger, also known as potential robber number three, and it made her cringe.

The alarming number of likes and shares sent a wave of dread coursing through her.

"Good grief," she muttered to herself. "This is going viral."

She couldn't believe her bad luck. Once again, she found herself trapped in an embarrassing moment caught on camera by some random smartphone-wielding bystander. Sighing heavily, she dropped her head into her hands, momentarily giving in to a wave of self-pity. Another potential PR disaster. Another awkward phone call to her agent. But this time, she had a sliver of redemption. This time, she had a solid excuse for wielding the candy cane—it was an act of self-defense.

Taking a deep breath, Hope reached for her phone and braced herself for the uncomfortable conversation with her agent. However, just as she was about to dial, a glimmer of hope emerged. There was a silver lining in this looming catastrophe. Not only was she captured in the photo, but so was the mysterious stranger who had invaded her personal space. The police would be able to hunt him down and put an end to this nightmare.

She had to show Detective Reid the video.

After rushing to shut off her computer, she was heading out of her house when her phone rang. The ringtone was Claire's.

"I can't talk now," Hope said as she slipped on her jacket. "I'm heading to the police department."

Claire's response was laughter. Deep belly laughter.

"You saw the video." Hope pulled the mudroom door closed behind her. "You can stop laughing now."

"I . . . I'll try." Claire got quiet for a moment and Hope suspected her sister was trying to compose herself.

"Did you call just to laugh at me?"

"No. The video just came up as I was making the call. It's about Nora. I just found out she's returned to work. I find that a bit suspicious. The woman just buried her husband."

Hope's steps hesitated. "Everyone deals with grief differently."

"You're telling me you don't think there's anything suspicious about her behavior?"

"I'm trying not to jump to conclusions." Hope entered her garage. "Look, I have to go. Thanks for letting me know about Nora." She disconnected the call and got into her vehicle.

• • •

On the drive to the police department, she made a last-minute decision to take a detour to Town Hall. Maybe there was a chance Nora could identify the stranger. Then she could tell Reid who he was looking for.

Inside the two-story building, Hope strode purposefully along the corridor as she made her way to the Economic and Community Development office. She knocked on the open door, announcing her presence as she stepped inside. Nora, the deputy director of ECD, looked up from her desk.

Clad in a dark gray sweater dress, Nora met Hope's unexpected entrance with a mixture of exhaustion, evident in the dark circles beneath her eyes, and an overall air of sadness. She furrowed her brow as she asked, "Hope, what are you doing here?"

"I'm on my way to the police department, and I wanted to stop by to talk to you." Hope stepped farther into the office. "Yesterday, I paid a visit to Ruth, and she showed me a folder she'd found in an old chest. It wasn't hers, so it must have belonged to Mitty. Inside, there were newspaper clippings about a jewelry store robbery."

Nora's response was a mix of confusion and irritation. "I'm sorry, I don't have time to discuss newspaper clippings. I really need to get back to work."

Undeterred, Hope continued. "Nora, aren't you even a bit curious about why Mitty had those newspaper clippings about a robbery? I don't think we're talking about hoarding old articles. There must have been a reason why he kept them."

Nora shook her head and shrugged simultaneously, her eyes wide with uncertainty, clearly at a loss for words.

"The robbery happened at the same time Ruth was battling cancer. Three robbers were involved, but only one was caught and convicted. He died in prison. His name was Denny Beyer. He and Mitty had stolen cars together years before."

"What's your point?"

"My point is what if Mitty was involved in that robbery?"

"That's absurd," Nora said.

"Is it?" Hope's gaze locked on to Nora's, whose nonchalant reaction seemed odd. "You don't seem surprised by this news . . . because you knew about his criminal past?"

"Of course I did. We didn't keep secrets from each other."

"He never mentioned Denny Beyer?"

Nora's jaw tightened. "No."

Hope pulled her phone from her tote, displaying a photo. "Have you seen this man before?"

"No." Nora rose, her composure faltering. "I don't appreciate being interrogated."

"I'm not interrogating you, Nora."

"Could have fooled me."

"I'm just trying to find out who killed your husband."

"*My* husband's murder is none of your concern." A touch of bitterness had crept into Nora's voice. "I should have never asked you to help. The police are investigating."

"Nora, I discovered his body."

"And *I* became a widow moments later," she whispered.

Hope took a deep, resolute breath. This wasn't going as she'd hoped.

"It's not my intention to upset you," Hope said, her voice steady. "I'm trying to find answers that will lead us to the person responsible for Mitty's death."

Nora's eyes narrowed, her suspicion apparent. "It seems more like you're attempting to ensure Mitty's killer goes unpunished. The police have made an arrest. But you're going out of your way to find another suspect? Another motive? Tell me, is it just a coincidence that your boyfriend happens to work for Ralph's lawyer?"

Hope felt a flicker of defensiveness at the accusation.

"I had no part in Ralph hiring Matt. I wasn't even aware until afterward. Do you really think I'd conspire to clear a murderer?"

"Hope Early." Suddenly, a grating voice pierced through the tension, causing Hope to snap her head around. Maretta Kingston, with her abrasive tone, barged into the office from the hallway and positioned herself in front of Nora's desk. "Quite a scene you made yesterday."

"What in the world are you talking about, Maretta?" Nora asked.

Maretta raised a slender eyebrow, her voice dripping with disbelief. "You haven't seen it? Well, in that case, you must be the last soul on Earth who hasn't." She turned her gaze toward Hope. "I must say, I'm utterly flabbergasted by the spectacle you created with that candy cane at the church, no less. What on earth were you thinking?"

"I was thinking I needed to protect myself," Hope replied. "I warned that man to stay back, but he didn't listen. While I regret that the incident was caught on camera, it provides me with evidence to show Detective Reid."

Maretta appeared baffled. "Evidence? What are you talking about?"

"I spotted that man near the crime scene. He was there when Mitty met his tragic end. Who's to say he's not the real killer?"

Nora sank into her chair, disbelief washing over her. "Wait, you mean the police arrested the wrong person? Mitty's murderer is still out there, roaming the town?"

Maretta quickly moved toward Nora, her protective instinct kicking in. "Look what you've done now! Hope, why can't you let the police handle this? Leave well enough alone." As tears welled up in Nora's eyes, Maretta gestured for Hope to leave.

Nora's voice trembled as she implored, "You should go, Hope." She reached for a tissue, visibly shaken.

With a resigned nod, Hope exited the office, glancing back to see Nora wiping away tears and Maretta whispering something indiscernible. She couldn't help but imagine the mayor's unflattering thoughts about her. Pushing aside those unhelpful assumptions, she hurriedly headed for the exit.

"Hope! Wait up!" Maretta's urgent voice echoed through the corridor, catching Hope off guard.

Hope, realizing her escape had been short-lived, let out a sigh. She gathered her composure and turned to face the older woman, who breezed down the hall in her flowing maxi skirt.

"Do you truly believe that man you had that altercation with could have killed Mitty?" Maretta asked as she came to a stop.

Hope shrugged. "I can't say for certain, but his behavior is suspicious. I've spotted him around town, and I even saw him lurking outside Nora's house the day after the murder."

"He then showed up at the funeral? Nora might be in danger! Why didn't you detain him and call the police?" Maretta's concern was evident in her voice.

"How exactly was I supposed to detain him?" Hope asked.

Maretta crossed her arms, looking slightly disappointed. "Well, perhaps if you'd wielded that candy cane with more finesse, you could've at least knocked him down."

"Thanks for the tip. I'll work on my candy cane combat skills in my spare time," Hope remarked sarcastically.

Maretta scowled. "No need for snark, young lady." She unfolded her arms. "You're going to fill Detective Reid in on all of this, correct?"

Hope nodded. "He already knows about what happened yesterday, but I'm going to show him the video. Although, I suspect he's probably seen it already, like everyone else."

"Good. Good. In the meantime, I'll ensure Nora isn't left alone."

With that, she pivoted and strode off purposefully.

Hope turned around and continued her departure from Town Hall, her mind brimming with the so many questions she was certain Detective Reid wouldn't answer.

• • •

Disappointment gnawed at Hope as she left the police department. Detective Reid was out, not due back for another thirty minutes. The receptionist offered a choice: wait in the sterile lobby or return later. Hope chose the latter.

Stepping onto Main Street, she pulled out her phone, scanning her to-do list for a quick errand. Nothing local fit the bill, and the mall was too far for a round trip. Glancing up, her gaze landed on the Coffee Clique's inviting awning. Coffee. Perfect. Her pace quickened, and minutes later she emerged, a steaming cup of hazelnut latte warming her hands.

A quick check of her watch revealed she had time to spare before she had to head back to the police department. With no particular destination in mind, she strolled along Main Street at a leisurely pace, sipping her coffee and nodding to familiar faces that crossed her path. The storefront displays beckoned to her, and she couldn't resist a bit of indulgent window-shopping. Christmas was just around the corner, and she still had a few gifts she needed to purchase.

As she walked and window-shopped, her thoughts were consumed with plans for Christmas and beyond. She wondered if she and Ethan would find an opportunity to escape together for a few days after the new year. Lately, they hadn't had much quality alone time. Just as she began compiling a list of potential destinations, her path led her to the Antique Alcove. Suddenly, a bone-chilling scream erupted from within, causing her to come to an abrupt halt.

Without hesitation, she flung open the door and dashed inside, only to be greeted by a heart-stopping sight. Alena, standing distraught in the center of the shop, quaked violently while pointing a shaky finger at the floor.

There, sprawled out before her, was the lifeless body of a man, his head surrounded by a pool of blood.

Chapter Eleven

Hope tore her gaze from the man on the floor and back to Alena. On an initial inspection, the young woman looked unharmed. And terrified. Who could blame her? There was a person lying on the floor who looked very much dead.

He also looked very much like the man Hope had confronted at the church and took a swing at with a giant candy cane.

What on earth was he doing in the antique shop?

"I . . . I . . . came out from the back room and there he . . . what happened?" Alena's voice shook as much as her body.

"You tell me," Hope murmured, her gaze fixed on the motionless figure. Despite the eerie stillness, she had to confirm whether he was alive or not. A tremor ran through her as she cautiously lowered herself to the floor. Heart pounding, she tentatively extended two fingers to his neck.

No pulse. He was gone.

"Is he . . . dead?" Alena's voice broke the silence.

Hope nodded as she withdrew her hand from the man's neck. That's when she noticed a menacing metal object nearby, stained with what looked like blood. A chill ran down her spine.

"What is that?" Hope asked.

"A mace. It's a Medieval weapon used in warfare. We have several Medieval objects. They're quite collectible. Is that what was used to . . ."

"To kill him? Possibly." Hope stood up. "There appears to be blood on the mace."

"I didn't do it, I swear," Alena declared, raising her hands.

"I'm not accusing you. But you will need to tell the police everything that happened from the moment this man walked into your shop. We have to call them." Hope dug into her tote, and just as she pulled out her phone, Lexi burst into the shop.

"Is everything okay? I saw you run in here, Hope . . . oh, my goodness." Lexi stopped in her tracks the moment she saw the man on the floor. "What happened?" She looked to Hope in disbelief.

"I only went back there for a minute to call Brody to tell him I made a deal." Alena dropped her head into her hands.

"What kind of deal? With him?" Hope asked. "Do you know his name?"

With tear-stained cheeks and smudged mascara, Alena looked up at Hope and Lexi, her voice trembling with fear. "Gus Wharton. He was fine just a few minutes ago." She gestured toward an antique-looking clock perched atop the sales counter. "He brought this with him."

Lexi shivered, wrapping her coat tighter around herself, her petite frame shrinking as she absorbed the gravity of Alena's words. "Another murder?" she whispered.

"Alena, when you left to call Brody, was anyone else in the shop?" Hope asked, her voice steady but firm.

Alena shook her head, her eyes downcast.

"And you didn't hear anything unusual while you were talking with Brody on the phone?" Lexi pressed, her voice tinged with disbelief and fear.

Again, Alena shook her head.

Hope glanced at the mace and then at Gus Wharton. She couldn't shake the image of the impact and imagined the pain he must have felt. He must have screamed when he was assaulted. How could Alena not have heard that or him fall? For now, she kept the questions to herself. Their priority was to get the police there. She dialed 911 on her phone and reported the incident to the dispatcher. After ending the call, she instructed Alena and Lexi not to touch anything.

Within minutes, Officer Roberts arrived on the scene and immediately removed Hope and Lexi from the antique shop. Hope wasn't sure where Lexi was moved to, but she was ushered into the backseat of the officer's patrol car. Alena remained in the shop and was admittedly confused about being separated from Hope and Lexi. Hope, however, was a seasoned player in the separation game—she knew the drill. The officer's priority was to make sure that the three of them would not influence each other when giving their statements.

Hope waited patiently in the patrol car. When Officer Roberts returned, he slid into the driver's seat and took her statement. He spoke sparingly. Instead, he nodded and scribbled notes. Once they were finished, he said, "You can go home, Hope. But you'll need to come to the police station tomorrow morning to give a formal statement."

Relieved to be done for now, Hope exited the vehicle. But instead of going to the police department to see if Detective Reid had returned, she lingered outside the antique shop, watching as the police meticulously processed the crime scene. A crowd of curious onlookers had gathered, drawn by the blaring sirens. Whispered theories swirled through the huddled group.

"Officer Roberts gave me the all-clear," Lexi announced, joining Hope with a weary expression. "I don't know how you handle it."

"Handle what?" Hope inquired, turning her attention to Lexi.

"You know, stumbling upon dead bodies," Lexi confessed, her voice tinged with unease. "After what happened today, I hope I never have to experience it again."

"Believe me, I feel the same way," Hope admitted. Despite encountering her fair share of corpses, she found the experience unsettling every time. "It's something I hope to never get used to."

Lexi offered a weary smile. "I'm going to head home and drink some wine." With that, she turned and disappeared down the driveway leading to the communal parking lot behind the storefronts.

Suddenly, a commotion seized Hope's attention. Nora tore up the street, panic contorting her face. She reached the perimeter of the crime scene, marked by yellow tape, but an officer held her back despite her pleas to speak with her daughter.

Hope wove her way through the crowd, coming up beside Nora. "They're still investigating so they won't let you in."

"She's my daughter! I demand to see her. If they won't let me in, I'll call Maretta. They have to listen to her." Nora was opening her purse.

"No, they won't. They have a specific protocol to follow when investigating a crime scene." Hope didn't want the situation to escalate and end up having Nora charged with interfering with a police investigation. "I spoke with Alena and she's okay. She wasn't hurt."

"Thank goodness." Nora placed a hand over her heart. "She called and said there was a murder . . . I can't believe this is happening. First Mitty and now this, with Alena present. Hope, my family is in danger."

"From what Alena told me, it seemed like the killer waited for Alena to leave the front of the shop," Hope said. "It appears she wasn't the intended target."

"Are you certain of that?"

"Not entirely," Hope conceded.

"Maybe the killer intended to harm Alena, but the customer, or whoever he was, got in the way." Nora gazed at the white clapboard building. "I wish Mitty had installed security cameras. It had been on his to-do list for ages."

Hope considered Nora's words. "If someone is indeed targeting your family, can you think of anyone who might have a motive?" This time, she was certain that Ralph Lang was not involved. As far as she knew, he was still in police custody.

Nora's brow furrowed as she pondered Hope's question, her expression growing more serious by the second. Then, with a slow shake of her head, she responded, "If I knew anything, I would have immediately reported it to the authorities."

"Does the name Stan Baby mean anything to you?" A nagging suspicion lingered in her mind, wondering if the deceased man could be the mysterious Stan Baby who had called Alena. She couldn't shake the feeling that the name Gus Wharton might not be real.

Nora's reaction was a mixture of incredulity and confusion. "Stan Baby? Seriously? What a preposterous nickname. Where did you come across it?" she inquired, her interest apparently aroused.

Hope leaned in closer, her voice tinged with intrigue. "I noticed a call on Alena's phone the day after Mitty's death. It was from someone using that name. The day before, I overheard her speaking to someone at the tree lot about the antique shop and the possibility of her taking it over."

"But there's never been any plan for her to take over. She and Brody are meant to work together as partners." Nora paused, her eyes wide as realization washed over her. "Could it possibly be . . . Stanley Burrows Jr.?"

Hope was perplexed. "Who's he?"

"His family owns a prestigious antiques business with locations in both Litchfield and Greenwich. Could they somehow be involved?" Nora questioned, a sense of urgency creeping into her voice.

"Mom!" Alena's voice rang out in the chilled air as she broke into a run from the front door of the antique shop. "It was horrible. Absolutely horrible," she said, throwing herself into Nora's embrace.

"I'm so relieved you're not hurt." Nora held her daughter tightly, patting her head. "I'm so sorry you had to experience something like that."

Alena pulled back from her mother's hold. She wiped her eyes with a tissue and did her best to compose herself. "I'll be okay," she said. "I'm grateful that Hope came in. She checked his pulse and called the police. Thank you."

"I'm sure finding Mr. Wharton's body was a shock. Had he been in the shop before?" Hope asked.

Alena shook her head.

"Because I saw him yesterday only a few feet away from here," Hope said. "I also saw him outside your house, Nora, the day after Mitty's death. And at the church on the day of the funeral. He's the man in the photo I showed you."

Nora and Alena looked at each other, both perplexed.

Hope believed neither woman knew Gus Wharton.

"The police said I could go home," Alena said.

"You're coming to my house and staying the night. I'm not letting you out of my sight until the killer is caught," Nora said.

Alena looked as if she was about to argue but she acquiesced and simply murmured, "Okay, Mom."

"Just one thing before you leave, Alena. Nora and I were just talking about Stan Barlow Jr. He's your boyfriend, correct?"

"What? How do you know?" Alena asked.

"Since when?" Nora demanded.

"It's been a few months," Alena admitted. "He's a great guy, Mom. Stan wants to break free from his family's control and open his own shop. We've been talking, and we think it would be great if he could become a part of running the Antique Alcove." All the distress from finding a lifeless body had been replaced with the look of a young girl in love with a boy.

"Does Brody know about that?" Hope asked.

"Well, that's a discussion for another day. For now, we're going home." Nora grabbed her daughter's hand. "Goodbye, Hope." She and Alena walked away.

Hope stepped back, removing herself from the crowd, where speculation ran rampant among the onlookers and she couldn't help but do some of her own. From what she overheard at the tree lot, it hadn't sounded as if Stan Jr. would have been content with just being a part of the Fitzgerald family business, being partners with Brody. If he planned on taking over the antiques business, then he had a motive to kill Mitty. But what about Gus?

Another thought settled in her brain, and she wished it hadn't because it was a horrible thought.

Alena and Stan Jr. could have conspired to commit both Mitty's and Gus Wharton's murders. Perhaps Alena orchestrated an alibi by being on the phone with Brody while Stan Jr. carried out the latest killing. But the question still lingered of what motive they had to kill the stranger.

Knowing about Mitty's criminal history, particularly the jewelry store robbery, they might have believed he had hidden valuable jewels. Suspecting that Gus Wharton was searching for them, they could have eliminated him to prevent any claims to the stolen goods. Hope paused, her mind grappling with the implications of her theory. It was all based on circumstantial evidence, with nothing concrete to support it. If the police had suspected Alena's involvement in Gus Wharton's death, they would have detained her for further questioning. Yet, they had let her go. Maybe it was time for Hope to follow suit and head home.

• • •

Once back in the comfort of her home with a hot cup of tea in hand, Hope called Ethan. She wasted no time in telling him what she'd walked in on at the Antique Alcove. A heavy silence settled on the line, and Hope could almost hear Ethan's unspoken thoughts: *Not again.*

"Are you okay?" Ethan's voice broke through the silence and it was filled with concern.

Hope managed a small smile, despite the weight of the situation. "I'm holding up," she reassured him. Then, she shared the details of the victim and her suspicions about the murder weapon. Although she expressed doubts about Alena's claim of not hearing anything during the incident, she chose to keep her theory about Alena and Stan Jr. conspiring together to kill Gus Wharton to herself. However, she did confess she was exhausted. The day's events had taken their toll.

Being the great guy he was, Ethan suggested they go out for dinner, and she didn't hesitate to say yes. Now they were seated at a table for two at Donnelly's Steak House with menus. The restaurant had been a fixture in Jefferson since Hope's childhood and where she and Ethan had their first date.

Ethan set his menu aside confidently and declared, "I already know what I'm having."

Hope peered over the top of her menu. "Let me guess," she teased, "prime rib with a baked potato and green beans?"

He grinned. "You know me too well. What about you?"

She scanned the menu, her mouth watering at the array of tempting dishes. "I think I'll have a New York strip steak with wild rice," she said, closing the menu with a satisfied sigh. She leaned back into the chair and allowed every muscle in her body to relax as she soaked up the restaurant's atmosphere. It had been a long time since she and Ethan had a date night. Though, considering the circumstances, it wasn't the best night for romance. Her thoughts were consumed by theories about the murders, and she couldn't shake the intermittent flashbacks of discovering Gus Wharton's body.

"You okay, babe?" Ethan's concern was evident in his voice as he reached across the table, gently covering her hand with his own. "You seem to have drifted off for a moment."

"There's a lot on my mind."

"We can go home if you'd like," he offered.

"And miss getting my delicious steak? Not a chance," she replied with a grin, giving his hand a reassuring squeeze before letting go. "I'm going to run to the restroom really quick. I'll be back before you miss me."

She stood and, as she passed by Ethan on her way to the restrooms, he reached for her hand, placing a soft kiss on its back.

"I'll be waiting," he said, his eyes filled with warmth.

Hope's heart swelled with happiness, and she continued her stroll through the dining room, her memories entwined with this familiar place, a locale that had been part of her life since her earliest days, where her family had celebrated their most significant milestones.

As Hope ventured out into the bustling front of the steak house, the warm aroma of sizzling meats enveloped her senses, and the low hum of patrons filled the air with the promise of hearty meals and good company. Her eyes scanned the group of patrons waiting for a table and found a familiar face. She spotted Brody hunched over on a rustic bench near the front door, his shoulders slumped and his face obscured by a disheveled shock of hair. His hands were clenched tightly together. She could only imagine the kind of day he'd endured after that fateful call with Alena.

Approaching him with a sympathetic smile, Hope offered a friendly, "Hey, Brody."

Brody's head snapped up, his eyes widening in surprise at the sight of Hope. He quickly straightened up, his hands unfurling from their tense grip. "Hope, I didn't expect to see you here. I'm just waiting for a to-go order."

"I wasn't expecting to be here either. It's been a rough day. How is Alena doing?" Hope joined him on the bench. "When she left the shop, she was still pretty shaken up."

Brody sighed, his voice heavy with remorse. "Yeah, it's hard to believe that someone lost their life in our shop. You know, I've been meaning to install security cameras for months. I wish I had done that sooner."

"Having security footage would have been helpful for the police," Hope said.

"Nora mentioned something," Brody continued, his expression thoughtful. "She thinks the dead guy was stalking our family. I'm not too sure about that, though."

"Why not?"

"I think the dead guy was just trying to sell that clock," Brody explained. "He approached me after the funeral reception, claiming he and my dad had made a deal months ago. He wanted to bring the clock to the shop, but I turned him down."

"How come?"

"I can't quite put my finger on it. There was just something off about him. If nothing else, I've learned to trust my instincts."

Hope couldn't help but ask, "Do you think he might have been connected to your dad's past?"

"What are you talking about, Hope?" His tone sharpened as he squared his shoulders.

"I know your dad had a criminal record," Hope explained, her voice calm despite the tension that was building. "And that one of his colleagues went to prison for a jewelry store robbery. Could Gus Wharton be someone from that time in your dad's life?"

"Hope?" Ethan's voice interrupted. "I thought you were going to the restroom."

Her head whipped up, her heart racing in her chest at the sight of Ethan standing there with his arms crossed. "Uh-oh," she muttered.

"Look, I don't know what you're doing, but I won't have you badmouthing my dad." Brody's jaw clenched tight, his skin flushing a deep red. "Whatever his past was, he was a good father!" With that, Brody bolted to his feet and stormed out of the restaurant, leaving Hope and Ethan in stunned silence.

Ethan, though displeased, took Brody's vacated spot on the bench and draped his arm over Hope's shoulders. "So, is that how you conduct your interviews?" he asked, a hint of amusement in his voice.

She rolled her eyes and dropped her head onto his shoulder. "Guess I need to work on my technique."

Chapter Twelve

As the crisp morning air surrounded her, Hope stood outside her red barn with her gaze fixed upward on Ethan. He was hanging the enormous wreath she had custom-made from the hayloft.

Golden rays of sunlight filtered through the snowy branches, casting a soft glow over the winter landscape. The barn stood proud against the backdrop of her three-acre property, its weathered wood adorned with a dusting of snow, creating a picturesque scene straight out of a holiday card. Hope couldn't help but smile as she admired Ethan's handiwork, knowing the festive wreath would be a heartwarming sight for anyone passing by her home on the quiet road.

It had been the tradition since she moved back to Jefferson that Ethan hung the wreath. That morning, he stopped by on his way to take his girls to school and went straight to the barn to take care of the chore.

Hope, cradling Poppy in her arms, gave a thumb-up. Her eyes met his through the small hayloft opening, and a smile bloomed on his face. He pulled back, shutting the door with a soft click, and vanished momentarily. Then he emerged from the building, his breath forming a fleeting cloud in the cold morning air.

"How does it look?" he inquired, rubbing his hands together to ward off the morning chill. The overnight temperature drop had left a frosty veil over the surroundings, and the day seemed reluctant to warm up. "What's your verdict, Poppy?" he added, giving the chicken's head a gentle pat.

Hope smiled. While she loved all her chickens, Poppy had a special place in her heart. She couldn't imagine her home or her life without the sweet bird.

"I think Poppy approves. What about you?" Ethan's gaze locked with Hope's, searching for her reaction. When she remained silent, he furrowed his brow. "Hey, what's wrong, babe?"

Hope exhaled heavily, her shoulders sagging with the weight of her thoughts. "It's perfect. It's just . . . I don't know. It feels like the spirit of

Christmas is slipping away, no matter how many decorations I put up or cookies I bake." Seeking comfort, she turned to Ethan, finding solace in his dark eyes. With gentle strokes, she caressed Poppy's feathers, receiving soft clucks in return. "Everything is changing. Mitty was murdered while dressed as Santa. For heaven's sake, we were out caroling and children were there. And then yesterday . . . What kind of world do we live in?"

"An uncertain world, where evil has always existed," Ethan began, his arm encircling Hope's shoulders, drawing her close. "We can't let it dictate our lives. We can't allow change to paralyze us either. We have to believe in the good and find joy not only during the holidays but in the everyday."

Suddenly, the lively laughter of Molly and Becca caught their attention. The girls bounded toward them, their arms flailing in playful excitement, their vibrant mittens glinting in the sunlight. Bigelow joined in the chase, his tail wagging exuberantly as he romped through the snow.

"Life is changing, and I couldn't be happier about it," Ethan said, giving Hope a reassuring squeeze. "I think it's time for a cookie break."

A smile spread across Hope's face as a sense of contentment and warmth washed over her. "I happen to have a fresh batch cooling in the kitchen," she replied.

After handing out warm gingerbread cookies, Hope waved goodbye to Ethan's rumbling truck as it drove away. She then dashed back into her house. With one more Christmas task down, she sprinted upstairs, shedding her cozy sweats for an outfit more appropriate for the police station. She was scheduled to meet with Detective Reid to go over and finalize her statement regarding yesterday's murder. It would also be her chance to ask the questions that had been nagging at her, though she knew she might have to brace herself for the possibility of leaving without any answers.

• • •

Seated behind his desk, Detective Reid reviewed the statement Hope had just signed, then set the paper down. Removing his reading glasses, he reclined in his chair, fingers drumming lightly on the armrest.

"I don't know how you do it, Hope," he remarked wryly. "It's like you have a sixth sense for crime scenes."

"I'm not sure what to call it, but I don't exactly enjoy it." Leaning forward, Hope scanned Reid's face, searching for any hint of openness that might lead to him sharing information about the murders. She saw none. He seemed closed off. But that wouldn't stop her from asking. "Can you tell me if you found any connection between Gus Wharton and Mitty?"

Reid considered her request, and she anticipated him flat-out refusing. This prompted her to quickly craft a rebuttal, explaining why he should share the information. But before she could utter a word, he leaned forward, revealing a hint of openness. It appeared their relationship was shifting. He'd said in the past that he admired how Hope managed to get people to talk to her. It seemed that skill had worked on the detective himself.

"I guess there's no harm," Reid said, his tone guarded. "Mr. Wharton had a criminal record. I didn't find a connection between the two men. However, I found one between Wharton and Denny Beyer."

"You're not going to tell me the connection, are you?"

He shook his head, maintaining his professional disposition. Hope felt a twinge of frustration but persisted. "Any idea why Gus Wharton was in Jefferson?"

"Not at this time. And honestly, if I knew, I wouldn't be able to tell you. After all, this is an ongoing investigation, and you're a civilian."

"Are you going to follow up on Stan Barlow Jr.?" While reviewing her statement, Hope filled Reid in on the conversation she overheard between Stan and Alena at the tree lot days earlier. Reid seemed interested enough to make notes about it.

"I'll look into every lead that comes my way. Even from you," he quipped.

A slight smile tugged at the corner of her lips. "Thanks, I guess." She gathered her things as she stood. "I have one more question. Have you had a chance to authenticate the clock Wharton brought into the shop?"

"It's in evidence," Reid said, sliding Hope's statement into a folder. Okay, that was a non-answer, which she should have expected.

"Gus Wharton didn't strike me as an antiques collector," Hope said thoughtfully. "So, if the clock is truly an antique, where did he get it from? Or where did he steal it from?" Then a thought popped into her head. "Maybe he got it from Stan Barlow Jr.! Maybe Brody was the intended victim, but when he refused to meet with Wharton about the clock, they arranged for Wharton to go to the shop and lure him there!"

Reid's eyes narrowed. "How do you know Gus Wharton spoke with Brody?"

"He told me last night," Hope said. "I ran into him at Donnelly's Steak House."

Reid sighed and rubbed his temples. "This case is getting more complicated by the minute. Especially when I have you running a shadow investigation."

"That's not what I'm doing."

"Really?" Reid gave her an expectant look, his arms thrown wide open. "Then what do you call it?"

She shrugged. "I can't help it if people talk to me."

"And you can't help but be naturally curious, right?" he countered.

"Exactly." At least they agreed on something.

"Just don't forget that your curiosity almost got you killed a few times."

Hope gulped. "Point taken."

Reid stood and came out from behind the desk. "I know there's nothing I can say to stop you from talking to people, but promise me you'll be careful. There's a killer out there."

She turned and walked to the door. Before stepping out into the corridor, she looked over her shoulder at the detective. "I promise."

• • •

When Hope returned home from the police department, she immediately set to work setting up a hot chocolate bar for her company, who were due to arrive shortly according to her watch.

Yesterday, while waiting to be questioned by Officer Roberts, Hope sent her sister a text message letting her know what happened, that she was safe, and she'd call later, which she did after coming home from dinner. During the call, Hope went through it all, from hearing Alena's scream to finding Gus Wharton dead in the shop. Her next call was to Jane, and she went through the whole story again. By the time she had finished talking with Jane, she'd decided to invite Claire and Jane over to sort through the two murders. Previously, they'd put their heads together and managed to come up with a solid plan for investigating. She sent a group text, and by the time she was ready for bed, they'd set a time, and Sally would also be attending. Setting up a hot chocolate bar seemed a perfect idea for their murder discussion. Of course, she documented every step of the process for her blog.

Comprised of three tiers, which she made from scraps of wood, she showcased an array of temptations to add to the hot beverage.

The top tier housed glass jars filled with cocoa mix and mini-marshmallows, and red seasonal mugs. The second tier offered jars of chocolate and caramel syrups, hazelnut drizzle, and shakers of cinnamon and cocoa powder. The bottom tier displayed jars bursting with crushed peppermint, candy cane sticks, mini chocolate chips, and sprinkles—all adorned with red and white twine and handwritten labels. Plates of cookies, a carafe of homemade hot chocolate and a bowl of freshly whipped cream completed the inviting display.

Not long after Hope took off her apron, she welcomed her guests, and they filled the air with oohs and aahs as they marveled at the hot chocolate station. Without hesitation, after shedding their coats, all three filled their mugs, each customizing their beverage with enthusiasm.

"I feel like a little girl again," Jane exclaimed, adding a dollop of whipped cream and caramel syrup to her creation. "This is a marvelous idea, Hope."

Sally, dropping mini chocolate chips into her mug, chimed in, "We should do this at the inn. Our guests would love it."

"Brilliant marketing move," Claire remarked, pouring a steaming mug of hot chocolate and crowning it with a spoonful of whipped cream.

Once they settled around the kitchen table with their drinks and cookies, they began to discuss the two murders. Hope had her composition notebook opened to a blank page as she recapped yesterday's deadly events and then what she'd learned from Reid, which wasn't much.

"Let's review what we know about Mitty," Hope declared, pen poised over the page. "We've got a rap sheet that reads like a crime novel—criminal history, ties to the late Denny Beyer, who met his demise behind bars after a jewelry store heist, and let's not forget the sudden influx of cash to settle medical and other bills. Oh, and he's accused of selling Ralph a bogus antique."

Sally, reaching for a gingerbread cookie, chimed in, "Am I the only one who finds it hard to believe there's no link between Mitty and Gus Wharton? Both are pushing up daisies."

"Pushing up daisies? Really?" Jane admonished.

Sally crunched on her cookie, ignoring her sister-in-law's reprimand.

Hope updated the list by adding Gus Wharton's name. "Detective Reid hasn't found a connection between them. Though, I can't be certain about that. After all, I am a *civilian*, as he put it."

"A civilian who has helped solved how many murder investigations?" Jane asked.

Claire, her skepticism on full display, scoffed. She hadn't forgiven him for suspecting her of murdering a colleague back when she was a real estate agent. "I wouldn't trust Reid to find his own shadow."

Hope, undeterred, continued. "Drew hasn't found a connection between them either. But I'm with Sally and Claire on this—there's a missing link between Mitty and Wharton."

"Let's keep moving on. We may discover the missing piece as we talk this through," Jane suggested.

"Ralph was arrested for Mitty's murder." Hope jotted down his name and his alleged motive. "He doesn't have an alibi for the first murder, and I'm not sure of one for the second murder." On the next line she wrote *check for alibi*.

With the air of a seasoned amateur sleuth, thanks to her published mystery novels, Jane shifted the focus to another suspect. "Brody is such a nice young man. I'd hate to think he killed his father or that other man. But then again, isn't it always the one you least suspect?" A mischievous twinkle sparked in her blue eyes.

"They always were in your books," Sally teased.

Jane grinned in response, clearly pleased with the compliment. "But what would his motive have been? He'd already taken over the antique store. No, I don't think he had a reason to kill his father."

"Instead," Hope said, flipping to a new page in her notebook, "he may have been a target." She wrote down the word *conspiracy.*

"Conspiracy?" Claire raised an intrigued eyebrow, peering into her sister's notebook as if it held the key to the mystery.

"When I was leaving the police department, I realized something," she said. "Maybe Nora and Alena are conspiring to take over the business."

Jane, ever the curious soul, leaned forward, cookie in hand. "What makes you say that, dear?"

"Here's the juicy tidbit," Hope said, before sipping her hot chocolate. "Alena is dating Stan Barlow Jr. You know, of Barlow Antiquities—the folks who get their hands on the most prestigious antiques you can imagine." She'd done a quick internet search and was blown away by the rare and expensive pieces Stan's family dealt with.

Claire blew out a low breath. "Barlow Antiquities? The stuff of legend."

"Alena said that Stan is eager to branch out on his own," Hope continued. "And I overheard the conversation between them at the tree lot that made it sound like they were up to something involving Mitty's shop."

Claire finally reached for a gingerbread cookie and snapped it in half. Ever caloric-conscious, she always seemed to be mentally tallying the calories. So, Hope popped up from her seat to retrieve a bottle of water from the fridge for her sister. After one cup of hot chocolate and one cookie, Claire had reached her festive caloric intake.

Hope returned to the table and set the bottle in front of her sister. "Doesn't it seem odd that Wharton approached Brody to set up a meeting to sell the clock and when Brody refused, Wharton showed up at the shop anyway, and Alena conveniently called her stepbrother?"

Sally leaned forward, her eyes narrowed. "You think they were trying to lure Brody to the store to kill him?"

"Then what happened?" Jane asked, her brow furrowed. "Wharton was the one who ended up dead."

Claire shook her head. "Why go through all that trouble for an antique shop? It's not like Mitty's business is anything like Barlow Antiquities. Stan Jr. could easily open his own store. I think you're way off on this one, Hope."

Hope met Claire's gaze. "I don't think I am," she said. "I think there's more to this than we realize."

The four of them sat in silence for a moment, their thoughts swirling. Hope looked up from her notebook and glanced out the window. Snow had started to fall. It was a beautiful sight. Quite a contrast to what she had written in her book. *Motives. Conspiracy. Murder.*

"We haven't confirmed that Mitty and Wharton were involved in the jewelry store robbery," Sally said.

"True," Hope said, turning her gaze to Sally. "What if Mitty didn't spend all that robbery cash? What if there's a stash somewhere, maybe even a dazzling piece of jewelry hidden? Now, Wharton, Alena, Nora, and Stan hatch a plot to eliminate Mitty and Brody, and they divvy up the loot."

"That would have to be a lot of money to split four ways," Claire said. "That is, if there is money or jewelry."

Hope countered, "What if they cut Wharton out of the equation? Lured him to the shop and got rid of him?"

Claire reluctantly conceded. "That's definitely a possibility. Maybe they planned to get Brody to the shop and frame him for Wharton's murder. But something went wrong. Like you showing up!"

"You're getting the hang of this." Impressed with Claire's theory, Hope jotted it down and circled the words. "We absolutely must establish Stan's alibi for Wharton's murder."

After swallowing her last piece of cookie, Claire threw another name into the mix. "What about Ruth? Angry ex, potential motive?"

"Well, she was furious with Mitty, but that's not surprising considering they're divorced. However, she did mention wanting to reconcile when she first returned to Jefferson. But Mitty had moved on.

Could that be a strong enough motive?" Hope asked.

"Probably not," Claire said. "But there is a property up in the Berkshires that Mitty was refusing to sell. That could be a motive."

"What property?" Jane asked.

"While they were married, after they recovered from the medical bills they bought a few acres to build a weekend house." Claire wiped her hand on a napkin.

"Though, honestly, if she hadn't killed him by now because of that issue, she probably isn't our murderer," Hope said.

Claire then dropped a motive bomb. "Ruth needs cash for a van. To expand her business, she needs to go to craft shows and county fairs. How's that for a motive?"

Sally looked fascinated. "How do you do this?"

"People spill all sorts of secrets in my store while shopping for candles and pillows. You'd be amazed what you hear when folks don't realize they're speaking out loud," Claire said.

"So, what do we do now?" Sally drained the last of her drink and then reached for another cookie.

Hope rose from her seat, her eyes glinting with determination. "We start digging."

Claire immediately shot her arm up in the air, prompting a giggle from Jane. "I can visit Ruth and see if she found any more newspaper clippings. Who knows? There could be more robberies we don't know about. And I'll also reach out to my real estate contacts to see if I can get a status update on Mitty and Ruth's property in the Berkshires."

"Good idea," Hope replied.

Sally, armed with the seasoned skills of a former librarian, eagerly volunteered to research Gus Wharton, Denny Beyer, and Mitty. "I'm sure I'll come up with a connection between them," she said with a confident nod.

"Of course, I'll oversee her research to make sure she doesn't go down rabbit holes," Jane said. "Once she gets going, she doesn't know when to stop."

Sally shrugged. "It's a passion."

"I'm going to track down Stan Barlow Jr.," Hope declared from the island. "We're going to find out what Nora and Alena are up to, and we're going to stop them before it's too late. I don't want anything to happen to Brody."

• • •

With a satisfying click, Hope secured the dishwasher door and set the wash cycle in motion, the rhythmic hum filling the kitchen like a comforting lullaby. She then shifted her focus to the three wooden tiers stacked on the island. She swiftly gathered them and, as she made her way out of the kitchen, the continuing snowfall caught her eye. It seemed the forecast promising a fresh dusting of snow by nightfall had been correct.

With a light step, she padded out of the kitchen and paused at the threshold of her home office. The door swung open at her touch, revealing an unusually disorganized space. The prospect of transforming this disarray into a playroom for Becca and Molly filled her with anticipation. Once the barn renovation was completed, she'd have an office out there, so this room would become a play area. For now, it was her haven gone awry, with stacks of backdrops, camera accessories, and cookbooks vying for space. Among the clutter, she found a spot for the wooden tiers.

Returning to the kitchen, Hope grabbed a damp cloth and swiftly glided it across the cool expanse of the granite island. Her guests had left a half hour ago, each with their assignment. In the aftermath of goodbyes, she sent a text to Drew to ask him to help locate Stan Barlow Jr.

As she awaited his response, she zipped through the kitchen, tidying as she went. A basket overflowing with newspapers caught her eye. "Recycling," she muttered, gathering the stack. While tying them up on the island, she spotted the *Gazette*'s special fall insert, "Home and Antiques." Two articles had caught her eye previously, and now a third one held a particular allure—the author's name. Reaching for her phone, Hope knew exactly who could answer her questions about the antique world.

Chapter Thirteen

Hope tossed the folded "Homes & Antiques" section on the passenger seat of her Explorer. She'd nearly recycled it before remembering Kempner Russell's column. Kemp, the town's friendly antiques expert, was the perfect person to ask about the Higganum lamp, Ralph's supposed motive for murder. A quick call confirmed he was home, so she grabbed her tote and a tin of freshly baked cookies, and headed out to Kemp's antique saltbox house, which wasn't far from her own.

Emerging from her Explorer, she followed the snow-covered winding path to the front door, where Kemp stood waiting with the door ajar. She stepped over the threshold into his home and the familiar creak of the wooden floorboards greeted her like an old friend, instantly putting her at ease. Sunlight streamed through the lace curtains, painting the space in a soft golden hue that illuminated the carefully curated collection of antiques in every corner.

The foyer, though modest in size, exuded charm with its intricately carved mahogany coatrack, adorned with an array of vintage hats and coats. Beside it stood a gleaming brass umbrella stand, brimming with an assortment of umbrellas.

"Thank you for letting me come over. I'm sorry it's so last-minute," she said, slipping off her coat and handing it to him. "Of course, I couldn't come empty-handed."

Kemp's brown eyes lit up at the sight of the cookie tin she carried. "You and your delicious treats are always welcome guests." He took the container after hanging her coat on the rack. In his mid-forties, Kemp's tousled dark brown hair hinted at his need for a haircut, while his dark-rimmed glasses lent him an intellectual charm. Dressed in an Aran sweater, gray corduroy pants, and worn loafers, his outfit perfectly mirrored his relaxed attitude.

To the left of the foyer was the living room, its plush armchairs practically calling out for company. He motioned for Hope to follow, leading her into the cozy room.

"I must confess, I am intrigued by all the drama surrounding

Ralph's Higganum lamp," Kemp admitted as they entered. "Or should I say, alleged Higganum lamp? Please have a seat." He gestured toward a chair and set the cookie tin on the coffee table where among an assortment of carefully arranged antiques that included an ornate silver snuffbox and a weathered leather-bound book with gilt-edged pages. When not writing, Kemp hunted for treasures at tag sales and estate auctions.

"Your home is beautiful," Hope said as she settled into the chair, her tote finding a spot on the floor beside her. "Honestly, I don't know what to think. Mitty wasn't known for misleading customers. But why would Ralph lie about something verifiable?"

Kemp settled opposite her. "A perplexing situation indeed. However, Ralph was telling the truth about the lamp."

"How are you so certain?" Hope inquired.

"Because I saw it," Kemp disclosed, pushing his glasses up the bridge of his nose. "It's a good fake, but a fake nonetheless."

"He asked you to assess it because he suspected it was a fake?"

"No, quite the opposite," Kemp clarified, his gaze drifting around the room, lingering on his own collection of antiques. "Like many buyers, he lacked the expertise to discern a genuine antique. You see, his doubts were about the purchase, not about the lamp's authenticity. He told me that he'd bought it somewhat selfishly, as a tribute to his late wife's fondness for Higganum lamps. Yet, he felt someone who truly cherished them should possess it. He said his wife would have liked that. So, I offered to do an appraisal. I know a few collectors who would have jumped at the chance to buy the lamp. That is, if it was authentic."

"And you told him that the lamp wasn't the real deal. I presume he wasn't happy with the news."

Kemp shook his head. "No, he was not. He'd invested a substantial sum into what turned out to be a counterfeit."

"Surely he could have worked something out with Mitty," Hope said.

"That's what I suggested. But Ralph was too angry to listen."

"So, he went to the police after you confirmed it was a fake, but he didn't press charges? Do you know why?"

"He didn't tell me why." Kemp leaned back, steepling his fingers. "There may be more to this story, Hope. I believe Ralph isn't the only one who unknowingly bought a fake Higganum lamp."

Hope's eyes widened in astonishment. "Are you serious?" she exclaimed.

"Just recently I learned of someone who purchased a supposed Higganum lamp two months ago. They didn't buy it from the Antique Alcove," Kemp said.

"Do you know where it was purchased from?" Hope pressed eagerly.

Kemp leaned forward, his fingers clasped tightly together. "Fenn Antiques," he disclosed.

Hope's mouth fell open in disbelief. "Are you absolutely sure?"

Kemp nodded solemnly.

"Oh, boy. That is not what I expected to hear." Never in a million years would she have ever thought Diana Adams and Issy Leopold would be connected with antique fraud. No way, no how. Yet, that's what Kemp had just told her. "I can't believe you're saying that Drew's mother and aunt sold a counterfeit antique." Now she'd have to break the news to her best friend. A flashback to Halloween reminded her that the last time she had bad news to share about Drew's family, it nearly cost them their friendship. This wouldn't be good.

• • •

Hope knew exactly where she needed to go after leaving Kemp's house. When she arrived at Fenn Antiques, she paused to peer through the glass door. The shop was empty—a stroke of luck, given the awkward questions she needed to ask Diana and Issy. The last thing she wanted was for their conversation to be overheard and relayed to Drew before she could share the new information with him herself.

Hope pushed open the door and was greeted by a treasure trove of antiques, from delicate china teacups to a towering armoire that gleamed under the soft glow of the shop's lighting. Issy stood behind the counter, a vibrant presence compared to just a month ago, when her health had faltered. Now she looked revitalized and deeply engrossed in her work once more.

Issy glanced up from the file folder on the countertop, quickly closing it as soon as she spotted Hope. Darting out from behind the counter, she enveloped Hope in a warm hug.

"It's wonderful to see you, Hope," Issy exclaimed. Clad in sleek black pants and a sapphire-colored sweater, her white hair styled into a youthful bob, she had a rosy hue to her cheeks. "You just missed Diana. She had a few errands to run. What brings you by today? Some last-minute Christmas shopping, perhaps? You know you always get the family discount," she said and winked. Drew's aunt had known Hope since her childhood.

"I'm delighted to report that all I have left to shop for are stocking stuffers," Hope announced proudly. "But that's not why I'm here."

She hesitated, uncertain about the reception her news would receive. Delivering bad news was never easy, especially to someone as kindhearted as Issy. Maybe she should have sought out Issy's sister first. Then again, Diana's prickly personality made predicting her reaction nearly impossible.

"I have some unsettling news," Hope began tentatively.

"Really?" Issy's smile faded and she clasped her hands.

"I was just at Kemp Russell's home, and we were discussing the Higganum lamp that Ralph purchased from Mitty's shop. The alleged counterfeit," Hope began, carefully choosing her words. "Apparently, there might be another."

Issy's expression clouded. "Another one? You know, it's those things that give all of our businesses a bad name. Fortunately, Fenn Antiques has a wonderful reputation. Diana and I work every day to maintain that." She and Diana had inherited their love of antiques and the shop, a century-old Main Street staple, from their parents.

Hope took a deep breath. "I'm afraid Kemp believes a counterfeit Higganum lamp was also sold here, weeks ago."

"What?" Issy exclaimed in disbelief. "That can't be right. It's simply not possible. Diana and I personally authenticate every antique we sell, and for those beyond our expertise, we rely on trusted experts." With determination, she marched back to the counter. "This has to be some kind of mistake."

Hope followed Issy to the counter and watched as her fingers flew across the keyboard as she accessed the store's records.

"Let me see if I can find out who sold us that lamp," she said, her brow wrinkling in concentration. "Ah . . . here we go. Hmm . . ."

"What is it?" Hope inquired, her interest sparked. Too bad she couldn't see the computer screen.

Issy shot Hope a worried glance. "You know, we deal with many regular clients, but this one I don't recognize. Actually, I don't recall the lamp at all."

"The person probably came in when you were out sick," Hope suggested. "What's the seller's name?"

"Dennis Llewellyn. You're right, this happened when I was home recovering. Diana handled the sale, and it was a cash transaction." She bit her lip, clearly concerned. "If the lamp is indeed a fake, this could be disastrous to our reputation. I just don't see how Diana could have made such a mistake. This must be a misunderstanding."

"I have no doubt there's a reasonable explanation. Is there an address for Mr. Llewellyn?" Hope asked, pulling out a notepad from her tote bag. She flipped it open to a blank page and poised her pen.

"Yes, there is," Issy confirmed, glancing back at the computer screen. "Three Swamp Road. Why are you asking?"

Hope quickly jotted down the address, her mind already racing with possibilities. "Just gathering information," she replied vaguely.

Issy pulled away from the computer, fixing a stern gaze on Hope. "You're not thinking about going there, are you?"

Hope hesitated, unsure of her own intentions. "No . . . well, maybe," she admitted reluctantly.

"Listen to me, Hope," Issy said firmly. "I don't want you getting involved. I'm going to call the customer who purchased the lamp from us and have them bring it in for authentication. Then we'll go from there."

"Sounds like a plan." Just not Hope's plan. She tucked her notepad back into her bag. "I'll leave you to it. Please keep me posted, alright?"

Hope had barely stepped out of the shop before Ralph swooped in, catching her off guard. He linked arms with her, guiding her along the sidewalk with a sense of urgency. His gaze darted between her and the bustling activity on Main Street.

"Ralph! I had no idea you were out," Hope exclaimed, surprised by his sudden appearance.

"This is a complete outrage," Ralph hissed, his grip tightening on Hope's arm as he pulled her along. "Can you believe that idiot Sam Reid thinks I killed Mitty?" His pace quickened, his anger evident in every stride.

"Ralph, please let go." Hope attempted to free her arm from his grasp. "Let's go to the coffee shop and discuss this."

Ralph remained silent, his determination evident as he abruptly turned down the driveway behind the stationery store, leading to the communal parking lot.

Scanning the deserted lot, Hope felt a knot of unease tighten in her stomach. Ralph's grimness was out of character, and his behavior was unacceptable. Being alone with Ralph in his current state didn't feel safe. She had given him the benefit of the doubt for too long. It stopped now.

"Ralph, listen to me," Hope asserted, her voice firm as she struggled to break free from his grip. "I don't appreciate your behavior. You can't just grab me like that."

Ralph released her, and in a flash his attitude shifted. He lowered his head and said quietly, "I'm sorry, Hope. I didn't mean to scare you."

"What exactly did you mean?" Hope demanded, her arms folded tightly across her chest, her gaze fixed on Ralph. Whatever explanation he had, it had better be good.

"I'm not sure," he admitted, his voice tinged with uncertainty. He appeared to have aged a decade since she last saw him, his once calm blue eyes now resembling a stormy sea of chaos. "Julia mentioned that you've been conducting your own investigation to clear my name."

"I wouldn't exactly call it my own investigation," Hope countered, though she couldn't deny the truth in Ralph's words. Reid had referred to her efforts in much the same way—a shadow investigation.

"The whole situation has me going crazy. I mean, for goodness sake, I was arrested!" Ralph exclaimed, throwing his hands up in exasperation. "I have a mug shot!"

"I can't even imagine what that must have been like," Hope replied sympathetically. However, she couldn't ignore Ralph's current actions. Just like when he had lunged at Mitty that day at the Snowflake Market. She was witnessing a side of Ralph she never thought she'd see.

"I never thought I'd find myself in this situation again," Ralph confessed, his agitation evident as he began to pace back and forth.

"Again? You've been arrested before?" Hope's eyebrows shot up in surprise. But then maybe she shouldn't have been shocked. She'd had a hunch that both men's past might shed some light on why Ralph was so quick to believe Mitty was dealing in fake antiques. Well, that begged the question why Ralph would have trusted Mitty in the first place. Honor among thieves? Whoa! Could Ralph have been involved in the jewelry store robbery?

"It's something I'm not proud of," Ralph admitted, his voice tinged with regret as he looked away. "But it was a long time ago. Back when I was young and foolish."

"You knew Mitty when he was running with the wrong crowd, didn't you?"

Ralph nodded solemnly. "That's why I couldn't believe I trusted a guy like Mitty. Because he'd been a thief. Just like me."

"Were you involved in the jewelry store robbery?" she asked.

He shook his head. "What jewelry store? What are you talking about? It doesn't matter. I thought Mitty had turned his life around, just like me, but all this time he's been scamming people. Including me!" The frustration in Ralph's voice was clear, mirroring the sense of betrayal Hope felt.

"Hey!" a deep voice rang out from several feet away, catching Ralph's attention.

"Ethan?" Hope's brows knitted together in confusion. What was he doing there?

"What's going on?" Ethan's steps were purposeful as he closed the distance between them, his expression serious. "Hope, are you okay?"

She nodded, grateful for his arrival.

"I asked what's going on." Ethan turned his focus to Ralph, his gaze piercing and demanding answers.

"We were just talking," Ralph said, his eyes darting between Hope and Ethan, silently pleading for her support.

"Really? Because by the looks of how you laid hands on her, it looked like she didn't want to have a conversation with you," Ethan retorted, his tone firm. His stance conveyed authority, leaving no room for debate.

Hope wondered where Ethan had come from to witness Ralph's approach outside Fenn Antiques.

"I just wanted to talk to her in private," Ralph muttered, looking sheepishly at Hope. "I'm sorry if I startled you. That wasn't my intention. I'll leave now." But before Ralph could make his escape, Ethan grabbed his shoulder, preventing him from leaving.

"Remember what Matt told you? There's no discussing your case with anyone, and that includes Hope," Ethan reminded him firmly.

Her jaw dropped in disbelief. "I'm only trying to help him."

Ethan shot her a "not now" look before turning back to Ralph, leaving Hope feeling frustrated and belittled. She didn't appreciate being treated like a child.

"Got it." Ralph shrugged Ethan's hand off his shoulder and continued on his way out of the parking lot, his steps heavy and slow.

"I was handling Ralph fine by myself," she said, her tone tinged with irritation. "I didn't need you to rush in and save the day."

Ethan shifted his attention to Hope, looking vexed. "Actually, it was Ralph who needed the day saved. We can't risk jeopardizing his case. Why can't you understand that?"

"I understand," she replied, taking a deep breath to calm her frayed nerves. Between being grabbed and shuffled about by Ralph, who then dropped a bomb, and Ethan charging in to take over, her nerves were beyond rattled. "What I don't understand is how my helping him can hurt his case."

"I'll have Matt call you and give you a detailed explanation," Ethan said, his tone firm. "And maybe a restraining order."

"Ha-ha." Hope rolled her eyes. "Oh, shoot. Because you barged into our conversation, I didn't get a chance to ask Ralph about what he knew about Gus Wharton or Denny Beyer."

"How do you know about Denny Beyer?" Ethan asked, closing the distance between them. "What exactly do you know? And how much?"

"Well, I didn't know Ralph had a criminal past and was involved with Mitty back in the day. As for Denny, I read his name in an article about a jewelry store robbery. Ruth showed it to me," she said.

"I know you want to help, but you have to leave this case to me and Matt and to Sam Reid. I don't have all the answers yet, but my gut tells me that Gus Wharton's death isn't going to be the last. Either someone is cleaning up the past or seeking some kind of revenge, and I don't know who all the players are. Not yet."

Hope's phone pinged, and she quickly dug into her tote for it. It was a text from Drew.

He'd gotten Stan Jr.'s address and now she had it.

"Hope, we're not finished talking," Ethan said.

"You're very bossy this afternoon, and I don't appreciate it," she shot back.

Ethan raked his hands through his dark hair, a sign his frustration was ratcheting up. "You're right. I shouldn't be telling you what to do since you never listen anyway."

"I also don't not appreciate your tone with me," Hope retorted, her voice tinged with irritation, and she wasn't one bit sorry for it. "I am a grown woman who can take care of herself. Now, I have to go, and I'm sure you have to get back to work. You know, to get that restraining order started." She managed to crack the smallest of smiles, but it was done grudgingly.

"You're right, I do have to get back to work. See you tonight. I'll give you a call before I leave the office." Ethan leaned in and gave her a kiss on the cheek before turning and walking away.

Once Ethan was out of sight, Hope returned her attention to her phone and initiated a quick internet search. She discovered that Stan Jr. resided right on the border of Jefferson, a fifteen-minute drive away. After calculating how long she needed for the drive and a conversation with Stan, she determined there was enough time to spare. However, she couldn't shake the feeling of falling behind in her work schedule, another reason why she should consider dropping her "shadow" investigation.

As she settled behind the steering wheel, a sense of unease crept over her, fueled by Ethan's ominous words: "Either someone is cleaning up the past or seeking some kind of revenge." She wished she knew what she had stepped into the middle of.

Chapter Fourteen

Braving the sleet-slicked roads, Hope arrived at her destination later than anticipated. The picturesque afternoon snowfall, now transformed into a treacherous glaze, had slowed traffic to a crawl. Upon reaching Stan's address, she found herself at an old mill building, its rustic charm repurposed into modern apartments. The driveway snaked down to a parking lot along the river, its steep incline made less daunting by her trusty SUV. With a grateful nod to her vehicle, Hope expertly navigated the descent. The lot was sparsely populated, with a designated section for visitors. After securing a spot and retrieving a pastry box brimming with gingerbread cookies she'd picked up on a quick stop at home, Hope made her way toward the building's entrance.

Moments later, she found herself at a standstill before the imposing locked wooden door. The absence of residents' names on the intercom left her clueless about Stan's unit—a glitch in an otherwise well-thought-out plan. Just as her uncertainty reached its peak, the door swung open, revealing a flustered mom navigating a stroller and a fussy toddler. Seizing the opportune moment, Hope grabbed the door, concealing her surprise with a quick, welcoming smile.

"Perfect timing," she remarked.

"Thank you so much," expressed the mom, making her way out. "Have a nice day."

"Thank you." Hope hurried into the lobby, which seamlessly blended the historical charm of the old mill with contemporary touches. From its exposed brick walls to the high ceiling that now accommodated modern lighting fixtures, which cast a warm glow over the space, Hope appreciated the building's industrial heritage and the care taken in the restoration.

"I'm inside, now what?" She looked around the lobby. The elevator was to her right, while a bank of mailboxes with a shelf cluttered with packages was off to her left. She had a thought.

She dashed to the packages and did a quick scan of each one, hoping to find one belonging to Stan. Surely the mailing label would have his apartment number on it, right? She hoped so. And there it was! A small box addressed to Stan. Apartment 2A. With that information, she dashed over to the elevator and up to the second floor.

When Hope stepped out of the elevator, she was pleased to find Stan's apartment conveniently located just opposite. With only a few steps, she stood before a solid wooden door boasting an awesome transom window. As she raised her hand to knock, she couldn't help but marvel at the building's overall charm.

With a creak, the hefty door swung wide, revealing a figure in his early twenties. Towering and relaxed, clad in a loose T-shirt and sweatpants, his curly, dark blond hair contributed to his effortlessly cool vibe.

In her most hopeful tone, she introduced herself. "I'm Hope Early, a friend of Alena's."

His eyes narrowed, a hint of suspicion clouding his gaze. "If you're selling something, I'm not interested," he stated flatly.

Quick to reassure, Hope shook her head. "No, no selling here. This is for you. I baked gingerbread cookies. They're a favorite of my family and friends." She extended the box. "I was with Alena right after she found Gus Wharton's body. It was quite a shock for her. And me."

He nodded curtly, his expression unreadable. "Yeah, she told me. So, what do you want, Ms. Early?" His tone was brusque, devoid of any warmth or any sign of engagement.

Considering Stan's potential involvement in a murder investigation, Hope figured it was safer for her to remain in the hallway. She decided to cut to the chase, determined to make the most of the limited time she had.

"I was at the tree farm the day you and Alena were there, and I couldn't help but overhear a portion of your conversation. To be honest, it sounded a little . . . cryptic."

"Cryptic? How so?"

"You were discussing the antique shop."

Stan's eyes narrowed, a hint of amusement flickering across his face. "Ah, so you think I had something to do with Alena's stepfather's murder?"

"Alena mentioned you wanted to strike out on your own from your family's business and maybe join her and Brody in the Antique Alcove."

"You're here looking for an alibi." He chuckled. "This is a first."

"First?"

"Being suspected by a busybody of murder," he elaborated, his tone dripping with disdain. "Look, I don't know why you're poking your nose into this matter, but I will be more than happy to humor you. I was home alone the night of Mr. Fitzgerald's murder. And as for the other unfortunate incident at the antique shop, I was attending two estate sales that day and didn't return home until nine o'clock in the evening. So, I suggest you update your murder board, or whatever you're using to keep track of your amateur sleuthing and take your leave." With a swift motion, he shoved the pastry box back into Hope's hands and slammed the door shut with a resounding thud.

Hope stood momentarily stunned by the abruptness of his dismissal. "Busybody? Murder board?" she muttered under her breath. Though, she did use a notebook to keep her thoughts about the murders organized, so Stan wasn't too far off. Turning on her heel, she marched back to the elevator.

She emerged from the building, the fading sunlight casting long shadows across the now-slick pavement. Although she'd secured his alibi for one murder and possibly another for the second, she had hoped to glean more information from Stan, particularly regarding his plans for the Antique Alcove.

The deserted parking lot, shrouded in the twilight gloom and battered by the relentless sleet, exuded an eerie atmosphere that sent goose bumps up her arms. The limited lighting did little to dispel the growing unease in Hope's stomach. She forced herself to focus on navigating the treacherous surface, reminding herself that a fall was the last thing she needed now. First, she was alone. Second, she had recipes to make. Third, Christmas was days away. No, she needed to tread carefully.

Just a stone's throw from her parked vehicle, she swiftly extracted her key fob, aiming it toward the SUV. The familiar beep chimed in response, signaling the driver's door unlocking. As she closed the distance, a sudden interruption echoed through the chilly air—her phone's lively ringtone, unmistakably Claire's.

Against her better judgment, Hope attempted to unearth the device from the depths of her bag. Juggling the precariously perched pastry box and the key fob, she found herself in a clumsy dance, resulting in her stumbling and the key slipping from her grasp.

"Shoot," she muttered under her breath, snatching her phone from her bag as the key clattered to the pavement. With a tap, she answered the call, her voice trembling. "Hey, Claire."

"Where are you?" Claire's concerned voice crackled through the connection. "The roads are getting bad. I'm thinking about closing the shop early."

"I'm heading home now." Hope swept up the key fob and an unexpected, agonizing surge of electricity jolted through her body, sending a thousand searing needles pricking her skin. The pain was so intense it felt like her very bones were being shattered. The key fob and phone flew from her grasp as her muscles contracted with a force beyond her control.

In the chaos, a single, bewildering thought echoed in her mind—*what is happening to me?*

In a heartbeat, her reality narrowed into the overpowering sensation of electricity coursing through her, the air crackling with an otherworldly energy. The assault on her senses was profound, an acrid, metallic taste assaulting her palate as her vision blurred into a disorienting darkness at the edges.

"Hope? Hope!" Claire's voice echoed from the phone, laced with panic. "Hope!"

But Hope was unable to respond. Immobilized and speechless, her world narrowed down to the overwhelming electricity moving through her veins. She teetered on the fragile edge between consciousness and the encroaching darkness, the pain wrapping around her like a haunting cloak.

After what felt like an eternity, the electrifying charge gradually subsided, leaving behind a lingering numbness and the faint echo of pain. Gasping for breath, she shuddered with the aftermath of the shocking ordeal. As her senses slowly came back to her, Hope, disoriented and weakened, found herself on the cold ground of the parking lot, struggling to make sense of what had just unfolded.

A flash of light pierced her half-opened eyes, followed by the jarring sound of a car door slamming shut. Heavy footsteps crunched against the pavement, growing louder and more urgent.

"Hope!" a voice, thick with concern, cut through the haze clouding her mind. She recognized the voice. It was Detective Reid. He dropped to his knees, his hands swiftly scanning her body, cursing under his breath.

Struggling to find her voice, Hope attempted to speak. "Shocked . . . back," she managed to whisper, barely audible.

"Stay still, Hope. I'm calling for an ambulance," Reid instructed, his voice firm yet gentle. "We'll get you to a hospital in no time."

Claire's voice pierced the silence, crackling from the abandoned cell phone, "Hello! Hope! Say something! What's going on?"

Reid scanned the surroundings and then saw the phone. In a swift motion, he retrieved it. "Claire, it's Sam Reid. I just found Hope . . . Yes, she's alive . . . I'm calling for an ambulance . . . I'll keep you updated." He ended the call, tucking the phone into his coat pocket.

Hope heard him call for the ambulance, and despite his warning not to move, she found herself shifting her arms and legs. She tried to piece together the events that led to her current state, and one chilling realization dawned upon her.

"Sam," she called out, her voice gaining strength. When he returned to her side, she asked, "Was I hit with a taser?"

Chapter Fifteen

Hope bounced her legs impatiently against the edge of the bed. It was all she could do to stay still. The bland white walls of the emergency exam room did nothing to soothe her frayed nerves. She wanted out of the sterile prison and to get back to the normalcy of her life. Having Detective Reid standing by the door wasn't helping. He'd been allowed in the room once he'd identified himself.

She told him why she was at the old mill, who she visited and what she remembered when she left the building. During her statement, she paused frequently, expecting a lecture, but none was forthcoming. The detective just listened.

"I can't believe someone did that to me. Why?"

"Is that a rhetorical question?" he asked with a touch of dry humor.

"You think it has something to do with the murders?" Hope asked, her mind racing to connect the dots. She suspected a connection to the ongoing investigation but couldn't fathom why, considering she was nowhere near identifying the killer.

"It's not uncommon for us to hold back information about a crime. A detail we've kept from the public is that we discovered two taser prongs in Gus Wharton's back when we found his body. This certainly raises the possibility that your attack is connected to the murders," he acknowledged, his expression grim.

A gasp escaped her lips. "He was tased before being killed?"

"It likely made it easier for the assailant to overpower him," he explained.

"Then the killer could have been a woman," Hope mused as she sorted out her thoughts about Wharton's murder. Her mind was still fuzzy. "Alena? I mean, how probable is it that someone else entered the antique shop and killed Wharton without her knowledge? She claimed she didn't hear anything, but I think I may have screamed when I got tased. Honestly, I'm not even sure."

The detective nodded thoughtfully. "It's a possibility we're considering," he admitted. "But we can't rule out other suspects until we have more information."

Reid withdrew his hands from his coat pockets and approached the bed. "Are you holding up alright?" he asked, sounding genuinely worried.

Her eyes darted around the compact, clinical space, absorbing every detail as she took a deep breath, the scent of disinfectant filling her nostrils. Just moments ago, she'd been a tangle of wires and tubes, her vitals displayed on a cold, flickering monitor. The doctor and nurses had reassured her of her well-being, their words punctuated by hushed exclamations of her fortunate escape.

"Kinda feels like I was lit up like a Christmas tree with a short."

He cracked a grin. "Get some rest and please leave the investigation to us," Reid instructed, his voice turning serious. "We'll handle it from here."

Just then, the door swung open with a flourish, and Claire burst into the room like a dynamo. The murmur of the bustling emergency room trailed behind her, a stark contrast to the hushed confines of the examination room.

"Mom's going to call you as soon as we get home. Have the discharge papers come in yet?" Claire inquired, her voice buzzing with a mix of concern and relief. She abruptly stopped in her tracks when she saw the detective.

An unusual silence descended upon the room. Then, to everyone's surprise, Claire lunged forward and wrapped her arms tightly around the detective, pulling him into a bear hug.

Reid's eyebrows shot up in astonishment, his expression a mix of confusion and amusement. Hope's mouth agape, she stared at her sister in disbelief, her mind struggling to process the unexpected display of affection.

"Thank you, thank you, thank you," Claire gushed, squeezing the detective tighter. "I'm so grateful you found my sister and helped her. She could have died."

"Claire, I was only tased," Hope interjected, trying to dispel her sister's exaggerated fear. "And I was starting to come around when he arrived."

"She could have frozen to death." Claire pulled back but maintained a grip on the detective's arms. "I'm so sorry for all the names I've called you. I really am."

"Names?" he inquired.

"Barney Fife once or twice, or maybe more," Claire admitted, her cheeks flushing with embarrassment. "But that was a long time ago." She let go of Reid and moved toward her sister, gently tucking a stray lock of hair behind Hope's ear. "There were a few others, but let's not dwell on them. I'm just glad I can take my sister home."

Reid chuckled softly, then quickly composed himself, his expression shifting back to that of the seasoned detective. "While I agree with Hope that the taser was not lethal, I did find piano wire near her when I arrived," he revealed, his voice grave.

"Piano wire? I don't understand," Claire said.

Hope locked eyes with her sister. "To strangle me. Right, Sam?"

Reid nodded solemnly. "That's my assessment."

• • •

Standing in her bathroom, Hope ran her fingers along her neck, a chilling reminder of her brush with death. She'd been mere moments from being strangled. Had Sam not intervened, the paralyzing effects of the taser would have ensured her fate. A fresh wave of terror washed over her—she'd been so close to dying.

Her reflection in the bathroom mirror stared back at her, a face revealing both fear and determination. She weighed the advice she'd received—Claire's pleas to abandon their rogue investigation, Jane and Sally's echoing concerns. As she turned off the faucet and patted her face dry, Hope couldn't shake off the unsettling feeling of vulnerability.

When she'd returned home, Claire had settled her in and reheated soup for dinner. She then stayed until Ethan arrived before leaving. Despite their protective presence, the knowledge that her attacker was still at large cast a shadow over the evening.

In the solitude of her bathroom, Hope's resolve hardened. The pain from the taser might have subsided, but the memory of her helplessness in that parking lot remained vivid. There was only one way to reclaim her power, to shed the fear that threatened to consume her—it was to find the person responsible for these heinous acts, to bring justice for Mitty and Gus Wharton.

With a newfound determination, Hope set aside her moisturizer, closed the medicine cabinet, and flicked off the light switch. The darkness enveloped her, but within it a spark of defiance ignited. She would not be a victim anymore. She would be the pursuer, the relentless force for justice.

The bedroom light abruptly pierced the comforting darkness, revealing Ethan sitting upright in their bed. "Ready to get some sleep?" he asked.

Hope managed a faint smile. The thought of slipping into his embrace, of finding solace in the safety of his arms, was the only thing that could tempt her from the clutches of exhaustion. She padded across the room, the carpet muffling her footsteps, and gently pulled back the inviting covers.

With a sigh of relief, she shed her robe and slid into bed, sinking into the cloud-like comforter that enveloped her like a comforting cocoon. Her luxurious bedding, along with her top-notch kitchen appliances and gadgets, were her most prized indulgences. After a grueling day of recipe testing and cooking, she craved a sanctuary for her weary body, a haven where she could shed the weight of her worries and drift off to sleep.

Ethan shifted beside her, his strong arm instinctively circling her shoulders, a silent gesture of reassurance and affection.

"Are the girls tucked in?" Hope asked, her voice barely a whisper. It was hard to believe that her bedtime now mirrored that of Molly and Becca, but the fatigue weighing her down was undeniable.

"They're out like a light," Ethan replied, his tone laced with amusement. "You were pretty quiet during dinner."

"There's not much to say. Someone out there thinks I know more than I do."

"Maybe not," Ethan countered.

Hope turned her head, her gaze searching his. "What do you mean?"

"If we accept the assumption that the person who attacked you is also the killer, then we have to consider that they know you lack knowledge of their identity. However, by you going around and asking questions about the murders, you're increasing the likelihood that they'll be exposed."

"That's not exactly a comforting thought," she said.

"It's a realistic thought," he murmured, a soft kiss brushing her forehead. "Babe, once again, you've gotten yourself caught up in a murder investigation. You know from experience how dangerous it can be."

Hope nodded. The dangers were all too familiar, a chilling reality she'd confronted before.

"You're scaring the heck out of me. You know that, right?" he asked.

She nodded again, fully aware.

"I want to protect you, Hope, but you make it incredibly challenging."

Their eyes met, and she couldn't help but smile, even letting out a small laugh. The moment of levity felt remarkably comforting.

"I know I do," she confessed, her voice soft. "And I'm sorry for that."

"Though, I have a feeling you're not abandoning this pursuit."

She shook her head. "I can't. Not now. When I was tased, I was vulnerable. There was no way I could defend myself. If I don't follow through on what I set out to do, then I worry that I'll never get over that feeling of being defenseless. Claire would say I'm taking back my power. Do you understand?"

He remained silent for a moment, appearing deep in thought. "I think consulting with a therapist would be a sensible and safer approach to handling this."

Hope cupped his face with her hands, her touch tender and reassuring. "I know you think so. And I'm not dismissing that option. But I'm determined to finish what I started—to find out who killed Mitty and Gus Wharton. I promise not to confront any potential suspects alone, and if I get a lead, Sam is just a speed dial away."

"Sam now, is it?" Ethan teased, a hint of amusement flickering in his eyes.

"What can I say, we're bonding." She nestled closer to Ethan's body. "I'm really tired."

Without a word, Ethan turned off the bedside lamp and enveloped Hope in a tight embrace. Hope closed her eyes, attempting to drift off to sleep, but one persistent thought kept pulling her from the depths of the rest she craved: which person she had been in contact with since Mitty's murder was the killer?

• • •

The next morning Hope eagerly tore open the Advent calendar, a delightful gift from Bank Street Chocolates. One of the perks of being a food blogger was that she received PR packages from brands, and anything chocolate was always welcomed. The rich aroma of dark chocolate wafted through the air as she unwrapped a decadent truffle, indulging in the sweet temptation. While starting the day with chocolate might not be the healthiest choice, the previous day's shock still lingered, making a morning treat seem entirely justified.

With a satisfied sigh, she returned the box to its place on the counter. She then cast a sweeping gaze across her kitchen, her mind buzzing with the countdown to Christmas. This year was different, she realized. It was the first of many holidays to be celebrated as a family, and she wanted to make it perfect for Ethan and the girls. The pressure was on, and she was determined to rise to the challenge.

She grabbed a sheet of paper and meticulously listed all the tasks she needed to do before Christmas. Among them was the library's annual gingerbread house contest. It was an event she cherished and wouldn't miss for the world. And this year she couldn't pass on because she'd volunteered to be a judge. While Ethan and Claire didn't object, Sam had expressed concern. He conceded, however, and arranged for regular patrol car drive-bys around her house and the library, bolstering her feeling of security.

As she wrote her last item, the smart doorbell chimed, a jarring contrast to the quiet solitude of her kitchen. She'd promised to keep all the doors and windows locked, a precaution that felt both necessary and somewhat isolating.

Glancing at her phone, she spotted Drew waiting at the mudroom door. Hastily, she made her way through the kitchen to let him into the house. With a warm hug, he apologized for not seeing her the day before, citing a chaotic day due to a pile-up on Jerry's Hill Road because of the icy conditions.

"I heard about the accident when I was in the emergency room," Hope replied as she led him into the kitchen. "Do you have time for a cup of coffee?"

He dropped his messenger bag onto the kitchen island. "Yes, please. Filled to the brim."

Hope nodded understandingly and prepared a cup of coffee for Drew, handing it to him with a warm smile. "Another late night with Trixie?"

"Training a puppy is hard work. But she's so darn cute. And smart." Drew took a sip of the coffee as he leaned against the island. "How about you? Are you okay? I can't believe you were tased." His concern was evident in his voice.

Hope poured herself a cup of coffee, her mind still reeling from the events of the day before.

"It appeared it was the best way to make me incapacitated," she said.

Drew's eyes widened in disbelief. "Incapacitated? I don't understand."

"This has to be off the record. It's just between us."

"Of course, Hope. What is it?"

"The police are keeping the detail of the piano wire out of the press."

Drew's face turned ashen, his expression one of shock and horror. "Piano wire? You mean they intended to use it on you? To strangle you?"

"If Sam hadn't shown up when he did, I would . . ." Hope began, her voice trailing off.

Drew set his cup down and reached out to comfort Hope, pulling her closer, his hand rubbing soothing circles on her back. "Hey, hey. Don't go there."

"I'm trying hard not to," Hope confessed, her voice trembling. She took a deep, steadying breath, forcing herself to focus on the present. "I'm okay," she reassured him, though the memory of the close call still sent shivers down her spine.

"Since you're okay, do you want to hear what I found out?" Drew grinned mischievously. "It's very interesting."

"Absolutely, I want to hear it. But first, there's something we need to talk about."

"Sounds serious," Drew acknowledged.

"It is." She grabbed her mug and led Drew to the table. After they both settled on their chairs, she took a deep breath and hoped this news about his family wouldn't upset him too much. "Yesterday I spoke with Kemp Russell about Ralph's Higganum lamp. He told me that he'd seen the lamp and confirmed that it was a counterfeit. Ralph didn't take the news very well."

"No surprise there, considering his behavior outside the Snowflake Market." Drew took a drink of his coffee and then leaned back. "What else did Kemp say?"

Hope felt a knot form in her stomach. "Apparently, Ralph isn't the only one who unknowingly bought a counterfeit Higganum. Kemp recently discovered another instance at a local antique shop." Hesitantly, she met Drew's gaze. "The thing is, that shop was Fenn Antiques."

Drew shook his head. "No. That's not possible. Both my mother and aunt are experienced antique dealers. They would know a fake when they saw it."

"That's exactly what I thought when Kemp told me. But the lamp was sold when Issy was out sick, and your mom was running the shop and overseeing Issy's care. Diana was doing so much at the time. Mistakes can happen."

He was silent for a moment, and that unnerved Hope. She desperately wanted to know what he was thinking. Yet, she couldn't push him. So, she sat on pins and needles waiting for him to say something.

Finally, he spoke. "Given the circumstances, the error is understandable. I should talk to Aunt Issy and Mom."

"Actually, I spoke with Issy yesterday," Hope admitted hesitantly.

"Before telling me? They're my family, Hope."

"I know, and I'm sorry for not keeping you in the loop, but I'm looping you in now." A strained smile played on her lips.

Another bout of silence stretched between them.

"Are you upset with me?" she asked.

Drew raised his coffee cup. "Nah. How could I be? You almost got electrocuted yesterday, remember?" A genuine smile played on his lips.

"Very funny." She playfully rolled her eyes and then lifted her cup. "There's something else you should know. It's confidential so you can't write about it. At least not yet."

Drew's eyes sharpened with intense interest, his lighthearted disposition vanishing in an instant. "You know I hate that condition but I'm dying to know what you know."

"Gus Wharton was tased before he was killed."

Drew slapped his hand down on the table. "No way!"

"Yes, he was," Hope continued, her voice laced with suspicion. "And here's the thing: Alena couldn't have missed hearing that. Their shop is tiny. She had to hear him scream when he was tased and when he hit the floor."

"You think Alena is involved?" Drew asked.

Hope shrugged. "It's hard not to. Oh, I almost forgot this," she added, her voice regaining its urgency, "Issy gave me the address of Dennis Llewellyn, the person who sold her the fake lamp."

She sprang from her chair and hurried to the counter, where she rummaged through her tote for her notepad. Back at the table, she opened the pad and showed Drew.

"That's close by. I'll head over and check it out," he declared, downing the last of his coffee.

"Not so fast. I'm coming too," Hope announced, reaching for her mug.

"Seriously? What about work? The gingerbread house contest? Recovering from being zapped with a jolt of electricity?" Drew raised an eyebrow. "You have plenty of things to do."

"They can wait," she stated, a determined glint in her eyes. "I can't focus on anything else right now."

Drew chuckled. "You know what Sally will be like if you show up late for the gingerbread contest. She doesn't like tardiness."

"There's plenty of time," Hope insisted. "Come on, let's go find the lamp seller."

With newfound purpose, she marched toward the mudroom door. Drew followed suit, and after grabbing their coats, they opted for Hope's SUV due to the slick roads. He offered to drive, a silent acknowledgment of her still-shaken state.

As Drew skillfully guided the vehicle through the familiar yet treacherous streets of Jefferson, Hope found herself consumed by a blend of anticipation and apprehension. The gentle hum of the engine lent a calming rhythm, and she was grateful for it.

Glancing at Drew's profile, Hope couldn't help but notice the determined set of his jawline. With his blond hair catching stray beams of sunlight and his piercing blue eyes concentrated on the road ahead, he exuded an air of quiet confidence.

"Before I mentioned the fake lamp that Dennis Llewellyn sold to your mom, you said you had something to share," Hope reminded him, breaking the silence.

Drew eased the car to a stop at the intersection, taking advantage of the pause to steal a glance at Hope. "The clock Gus Wharton brought into the shop wasn't an antique. It was about twenty years old, if that."

"That's what we suspected anyway," Hope remarked, her tone less than impressed. She shifted her attention to the empty intersection, contemplating the possibility of the gingerbread house contest being canceled in the aftermath of yesterday's sleet storm.

"Right." Drew flicked on the turn signal and executed a left turn. "But here's the kicker—it was stolen and worth about five thousand dollars."

"What?" Hope's head snapped in Drew's direction. "Where was it stolen from?"

"Barlow Antiquities," Drew revealed. "They're not just into antiques; they also deal with pricey collectibles, like the clock."

Hope's brow furrowed. "Barlow's?" The pieces started to click, but the puzzle remained incomplete. "So, Gus Wharton stole the clock to use it to gain access to Mitty or Brody? That doesn't make sense. Why would he need the clock to talk to either of them?"

Drew tapped his fingers on the steering wheel, frustration etching lines on his face.

"Maybe it's a coincidence. Or, he could have needed someone to fence it. It's plausible that Wharton knew about Mitty's past. And with Mitty dead, maybe he thought with Brody that the apple didn't fall too far from the tree."

"Maybe," Hope murmured, unease prickling her skin. "But there's more. What if . . ." Her voice trailed off as she sorted out her thoughts. "What if it wasn't Gus who stole the clock? What if it was Stan?"

Drew's grip tightened on the wheel. "Alena and Stan . . . trying to bump off Mitty and Brody? That's a dark thought, even for them."

"But not beyond the realm of possibility," Hope countered, her voice gaining conviction. "And it might explain who zapped me. Think about it. Stan could have followed me out of his building and took off after Sam's car appeared."

"Did you notice any security cameras in the parking lot or at the front of the building?"

Hope shook her head. "No, but I'm sure Sam has already looked into that."

The address came into view on what used to be a mailbox post. Drew swung the vehicle into the driveway. The gravel crunched under the Explorer's tires as Drew steered it toward a detached garage mirroring the one-story ranch house. The garage's wooden panels sagged under layers of peeling paint, while the roof sported missing shingles. The house itself seemed frozen in time, its weather-beaten façade devoid of any signs of life. There was no mailbox in sight, and the absence of lights inside further emphasized the desolate nature of the place.

"Are you sure this is the right place?" Drew's voice held a hint of unease as he killed the engine. "It looks deserted."

"Positive," Hope replied. "Let's go knock on the door. Maybe someone's home. It's not exactly a great day to be out."

"If you say so." Drew pocketed the vehicle's key fob and exited the driver's side, swiftly making his way around the car to join Hope after she closed the passenger side door. "Stay close, okay?"

She nodded and trudged through the slushy snow, her boots sinking into the soft ground with each step. There was no visible path, and it was evident that no one had bothered to shovel recently. A stark contrast to the cleared driveway leading to the garage.

Reaching the chipped and battered front door, she rapped twice. Drew, meanwhile, inched toward the large bay window, peering into the gloom.

"Furniture, but no movement," he reported in a low voice. "Try again, harder."

"This definitely feels off," Hope remarked, moving toward Drew and peeking into the house. "See all that dust? And the furniture looks old. There's no way anyone lives here."

Drew nudged her shoulder, and she looked at him. "But the driveway," he said, his voice taut. "Look at those fresh tire tracks. Yet, no path to the house itself."

"I noticed that. Odd, right?" she asked.

"Unless there's no need to get to the house but there is one to get to the garage. Come on." Drew lunged forward, his steps quick and purposeful through the thick, wet snow cover.

Hope followed, keeping up with Drew's frantic pace. They passed the Explorer and headed straight for the door of the garage. The door had a bank of small windows, low enough for both to peer through. Though being a few inches shorter than Drew, Hope had to raise herself up on her tiptoes for a better view.

Through the grimy windows, the single-car garage looked like a neglected afterthought. Oil-stained blotches marred the concrete floor like old wounds, and faded paint splatters hinted at unfinished projects. Bare metal shelves lined the walls, empty and echoing the garage's overall emptiness.

"Seems like a dead end," Drew remarked as he stepped back from the windows, disappointment evident in his tone. "What's our next move?"

Hope mirrored his frustration, already making her way back to the car. "I think the fake lamps are linked to the murders. We need to find the source of Mitty's Higganum lamp—the one he sold to Ralph."

"I'd like to confirm that Dennis Llewellyn owns this property. And then find out where he is," Drew added, jogging back to the driver's side. He settled into the seat, glancing at Hope as she climbed in.

"Who are you texting?"

"Brody," Hope confirmed, hitting Send on her message.

Drew, already backing out of the driveway, cast her a concerned look. "I'm going to drop you off on my way—"

"On your way where?"

"Barlow Antiquities."

"You're not dropping me off at home. I need to go with you."

"I don't think so. You shouldn't even be out now. If Ethan or Claire finds out . . ."

"I'm a big girl." She crossed her arms and stated firmly, "I'm not letting you go without me." Her voice carried a clear challenge. She was going with him to Barlow Antiquities.

Chapter Sixteen

Drew knew better than to argue with Hope. However, during the drive to Barlow Antiquities, he attempted to persuade her to remain in the car. When she balked, he wisely backed off. Now they entered the high-end antique shop through ornate, brass-trimmed double doors. The air was laced with the subtle fragrance of polished wood and aged leather, causing Hope's nose to twitch. Her gaze swept across the showroom, taking in the mahogany display cases that lined the walls, each meticulously arranged with priceless antiques. The soft ambient light from crystal chandeliers overhead cast a warm glow on the merchandise, creating an inviting ambiance that made it almost impossible to resist browsing.

This was like no other antique shop she'd ever been in.

"I don't think I can afford to even step foot in here," Drew whispered. "Whoa! Look at that. It's stunning." He pointed to a Victorian chaise lounge in the center of the showroom.

"So is that gilded grandfather clock," Hope added, nodding toward the magnificent timepiece that stood tall and proud, its dignified tick-tock announcing the passage of time. "This place is truly amazing."

"You can say that again."

They moved forward, abruptly halting when they spotted Nora emerging from the back of the store with a tall, distinguished-looking man. Locking eyes, Hope and Drew instinctively ducked behind a nearby art deco leather sofa.

"What is she doing here?" Hope whispered.

"Why are we hiding?" Drew asked.

"We can't let her see us," Hope explained, slowly stretching up so her eyes just cleared the sofa's top. "Too bad we can't hear what they're saying."

Drew raised up, peering over the top of the sofa, but just then Nora and the man advanced, and Hope grabbed his arm, pulling him down with her to avoid detection.

"How long are we going to stay here?" Drew inquired.

"I don't know. It would be nice to find out why she's here."

"We could ask her."

"Do you trust her to tell us the truth?" Hope countered.

Drew nodded thoughtfully. "Good point."

Startled by the sound of more footsteps, they stole quick, cautious glances from their hiding spot, catching sight of another man joining Nora and her companion.

"Oh, my goodness," Hope said with a groan.

"What? Do you know him?" Drew asked.

"That's Stan Jr."

"The one who tased you?"

Hope shrugged. "I'm not sure he did."

After a warm greeting between Nora and Stan Jr., he vanished into the depths of the shop, the same area where Nora had emerged from mere moments ago.

"Now it's getting interesting," Drew said.

"I thought he was striking out on his own?" Hope questioned.

"Shocker. Alena lied," Drew declared.

Approaching footsteps sent Hope and Drew into breath-holding suspense as Nora exited the store without spotting them. After a collective sigh of relief, their tranquility was shattered by a sudden, "Is there something I can help you with?"

"Ah . . . ah . . . we . . . I lost an earring, and my friend was helping me look for it," Hope quickly improvised, thinking on her feet. "But I guess I lost it before I came into this lovely store. Right, Drew?" When he hesitated, she playfully slapped his shoulder as she straightened up. "Right?"

"Yes. You must have because it's not here," Drew said, standing.

"I see," the man replied dryly. "Was there anything in particular you were looking for, besides the earring?"

Hope cleared her throat, trying to regain her composure. "We're just browsing," she said, her voice gaining a hint of confidence. "Drew has just moved into an antique Cape Cod, and he's looking for furnishings. I've heard marvelous things about Barlow Antiquities and suggested we stop in."

The man gave them an appraising look, as if calculating whether they could afford the items in the showroom. They couldn't, but there were a few pieces that might complement Drew's house, though they would also wipe out his bank account.

"This is quite nice." Drew broke away from Hope and moved to a regal-looking chair with carved figural lion heads and claw feet. "Late-nineteenth-century Victorian."

"It is. You know antiques." The older gentleman smiled appreciatively. "Allow me to introduce myself. I'm Wallace Barlow."

"I'm Drew Adams. And I grew up around antiques. This is an exquisite piece."

For the next few minutes, Wallace Barlow and Drew engaged in a conversation about antiques. Hope's knowledge on the subject was limited, rooted in growing up in what was known as the antique capital of Connecticut and her few purchases since buying her house. None of which matched the caliber of Barlow's collection, and the language Drew and Wallace were speaking seemed foreign to her.

While they chatted, Hope explored the showroom. Playing it cool, she did her best to appear captivated by the carefully curated pieces that filled the space, while what had actually interested her was the doorway Stan Jr. had vanished through. A swift scan of the surroundings suggested the coast was clear for a bit of discreet exploration.

Navigating the corridor, she passed by closed office doors until she stumbled upon one that was slightly ajar, and she heard someone talking. Halting, she took a moment to eavesdrop.

The voice she heard belonged to Stan Jr.

"Yeah, she just left . . . Yeah, yeah . . . It was stupid of Wharton to take that clock from here . . . How could we have known he'd take that . . . Well, we couldn't not report it to the police . . . Like it or not, the Antique Alcove isn't going to work for us . . . We'll have to find another shop . . ."

Hope drew back, mentally replaying Stan's words. If she understood correctly, Barlow Antiquities had a connection to Wharton, and there seemed to be a plan involving the Antique Alcove. Lost in thought, Hope was jolted back to reality by a cheerful voice behind her.

"May I help you?"

"I . . . you startled me," Hope confessed as she spun around.

"Sorry," chirped the petite blond.

Once her heart rate settled, Hope's mind raced to concoct an excuse for being where she wasn't supposed to be. "I was looking for the restrooms. My friend is with Wallace, and I didn't want to interrupt their conversation."

"It's ahead on your right." The woman pointed down the hall. "Your friend is in good hands. Wallace Barlow is quite the expert on antiques."

"That's reassuring to know. My friend is particularly interested in a Higganum lamp. They're incredibly hard to find," Hope said.

"Not if you know the right person," she said with a grin.

"Good to know. This shop is charming. I'm grateful Gus Wharton recommended we stop by," Hope remarked, probing for any reaction from the employee.

The woman's smile vanished. "Gus Wharton sent you?" Her voice dipped low. "Who are you?"

"Just a customer," Hope replied, feeling her nerves flutter. Had she misjudged the young woman? Could she be more than a mere employee, possibly even a Barlow? A Barlow that was involved with counterfeit antiques? It was time to leave. "I'm sorry to have bothered you."

"Wait," the woman said.

"I can't." Hope dashed off, rushing through the showroom, her eyes fixed on Drew, who was browsing a dining set. She grabbed his arm with urgency. "We need to leave."

"What's wrong? Why?" He stumbled after her firing questions, but they were ignored.

Hope yanked open the front door, stepping outside and hurrying down the sidewalk until she deemed it safe enough. Drew was bombarding her with questions, finally refusing to take another step.

"What the heck happened in there?" Drew asked.

"They are dealing in fake antiques. From what I gather, they are selling them through smaller shops and somehow Gus was involved."

"Okay. Okay. But that doesn't explain why we bolted out of there. I really liked that dining set," he pouted.

Hope sighed. "I got caught eavesdropping by an employee, I think. Anyway, I said that Wharton told us about the shop . . ."

"What?"

"She got suspicious."

"Of course she did."

"But I don't think they knew that Wharton took the clock."

"Are you saying he really did steal it?"

Hope nodded. "You know that saying, once a thief . . . Come on, we have to let Sam know what we've learned here. And I need to get back to town to judge the gingerbread houses."

"What business do you think Nora had with Wallace and Stan Jr.?" Drew looked back at the storefront.

Hope followed Drew's gaze. "My gut tells me nothing good."

• • •

Back in Jefferson, Drew dropped Hope off in front of the library after their visit to the police department, where they had briefed Sam in his office. They relayed what they had uncovered at Barlow's, which, on the surface, seemed like little to the detective. He pointed out that Hope had only overheard one side of a conversation, and Nora was in the store of her daughter's boyfriend's family. No smoking guns there. Feeling somewhat deflated, Hope reluctantly agreed that they hadn't gathered much new information to assist with Sam's two open murder cases.

"You're sure you don't need a ride home? I'm going there anyway to pick up my car," Drew asked from the driver's seat.

"Thanks, but I don't have the time. Don't worry, I can arrange a lift home after the contest," Hope replied. The inclement weather of earlier in the day had cleared, and the sun had begun to peek out from behind the clouds, so she considered the possibility of walking home if she felt up to it.

"Call me if you need anything," Drew insisted as he started the ignition. "I'm going to swing by Town Hall and check the property records for that abandoned house on Swamp Road."

"Keep me updated. See you later." Hope stepped out of the

Explorer and made a beeline for the library's entrance. She'd spent countless hours there as a child and now she enjoyed the sense of community it brought to Jeffersonians.

Once inside the building, she made her way to a quiet corner in the research room to do a little internet digging. She settled at a table and logged onto a computer. She had a few minutes before the gingerbread house contest began and she chose to use that time to delve into the shady side of the antique trade.

When she and Drew spoke with Sam, he had mentioned that a common tactic among fraudsters was to utilize well-established and reputable antique stores as fronts to gain the trust of buyers and the antique community. Stores such as the Antique Alcove and Fenn Antiques were ideal candidates. The mere thought that Issy's shop had fallen prey to such deception, targeted by con artists, ignited a surge of anger that made her blood boil. However, as Sam had said before they'd wrapped up their conversation, everything came to an end at some point. And she was determined to ensure Barlow's scheme came to an end.

"What a scam it was," she muttered as she scrolled down the computer screen. If Sam still wasn't going to share with her the connection between Wharton, Mitty and Denny Beyer, then she'd find it herself. She had a hunch but needed to confirm it. She was coming up empty. Until she found an age-old newspaper article. If she was looking at an actual newspaper, she would most likely have had to blow off the dust.

Gus Wharton had been arrested with Denny Beyer for a robbery in New Haven years before the jewelry store heist. She continued searching but couldn't find any follow-up articles. Guess it wasn't very newsworthy.

"Hope," Lexi called out from the hallway. "Sally asked me to get you. Everything is ready."

Hope glanced over her shoulder. Lexi stood in the doorway wearing her event organizer badge and grasping a clipboard to her chest. A wince contorted her face for a fleeting moment before she forced a smile.

"Sorry. I got sucked into a black hole of research," Hope said.

"What kind of research?" Lexi inquired as she made her way through a row of tables. Her smile softened as she reached Hope's chair. "I love researching."

"You and Sally have that in common. What I'm doing isn't really important. I'll just be a minute."

"Actually, Sally says you're already late." Lexi tapped her watch. "Everyone is waiting."

"Punctuality is very important to her." And, very important to Hope. She hated being tardy. She tore her gaze from Lexi, and it landed on her workspace. It would take a few minutes to pack up her bag. No, she couldn't make Sally and everyone else wait any longer. "Okay. I'll pack up when we're finished." She stood and breezed out of the room and walked along the corridor with Lexi to the community room. Entering, she was overwhelmed by the spicy scent of gingerbread in the air and instantly enveloped in the warmth of holiday cheer. The room was adorned with festive decorations, from twinkling fairy lights draped along the walls to vibrant garlands that added a touch of merriment. At the center of the room stood three cloth-draped tables, each carefully arranged to showcase the creative masterpieces of the gingerbread house bakers.

"Our last judge is *finally* here," Sally announced to the waiting audience.

Sally's pointed *finally* grated on Hope's ears. With a mumbled apology, she hurried past the older woman to join Jane and Meg Griffin, her fellow judges. Together, they'd choose the grand-prize winner and runners-up. Surveying the vast display of entries spread before them, Hope felt a wave of trepidation wash over her. Choosing just three winners from this talented pool seemed an almost daunting task.

Sally handed Hope her clipboard with the judging paperwork, and then all three judges were given final instructions and off they went to appraise each creation.

Armed with their clipboards and a keen eye for detail, Hope and her fellow judges made their way around the room. The array of gingerbread houses varied in size and design, from traditional gingerbread cottages with candy cane trim to imaginative structures adorned with gumdrops and chocolate shingles.

Hope had no idea how they were going to pick a winner. All the entries were amazing.

Once they had inspected each house, Hope, Meg and Jane huddled as soft, festive music mingled with excited whispers that filled the room as participants and spectators waited for the winners to be announced.

"I didn't think you were going to make it today," Meg said, clipboard clutched to her chest. "From what I hear, your snooping got you into trouble yesterday."

"Thanks for your concern," Hope said. You never knew what you were going to get with Meg—snarky Meg, sneaky Meg, or playing-nice-for-the-time-being Meg. "There was no way I'd miss this." She smiled at Jane.

"I knew you wouldn't, dear." Jane patted Hope's arm. "Though, you need to fill me in on what's been happening. Perhaps you'll come for tea at the inn later?"

"A murder meeting?" Meg rolled her eyes. "It's like high school never ended."

Jane gave a shake of her head and ignored Meg's comment about the mystery book club she led for high school seniors back when Hope was a teenager. "Drew texted me that you two went somewhere this morning."

"An old farmhouse out on Swamp Road. It looked abandoned," Hope said as she reviewed her scoring sheet one last time.

"That's because its owner, Giselle Abernathy, passed away eight months ago," Meg said. "Her daughter and her husband are clearing it out. Why on earth did you and Drew go there?"

"Is his name Dennis Llewellyn?" Hope asked.

"Yes," Meg answered. "How are they connected to your *investigation*?"

Hope's train of thought was derailed by a sudden loud clap. Her gaze snapped toward the center of the room, where Sally stood beaming at the podium.

"Alright, judges," Sally's voice rang out, carrying a playful yet expectant lilt, "have we reached a verdict yet? We're all on the edge of our seats here!"

A ripple of murmurs and suppressed giggles danced through the room. Jane raised a hand in appeasement. "We're just finalizing the details," she assured Sally and the attendees. Then, leaning closer to Hope and Meg, she whispered, "Are we all on the same page?"

"I think we made our decision," Hope said. "Are we ready to let Sally know?"

Meg nodded. "There's no question who the grand-prize winner is."

"I agree." Jane glanced at the gingerbread replica of the Jefferson Library. "The detail Honey Travis put into her entry is astonishing."

Hope gathered their clipboards and handed them to Sally. The grand-prize winner, along with the two runners-up, were noted on the judging forms. The announcement was made, the prize ribbons were handed out and photographs were taken for the *Gazette*.

"Dear, now that's over, we can continue our chat," Jane said as she cupped Hope's elbow and led her away from the group that had gathered around the winners. "When Claire called us last night, we were horrified someone attacked you."

Hope shared the same sentiment.

"Though, it does tell us that we are on the right track." Jane's blue eyes lit up and she looked positively thrilled. "You know, when I was writing the Barbara Neal mysteries, she always became a target of the perpetrator the closer she got to identifying the person."

"I'm nowhere near ready to identify the perpetrator."

Jane clasped her hands. Her bright pink lips turned upright and the glint in her eyes intensified. "You must be on to something, or else you wouldn't have been attacked."

"Me being attacked was a sign of progress?"

"Yes, dear. Now, you must come for tea. As I said, we need to regroup and review our notes," Jane said.

"Absolutely," Hope reassured her, enveloping Jane in a warm hug. "I'll call you later." Leaving the community room, she exchanged waves with Sally and Meg before strolling down the corridor back to the research section. She returned to the table she'd been working at. "Well, that's odd," she murmured at the blank screen as she clicked the mouse. The tabs she'd had open on the browser were closed. A prickle of unease ran down her spine. A quick check of her tote confirmed that nothing was missing. Had she closed the tabs? Maybe during Lexi's interruption? Exhaustion, a tidal wave after a long day fueled only by a couple gingerbread cookies, crashed over her. It was time to go.

With her tote slung over her shoulder and her jacket zipped up, Hope navigated through the research area toward the lobby. Conversations buzzed around her, ranging from gingerbread house raves to holiday plans to the recent murder, as attendees spilled out from the community room. Skillfully dodging the chatter by keeping her head down and her stride purposeful, Hope made her way toward the exit. It was then that she spotted Alena entering the library, carrying a stack of books.

"Alena," Hope called out in a loud whisper as she darted across the lobby. "I'm glad I've run into you. There's something that has been bothering me about Gus Wharton's murder."

Alena skidded to a stop in front of Hope. Her previously carefree expression turned guarded as their eyes met. Her dark hair was tamed by a colorful knitted headband that matched her mittens. "Something other than the fact that he was murdered?"

"I'd like to know why you lied about not hearing anything from the front of the shop when it all went down?"

"How dare you accuse me of lying." Alena's raised voice caused heads to turn in their direction.

Hope pressed her lips together. The last thing she needed was to cause a scene and have someone pull out their phone to video her conversation with Alena. Her first instinct was to diffuse the situation by apologizing. Claire always said her biggest weakness was wanting to be liked by everyone. But she couldn't apologize for something she knew she was right about.

"There's no way you didn't hear something. A struggle. Wharton's fall. His scream. There was noise. The shop isn't that big." Hope glanced around the lobby. Several of the huddled groups had dissipated or had re-engaged in their conversations. Since she and Alena were no longer of interest, she continued with her questioning. "Are you covering for someone? Was it Stan who killed Wharton?"

"Why would he? He didn't know that man."

"That's not true. Wharton stole the clock, the one he had when he was killed, from Barlow's. He was supposed to do something else. Maybe sell fake Higganum lamps to unsuspecting antique dealers like Mitty?" Hope suggested, watching for Alena's reaction.

Alena's expression clouded with confusion.

Hope pressed on. "You thought being on the phone with Brody would give you an alibi."

Alena's breath hitched. "No, Stan isn't a killer. The truth is, when I called Brody, I was out back in the lot behind the shop, not in the office."

"You were outside? Why?" Hope pressed for clarification.

"Smoking." Shame flushed her cheeks. "Brody hates it, especially in the shop. I'm trying to quit, but with everything . . . it's been hard." Her voice trembled. "After Wharton showed me the clock and said how much he wanted for it, I grabbed my phone and a cigarette, figuring I'd have a quick smoke while I called Brody. I never thought . . ." Alena's voice trembled as she reached into her cross-body bag for a tissue, wiping away the tears that had begun to flow. "I lied because I didn't want him to yell again. It's my fault. If I hadn't left that man alone . . ." Her words trailed off as tears streamed down her cheeks.

A gust of icy air swirled in through the open door. Hope glanced toward the entrance, realizing it wasn't just the weather causing the chill. Maretta Kingston had entered the building.

Chapter Seventeen

Maretta hurriedly approached but screeched to a halt as she spotted Alena's tear-streaked face. "Alena!" she cried. Before Hope could utter a word, Maretta's arm was wrapped protectively around the young woman. "What's wrong? Why is she crying?" The questions, sharp and laced with accusation, were fired directly at Hope.

Frustration bubbled beneath Hope's skin. The last thing she needed was Maretta Kingston's suffocating fog of judgment.

"It's all my fault," Alena choked out, dabbing at her tears. "I shouldn't have left that man alone. I'll tell the detective everything."

"There, there," Maretta consoled Alena. "Hope, were you interrogating her about the murder at the Antique Alcove?"

"There was no interrogation," Hope clarified. "We were discussing the events around the time of the murder."

"She knew I lied," Alena admitted tearfully. "I shouldn't have. I've made a mess of things. Like I always do."

Maretta's tone sharpened. "Hope, why do you persist in meddling in police matters? Especially since your boyfriend isn't around to clean up your messes anymore." Her voice dropped to a dramatic whisper. "Speaking of which, filling his position is proving an absolute nightmare. Nobody understands the burdens I shoulder! And now I have to deal with this." Her voice rose and caught the notice of patrons as they mulled around the lobby. She instantly composed herself but shot a glaring look at Hope, as if it was her fault people were gawking.

Hope fought the urge to respond to Maretta's glare and her self-centered comments. She had a knack for twisting sympathy into self-absorption. Before Hope could say anything, a soft "psst . . . psst" came from behind her. She looked over her shoulder and saw Julia Lang waving her over. Hope seized the opportunity to escape her current situation and quietly disengaged herself from Maretta and Alena, crossing the lobby to join Julia.

"Should I ask what's going on over there?" Julia inquired.

"No. I'm afraid you missed the gingerbread house contest." While talking, Hope kept an eye on Maretta and Alena. It appeared Alena had composed herself enough to continue into the library, heading toward the circulation desk accompanied by Maretta.

"I heard what happened yesterday. I didn't think you'd be out and about. But I'm glad to see you're doing okay."

"I've had better days," Hope admitted. "I ran into Ralph yesterday, and he told me about his past troubles with Mitty. He also mentioned being arrested."

Julia's complexion turned pale. "Ralph has done so much good over the years, and now it seems inevitable that his past mistakes will destroy his reputation, erode the trust he's built with his customers. It's just not fair."

Hope sympathized with Julia's distress. Living in a small town had its advantages and drawbacks. On one hand, there was a close-knit community ready to support you through thick and thin, like when she'd participated in the reality show *The Sweet Taste of Success* and received overwhelming local support. But the flip side was a relentless memory. Mistakes clung to you like cobwebs in an attic, making big-city anonymity seem almost appealing.

"It's probably more important to make sure he doesn't go to prison for murder than to worry about how some people will view his past deeds," Hope said.

"It happened so long ago. I'd just started dating Albert when Ralph got caught stealing a car," Julia recalled as she unbuttoned her wool coat and removed her gloves. "It was a frightening time because we didn't know how to help him."

"So, the arrest was the turning point?"

"Yes and no. He and Mitty had a falling out over the same girl. He returned to Jefferson, alone, and enrolled in a trade school."

"And he stayed out of trouble after that?"

"He most certainly did. He truly turned his life around. That's why we were so nervous when Mitty reappeared," Julia confessed, stepping aside to let a patron shuffle past into the computer room. "Thankfully, Ralph steered clear of him. We all did."

"Why?" Hope inquired. "It sounds like Ralph was a different person by then."

"Because Mitty was the ringleader. Sure, Ruth and Nora believed he just got caught up in the wrong crowd, but from what Ralph said, Mitty was the one who put the crowd together."

A sharp *ahem* cut through the conversation. Hope turned to find Maretta standing there, arms crossed, a disapproving look on her face.

"I should get going," Julia said abruptly. "It's good to see that you're doing well, Hope." She breezed past Hope and Maretta, making a swift exit.

Hope understood. Maretta radiating disapproval was enough to make anyone flee. "Is there something you'd like to say, Maretta?"

Maretta uncrossed her arms, a flicker of vulnerability replacing the usual sternness. "Yes, there is. I've known you since you were a child, and I cannot say that I've ever been so disappointed in you before. You really upset Alena. Her mother is a close friend of mine, and seeing her so distraught . . ." The sentence trailed off, a hint of genuine concern peeking through Maretta's tough exterior.

Hope, surprised by the unexpected glimpse of empathy, softened. "I apologize if I upset her. But I do appreciate her finally coming clean about what happened at the shop."

Maretta's expression hardened once more. "After your own ordeal yesterday, I would think that you would leave the investigating to the police."

"Then you don't know me as well as you think. Have a nice day." Hope patted Maretta on the arm and then turned, heading for the exit.

The brisk air nipped at Hope's cheeks as she walked out of the stately two-story brick building. Gathering her jacket tighter, she started down the path, past the empty benches that, come spring, would overflow with patrons enjoying their latest finds.

"Hey, Hope!" Drew called out as he approached with a bulging bag from Good Day, Good Dog pet shop.

"Did you clear out the entire store?" she teased once he reached her side.

"Almost." He chuckled, a hint of sheepishness in his voice. "It's my first Christmas with Trixie, and I want to make it unforgettable."

Hope couldn't help but picture the upcoming credit card

statement. "Unforgettable for your wallet too, I imagine," she said, peering into the bag. A festive plaid coat lay among an assortment of toys and treats. "How many coats does she have now?"

Drew shrugged, a playful grin spreading across his face. "Maybe two, or four? I just want her to have everything."

"She's going to adore this one," Hope remarked, setting off with Drew falling into stride beside her. "Even if Santa only brings her one gift this year, it would still be a wonderful Christmas for her. After all, she has the greatest gift of all—a loving home with you."

Drew's cheeks flushed with a hint of embarrassment. "Thanks, Hope. I'm doing my best. Though, I have a lot to learn."

She offered a reassuring pat on her friend's shoulder. "You're doing fine. Well, except for bringing a squirrel into the house. Not really a good idea with a dog."

Drew groaned. "You'll never let me live that down, will you?"

"Nope," Hope replied with a laugh. They reached the corner, pausing as traffic flowed by on Main Street.

"Before I stopped at the pet shop, I did have success at Town Hall looking through property deeds," Drew said.

"Great. But hold that thought for a moment because you want to hear this."

"Ooh, I'm all ears."

"I learned two things just now. First, Alena said she was outside the shop when Wharton was killed, and second, Mitty and Ralph did know each other when they were younger and stealing cars but had a falling out over a girl."

"Guess I shouldn't have skipped the gingerbread house contest," Drew quipped.

Hope nodded, smiling. "You really should know better. I also found out that Giselle Abernathy owned the house on Swamp Road."

"That's what I was going to tell you!" He pouted. "Who told you?"

"Meg. She mentioned the family's been clearing out the house after Giselle passed. My guess is her son-in-law sold the lamp to your mom's shop and was clueless it was a fake."

The streetlight changed and together they crossed the street.

"Yeah, but my mom should have known," Drew mumbled.

Stepping up onto the curb, they headed in the direction of the Coffee Clique. Hope was debating getting a cinnamon roll. Normally it would be an easy decision, but she'd been doing so much baking and taste testing each batch, plus the recipes for the cookbook. She wasn't sure if she needed the extra calories.

Drew's phone buzzed, and he checked the text message. He stopped in his tracks and whistled.

Hope knew instantly something had happened.

"What's going on?" Hope inquired, leaning in to catch a glimpse of his phone screen. "Don't tell me there's been another murder."

Drew glanced at her before returning to his phone. "No murder. But someone has broken into the Antique Alcove."

"The shop's been closed since the murder."

"I have to get back to the office," he said, already starting to walk away.

"Wait! Do you know who broke in?" Hope called after him.

"Yes, they do. It was Ruth Fitzgerald." Drew juggled his phone and shopping bag, attempting to respond to a message.

Hope frowned. "Seriously? Why would she do that?"

Drew shrugged.

"Unless she was after something," Hope mused aloud.

"Like what?" Drew asked.

Hope's voice dropped to a conspiratorial whisper. "Money? Jewelry? Maybe she thought Mitty hid something from the jewelry store robbery."

• • •

Hope kicked off her boots in the mudroom, the crisp December air clinging to her clothes. She stepped into the warm kitchen and the sweet aroma of cinnamon and berries greeted her. A steaming bowl of creamy oatmeal sat on the table, a welcome reward after her morning chores in the chicken coop. A white chocolate truffle from her Advent calendar sat temptingly beside her plate.

"Hey, babe." Ethan entered the kitchen from the hallway with his backpack slung over his shoulder. On his heels was Bigelow. The dog quickly veered off to welcome Hope back inside, tail wagging furiously. Clearly ecstatic to have Hope back, he showered her with enthusiastic doggy greetings even though she'd barely been gone thirty minutes.

Hope showered Bigelow with grateful pats and a quick scratch behind the ears before settling into her chair at the table. "Thank you for making me breakfast." With a satisfied sigh, her eyes landed on the creamy oatmeal. Her spoon clinked against the bowl as she scooped up a generous portion, then glanced playfully at the white chocolate truffle. "Alright, breakfast of champions," she declared, popping the decadent treat into her mouth before diving into the oatmeal.

Ethan laughed. "I thought you'd go for the chocolate first." At the coffee maker, he filled an oversized mug for Hope and then his travel mug. "I wish you would have waited for me to help with the chickens."

"That's sweet but I'm feeling better. And I want to keep busy. Next up is some admin work." She gestured toward her laptop across the table. After swallowing another spoonful of oatmeal, she asked, "Will you be home for dinner? I was thinking of making a meatloaf."

Ethan screwed on the lid of his travel mug and then delivered Hope's coffee to her. "It's going to be a long day. There are some loose ends to tie up before the holidays. How about I call you later?"

Hope stirred her oatmeal, a wistful sigh escaping her lips. "I was hoping for a quiet evening in tonight. Why can't Matt just close the office until next year?"

"Ongoing cases. Believe it or not, some people get arrested during the holidays." Ethan leaned down for a quick kiss and headed out.

She hated to admit it, but he was right. Poor Ralph Lang was proof enough of that. Shaking off the distraction that was the murder case, Hope finished her breakfast. After clearing the table and refilling her mug, she returned to the table and turned on her computer. The familiar hum of the awakening machine filled the silence. Her eyes flickered to the composition notebook lying open on the table. The urge to delve back into her unsolved murder case was a constant itch, but the long list of to-dos demanded attention first. Still, there were recent updates that begged to be included in her notes.

Just a quick update, she convinced herself. It couldn't take more than a few minutes.

Taking a sip of coffee, she flipped to a clean page and scribbled down the latest developments since the taser incident.

"Second fake lamp appeared," she scribbled. "Drew called earlier, while I was at the chicken coop. He spoke to Giselle Abernathy's daughter yesterday. She revealed that her mother owned the lamp for decades. It had been a housewarming gift. They were clueless about its being a fake and felt awful about selling it to Fenn Antiques. This meant the Abernathy lamp wasn't connected to Ralph's purchase or the suspected Barlow scam, although that still needed confirmation."

Hope flipped to a new page, her pen scratching furiously. That note recounted Julia's disclosure from the previous day regarding Mitty and Ralph's shared love interest—irrelevant on the surface, but she couldn't discount it as a piece of the puzzle.

Her final notation reflected the conversation she'd overheard at Barlow's, revealing that Wharton had pilfered a clock from the establishment. Despite the Barlows' familiarity with Wharton, they were caught off guard by his theft. This left Hope pondering the nature of Wharton's involvement with them, prompting a string of question marks to litter her page. Each discovery seemed to spawn a multitude of further inquiries, rather than offering any concrete answers.

Staring at her notes wouldn't solve anything. It was time to return to her real job, the one that paid the bills and kept a roof over her head. First, recipe development—her editor had emailed about her progress. Hope was happy to report that despite the murders, the tasering, and the holiday chaos, she was on track. Yet, with a sigh, she bypassed the spreadsheet she made for her recipe development schedule for the *Gazette*'s website. "Just a few minutes," she muttered.

The website's home page displayed the breaking news story about the Antique Alcove's break-in. While Ruth's arrest was reported, there were no details about her motive.

That was disappointing. She'd hoped for some insight into why Ruth broke into the store.

She was just about to open her spreadsheet when the doorbell's chime disrupted the quiet of the house. Hope swiftly reached for her phone, quickly accessing the smart doorbell app to find Ruth standing on the porch. Although Ruth's unexpected visit caught her off guard, Hope welcomed the sight of her. She had a few questions for her. First, she needed to get control over Bigelow. Always alert, he erupted into a frenzy of barks and darted toward the door. Feeling the lingering soreness from the taser incident, she acknowledged that she might have overexerted herself the day before. She grasped the doorknob just as the bell chimed once more, sending Bigelow into an even greater frenzy. Finally, she managed to calm the dog down before opening the door to greet Ruth.

Hope's heart ached as she saw Ruth. The woman's once-vibrant energy had faded, replaced by a weary exhaustion. Her skin lacked its usual healthy glow, her hair hung limp, and her eyes were rimmed with red.

"Hope, I'm so sorry to show up unexpected," Ruth rasped, her voice cracking. "I heard what happened and . . . well, I just had to see you."

Bigelow let out a woof, his attention fixed on Ruth.

"Bigelow, sit," Hope commanded, and he obeyed, but his gaze remained on the distraught woman at the door. "Thank you, Ruth. I am feeling better."

Ruth's attempt at a smile faltered. "Better enough for some company?"

"Yes, of course. Please come in," Hope replied warmly, stepping aside to let her guest enter the foyer. Bigelow shuffled out of the way but stayed nearby to keep his eyes on Hope.

"I've made a terrible mess of things," Ruth confessed, her voice trembling like a leaf in a storm. "An awful mess."

"I'm sure it's not that bad." As soon as Hope said those words, she regretted them. How were things not bad? Ruth had been arrested. "Let me take your coat, and then we'll go into the kitchen for some coffee and talk."

Ruth shrugged out of her coat and gave it to Hope, who hung it in the hall closet. Hope then led Ruth to the kitchen, with Bigelow trailing behind.

"This kitchen is lovely." Ruth's fingers brushed lightly across the granite countertop as she passed the island on the way to the table. A wistful smile flickered on her lips, then faded. "Mitty and I attempted a similar project once. Needless to say, our DIY skills weren't up to the challenge."

"Remodeling a kitchen is more than a DIY project," Hope said as she retrieved a mug from a cabinet. Turning to the table to remove hers, she noticed the lingering evidence of her internet search—the *Gazette* website was still open on her computer. "I have some cookies, if you'd like them to go along with our coffee." She dashed to the table and closed her laptop before removing it to the island.

Ruth shook her head, her interest drawn to the bank of windows overlooking the backyard. "Just the coffee, please."

Hope filled the mugs and carried them to the table. "Have a seat," she said and gestured. Bigelow promptly settled by her feet. "Now, tell me what happened. Did you really break into the Antique Alcove?"

"One of the things I appreciate about you is your directness," Ruth remarked.

"Not everyone shares that sentiment," Hope replied in a lighthearted tone.

After taking a sip of coffee, Ruth finally said, "I did it. I'm so ashamed of my behavior. But I'm desperate." The word hung in the air, a weight pressing down on them both. Hope's heart lurched. Desperate? What could have driven Ruth to such a drastic measure?

Chapter Eighteen

"Desperate?" Hope leaned forward, intrigued. "Why did you do it? Help me understand."

"This is so embarrassing." Ruth's eyes darted toward the windows, avoiding Hope's scrutiny. "Honestly, I don't recognize the person I was when I broke into that shop. If I hadn't messed up putting in the alarm code, I wouldn't have been caught. Mitty never changed it."

"The alarm company notified the police," Hope said. That answered the question about how exactly Ruth *broke* into the shop. She had visions of the woman using a lock pick to gain access. "Tell me, does what happened have something to do with the fact you need to buy a van for your craft business?" Hope recalled what Claire had said about Ruth's financial struggles. "Since Mitty refused to sell the property you both own up in the Berkshires, you can't afford the van."

Ruth finally met Hope's eyes, bewilderment giving way to understanding. "You know? Right. You're investigating the murders. And you're spot on."

"Why did Mitty refuse to sell the property?" Hope inquired.

"I have no idea. He wouldn't discuss it with me. Mitty had been angry with me because of the divorce and intended to make everything a struggle for me."

"Why did you feel the need to sneak into the shop? Why not just go there when it was open?" Hope redirected the conversation back to Ruth's break-in.

"Then I would have had to tell Brody what I was looking for," Ruth said, her voice strained. "After you left, I went back down to my basement and searched for anything else that I might have overlooked when I moved into the rental house. You know, anything that belonged to Mitty but got mixed in with my stuff. I kept thinking about the jewelry store robbery."

"You were hoping to find money or jewelry," Hope said. "Then what? If you found jewelry, you would have pawned it?"

"I do know a few people who don't ask a lot of questions about things," Ruth admitted.

Hope leaned forward, her voice softer now, laced with concern. "Ruth, listen to me. It would have been wrong. There must be another way for you to get the funds you need."

"I know. I know," Ruth mumbled. "I'm so ashamed. What's worse is that Brody is so disappointed in me. It shattered my heart when he said that to me."

"Give him some time. He's been through a lot, and what you did was a shock to him."

"Thankfully, he's not pressing charges."

"That's a relief."

"Tell me about it." Ruth sighed, lacing her fingers around her mug. "I just wish that mug shot wasn't plastered everywhere. How am I supposed to live this down?"

Hope chuckled, a hint of empathy in her voice. "Public humiliation? Trust me, I get it. Remember the Birdie Donovan meltdown last year? It went viral in seconds. And then there's the whole candy cane assault incident that just surfaced."

Ruth's lips twitched into a smile. "Right, the candy cane. Though, at least that wasn't an arrest. This . . . this feels different."

"It is different," Hope agreed, her voice turning serious. "But trust me, the news cycle forgets fast. Now, tell me. Did you find anything at the shop?"

"No." Ruth sighed, sinking back into her chair. "Whatever money Mitty got from the robbery is probably long gone. We had so much debt. But even if he did something wrong, it was for us. For me. If only I hadn't . . ." Her voice trailed off, laced with guilt.

"You can't think like that. Getting sick wasn't your fault." Hope stood with her mug in hand. She set it in the sink as she passed by on her way to the refrigerator for a bottle of water. Holding it up, she asked if Ruth wanted one too. When Ruth declined, Hope returned to the table.

"While I was looking for nonexistent *treasure*, I did find something interesting." Ruth rummaged in her purse and pulled out an old photograph, sliding it across the table for Hope to see. "It's Mitty."

Hope pushed aside her bottled water and picked up the faded

image of a younger Mitty with his arm around a woman. "I can see why you fell for him. He was a handsome man."

"He was," Ruth said wistfully. "I'd never seen that photo before."

"No? What's so interesting about it?" Hope inquired, looking up from the photo.

"The woman he's with, doesn't she look familiar to you?"

Hope brought the photo closer so she could scrutinize the young blond woman's face. It took a few seconds for her to recognize her. "Nora?"

Ruth nodded. "I had no idea they knew each other before."

"Julia mentioned a woman had caused a rift between Mitty and Ralph." Hope set the picture down. "And now Mitty is dead and Ralph is accused of killing him."

Ruth stayed long enough to finish her coffee and brainstorm some ways she could get the down payment for her van. She'd been relying on consignment sales since starting her business. Having a van would allow her to travel to craft shows. Hope pointed out there was an opportunity for online sales and shared with her some tips on getting started. When Hope said goodbye to Ruth, she left with a box of cookies and a glimmer of hope she'd be able to expand her ornament business. When Ruth was walking toward her car, Hope shut the front door and replayed their conversation about Mitty, Ralph and Nora. How did that triangle play into Mitty's murder? Gus Wharton's murder? Or did it? There was a chance it was all a coincidence. When she entered the kitchen, her phone buzzed with a notification that Claire was unlocking the mudroom door. Perfect timing. It saved Hope a phone call.

The kitchen door swung open, and Claire, barely visible beneath the pulled-up collar of her faux fur coat and hat, entered. "Mom and Dad had the right idea about moving to Florida," she announced as she visibly shivered.

"I was just about to call you," Hope said, reaching for her apron. "You won't believe what I just found out."

Claire shrugged out of her coat and draped it over the chair where Ruth had sat just minutes ago. "About Ruth? I saw her as I turned onto your road."

Hope tightened the strings on her apron. "She showed up unexpectedly. She wanted to talk." Her planned recipe testing session was delayed by Ruth's visit, and she had to get moving if she wanted to be done by dinnertime. The next recipe on her agenda was a cheddar chicken and broccoli casserole. She retrieved the deep dish from a lower cabinet and gathered all the necessary ingredients from the refrigerator.

Claire poured herself a steaming cup of coffee. "Talk about what?"

"She regrets what she did." Hope retrieved a grater, a mixing bowl and several spoons from the large red crock on the island.

Claire scoffed. "Regrets breaking into the store? What she probably regrets is getting caught. She'll never live it down, even though Brody isn't pressing charges. That's all over town now. It is the right thing for him to do. After all, she's his mother."

"You were right about her needing money to buy a new van. She was desperate. So, she was looking for anything Mitty might have hidden from that jewelry store robbery."

"The robbery? That was ages ago." Claire added a drop of cream to her coffee before taking a sip. She returned to the table and sat, crossing her legs. "Why does it keep rearing its ugly head?"

"I believe what's happening now is connected to that robbery," Hope remarked, measuring out the grated cheese and adding it to the bowl. "Yesterday, I ran into Julia when I was leaving the library."

Claire shot her a glare that could have rivaled Maretta's infamous death stare.

"You were and still are supposed to be taking it easy," Claire scolded.

Hope, adding more grated cheese to the bowl because you could never have too much cheese, sheepishly defended herself. "Okay, so maybe the library wasn't exactly *resting*."

Claire's glare softened slightly.

"I couldn't just not show up. I was one of the judges at the gingerbread house contest. Anyway, Julia said that Mitty and Ralph knew each other when they were younger."

"Don't tell me, they were thick as thieves?" Claire interjected.

"Exactly," Hope confirmed. "There's more. They had a falling out over a woman," Hope revealed, returning what was left of the cheddar wedge to the refrigerator. Back at the island, she removed the lid of the cooked, shredded chicken she'd prepared in the slow cooker for the recipe. "Ruth found a picture of Mitty when he was younger with who I think was the woman who tore apart his friendship with Ralph."

"Don't tell me you recognized her," Claire exclaimed.

Hope nodded solemnly. "It's Nora."

Claire's jaw practically hit the floor. "Seriously?"

"Yes. And Ruth recognized her too."

"Interesting. Very interesting. Nora's husband is dead, and her ex-boyfriend has been arrested for the murder. And you saw her with Stan Jr. at Barlow's," Claire observed, standing. She approached the island, worry lines evident on her forehead "She's involved with all of this up to her surgically enhanced arched eyebrows. Hope, listen to me. This is getting out of hand. We, *you*"—Claire pointed a manicured finger at her sister— "need to stop investigating. It's too dangerous!"

"You can't be serious. I'm not going to stop now." Shaking her head, Hope reached into a drawer, retrieving a set of measuring spoons. Just as she did, her cell phone buzzed. When she glanced at the screen, she saw Albert Lang's name. After tapping on the phone, she said, "Hi, Albert."

Albert's voice sounded urgent. "Hope, I hate to bother you, but we really need your help."

"Is it about Ralph?" Hope asked.

"No. No. It's Julia. She took a tumble and broke her leg," Albert said.

"Oh, no!" She quickly tapped her phone and switched to speaker mode. "Albert, you're on speaker with me and Claire."

"Hey, Albert," Claire chimed in. "What's going on?"

"Julia broke her leg," Hope said. "Albert, other than that, is Julia okay?"

"Yes. But here's the thing. There's no one else who can bake, and you know how the farm depends on the sales of the baked goods. We have enough for today, but we don't think we have enough to carry us through tomorrow," Albert explained.

Claire immediately shook her head, silently signaling her

disapproval for what Albert was about to ask.

"I know the timing stinks since your plate is already so full, but is there any chance you could step in for Julia and bake just enough for us to get through tomorrow? Our daughter arrives tomorrow afternoon, and she can take over until Christmas," Albert requested.

"Well . . . it's a lot of food that needs to be baked." Hope hesitated, contemplating the request. "Would you be okay with paring down the offerings?"

Claire mouthed a definite "no" and gestured frantically. Hope swatted her hands away, moving down the counter to get away from her sister. What Alfred was asking was a monumental task in addition to everything else she had to do, but it was exactly what she needed to keep her mind occupied. Plus, it would give her content for a blog post. It was a beast that needed to be fed constantly.

"Absolutely," Albert agreed. "I'll send you over a spreadsheet of what we normally sell in a day. Thank you so much, Hope. You have no idea of how grateful we are."

"You're welcome. I hope Julia has a speedy recovery." Hope ended the call and set her phone down. Then she turned her attention to her sister. "What is your problem?"

"My problem? You're supposed to be recuperating, not baking dozens of muffins for a tree farm," Claire exclaimed.

"Baking helps clear my mind. You know it's my happy place. Besides, all they need are some muffins, brownies and reindeer munch. It's only for one day. I've got this," she assured Claire.

Claire folded her arms and huffed. "It's way too much for you to take on. You're still recovering from being tased, and you have so much to do for your own Christmas."

"Don't worry so much. I feel fine. You know how organized I am. Besides, I have plenty of time," she said confidently, more to reassure herself than Claire, as she mentally planned on how to juggle all the tasks that now lay ahead.

• • •

Hope wasted no time in shooing her sister out of her house once her cheddar chicken and broccoli casserole was in the oven and Claire had exhausted all her arguments against baking for the Langs' tree farm or for stopping Hope's investigation into the murders. There was no way she would curtail her sleuthing. She was in too deep, and despite the looming danger, Hope felt compelled to see the case through until the killer was identified.

When the timer went off and she pulled the casserole out of the oven, she found herself yearning for a moment of relaxation and the opportunity to plan her baking schedule. A nice soak in the tub and then a quick planning session in a cozy fleece outfit sounded delightful. Too bad her anticipation of a warm soak upstairs was abruptly interrupted by the persistent ringing of her phone.

Sally's voice, filled with excitement, greeted her on the other end. She explained that she had stumbled upon a captivating piece of information about Denny Beyer's past and urged Hope to join her for tea at the inn to discuss it. Hope was caught in a tug-of-war, her tub's serenity versus the case's urgency. With a sigh she descended the staircase, gave Bigelow a goodbye pat, and made a beeline for the mudroom, the investigation beckoning once more.

Her drive to the Merrifield Inn took a little longer than usual because of the holiday traffic on Main Street. When she finally reached her destination, she parked her Explorer in front of the Victorian home. Eager to escape the relentless bite of the brisk wind, Hope hurried inside the building and instantly found refuge from the cold.

Entering the lobby, she was surprised by the hum of conversation from the dining room. Peering inside, she discovered a lively scene. Maretta, seated at a table by the window, was surrounded by friends, while Hope's neighbor, Mitzi Madison, chatted with another group of ladies at another table. Teapots and plates of dainty finger sandwiches adorned the tables, creating an inviting atmosphere.

Sally, approaching Hope from the kitchen, couldn't contain her enthusiasm. "Isn't this marvelous?" she exclaimed. "Eliza had the brilliant idea of hosting a Holiday Tea, and despite it being last-minute, we're fully booked. Come, there's a seat for you, if you'd like to join."

Regrettably, Hope responded, "That sounds delightful, but I'm afraid my schedule is packed today. I thought we were going to talk about the case over a quick cup of tea." Although she would have cherished the opportunity to mingle with everyone, enjoying tea and delectable petite sandwiches, Hope needed to return home promptly and commence her baking.

Sally nodded in understanding. "Yes, I heard about Julia Lang. A terrible thing to happen, especially at this time of year." Leading Hope into the parlor, she continued, "You're truly going above and beyond to help the Langs out. Let's have our tea in the parlor. Jane had a tray set up in there."

Hope, following Sally into the parlor, readily agreed. "Sounds perfect." She shed her gloves and jacket, tossing them on the sofa.

Sally, a picture of practiced ease, poured two steaming cups. As she offered one to Hope and settled at a window table overlooking Main Street, her sleek laptop flickered to life with a keystroke.

Hope followed. "I'm dying to see what you've found."

Sally's smile broadened. "It took some digging, but I've uncovered something about Denny Beyer. Retirement hasn't dulled my research skills one bit. It turns out Denny was married to a Cecilia Beyer."

Hope leaned forward to read the old newspaper article Sally found. "Did she have any connection to Mitty or Gus Wharton?"

"Can't say for sure if she was involved in their schemes," Sally admitted. "I haven't found any arrest records. The last trace of her leads to New Britain five years ago. Interestingly, I haven't found any divorce records either."

Hope placed her cup and saucer down. "She stood by her husband even during his time in prison. There's a possibility she knows something about Mitty and Gus that could help lead to why both ended up dead."

Determined, Sally declared, "I'm not giving up. My research skills have never let me down."

Hope, impressed, nodded. "You're incredible, Sally. Now, listen to what I found out from Ruth . . ." She recounted Ruth's visit, detailing the love triangle between Nora, Mitty, and Ralph.

A sly grin stretched across Sally's face. "You saw the photo? You're certain it's her?"

Hope confirmed with a nod.

Sally steepled her fingers, her gaze fixed on a point beyond the window. A thoughtful frown creased her brow. "We're missing something . . ."

"Hope!" Eliza called out as she breezed into the parlor. "I heard the news about Julia and that you are going to do the baking for the tree lot."

"News does travel fast," Hope remarked with a slight smile. "Only until their daughter arrives tomorrow and she'll take over."

Sally chuckled. "It's been the talk of the town all morning."

"That's quite a load to take on, especially with Christmas just around the corner and you still recovering from the . . . incident," Eliza said, her concern evident.

"I'm alright, Eliza," Hope reassured her. "I couldn't refuse Albert's request."

"I can't let you tackle everything alone. I'd be happy to lend a hand," Eliza offered earnestly.

"That's a wonderful idea. Having an extra pair of hands would make the task much more manageable," Sally chimed in.

"While your offer is tempting," Hope hesitated, "you must be tired after hosting the tea party. I'm so sorry I can't stay for it."

"Nonsense! I'm still full of energy, and I genuinely enjoy baking. Please, let me help you," Eliza insisted.

"Your assistance would be amazing," Hope conceded. Accepting help wasn't her strong suit, especially in her kitchen. But the looming Christmas deadline was undeniable. "Are you free this afternoon?"

Eliza nodded eagerly. "Absolutely! I just need to wrap things up here and change into something more comfortable," she said, glancing down at her emerald green sheath dress. "I'll definitely trade these pumps for something more practical."

"Thank you, Eliza." With an extra pair of hands for the baking, Hope knew she'd make tomorrow's delivery time to the tree farm and that she'd be able to get back on track with her recipe testing. "I should head out. I'll see you later, Eliza."

"And I'll pass along the updates to Jane when she's finished with the tea party," Sally said as she gestured for Eliza to join her at the computer.

Hope gathered her jacket and gloves before leaving the parlor. Passing through the lobby, she slipped on her jacket and glanced into the dining room one last time, catching Maretta's eye. Instantly, the older woman's smile turned into a deep frown, which quickened Hope's steps as she hurried out of the inn. Outside she caught sight of her neighbors, Leila Manchester and Doric Baxter, hurrying along the sidewalk.

"Hello, Hope," they chimed in unison.

"Here for the tea?" Hope inquired as she pulled on her gloves.

"Yes, we are," Doric replied. A few wisps of her gray hair escaped the blue beret that was perched atop her head. Draped over her shoulders was a plaid ruana. "We didn't expect to see you here."

Leila, wearing a knit cap with a matching scarf tied around her neck and a winter white peacoat, inquired, "How are you feeling? We heard about the attack. At first, I couldn't believe it! Who on earth would have tased you? What is going on in this world?"

"I'm feeling much better, thank you," Hope said, determined not to get into a lengthy conversation with her chatty, gossip-loving neighbors. "I hate to rush off, but I must get home to start baking for the Maple Hill Farm."

Doric nodded, her expression sympathetic. "Yes, we heard about Julia's accident. A broken leg is never ideal, especially during the holiday season. So much hustle and bustle." With a sweeping gesture, she admired the festively adorned inn, where every corner exuded the spirit of the season. As her ruana unfolded, a glint of silver caught Hope's eye—a delicate initial necklace.

"That's a lovely necklace, Doric," Hope remarked.

"Thank you. It's an early Christmas gift from my niece," Doric replied, her fingers delicately tracing the charm.

Hope's gaze lingered on the necklace, a single initial glinting in the light. "D for Doric," she murmured, her mind snagged on a stray thought.

"Of course. What else would it stand for?" Leila asked.

Hope blinked, her thoughts snapping back into focus. She suddenly remembered where she had seen a similar charm. "I'm sorry, I really need to get going," she said abruptly, breaking away and retracing her steps back to her vehicle.

Reaching her SUV, she fumbled in her tote, pulling out her phone and swiftly composing a text to Drew:

Was the location of the murder weapon made public? I know Sam wanted it to stay quiet.

Sliding the phone away, a wave of unease washed over her. She forced herself to breathe, reminding herself not to overreact. There could be a perfectly reasonable explanation for what she was thinking.

Just then, a hand clamped down on her shoulder, sending a quake through her entire body and jolting her into a defensive stance. Whirling around, she prepared to swing at the unseen threat.

Chapter Nineteen

"Geez, Hope!" Heather Cahill exclaimed, regaining her footing. She'd stumbled back in shock at Hope's raised fists. Her heeled boots seemed a little impractical for the current weather situation, but then again, she had always been more interested in looking good than comfort.

"Heather! What in the world made you sneak up on me like that?" Hope gasped for breath, attempting to steady her wildly racing heartbeat. "You scared the daylights out of me!"

"Seriously? Were you really going to hit me?" Heather's voice carried a tone of stunned disbelief. Her body went rigid, the muscles in her jaw clenching tightly. Rapid breaths escaped through flared nostrils as she visibly fought for composure, lips pressed into a hard line.

"I . . . I don't know. Maybe." The realization of how close she had come to striking Ethan's ex-wife stunned Hope. Apparently being ambushed and tased had left her unnerved and deep down her subconscious had a plan to deal with a potential threat. Though Ethan's ex-wife wasn't exactly that danger. "What are you doing here?"

"I was doing some Christmas shopping and I saw you. I thought we should have a talk," Heather said, her voice calming and her scowl fading. In fact, she looked surprisingly put together—long waves framed her face and expertly applied makeup enhanced her features. Shades of the old Heather were visible. The once-popular high school cheerleader who'd snagged the star football player was starting to resurface after an addiction had led her to a dark place, causing her to lose her public relations job and custody of her children. Now, she was working to regain the lost trust and to rebuild her life.

"I am truly sorry about the Jingle Bell Stroll. There was no way I knew what was going to happen. But I promise you, the girls saw nothing. All the kids were far enough away," Hope reassured her.

Heather stepped forward and placed a hand on Hope's shoulder. "Hope, you don't need to apologize."

"I don't?" Hope questioned, feeling a surreal sense that perhaps she was still in bed, dreaming this improbable encounter with a non-angry Heather.

"No. You're right. There was no way you could have known that a man would be murdered. I came over to thank you for the wreath," Heather said. "It's lovely."

"The girls made it."

"I know. I also know you helped them with it. You didn't have to do that." Heather's gaze dipped momentarily, as if she was gathering strength. "I've been difficult since coming home from rehab. I think it's because I've felt like I've been dragged out of my life and replaced."

The pain in Heather's voice squeezed Hope's heart.

"No one could ever replace you as their mother," Hope said.

Heather's chin trembled as she shook her head.

"I appreciate you saying that. There are some days when I believe that. Other days? Not so much. I messed up badly, but I swear, I'm trying very hard. I'm going to be nicer and let people help me. I hope you'll accept my apology. I promise not to cause any more trouble for you and Ethan. I only want what's best for the girls and him. Honestly, you're what's best for them."

Hope's breath caught, the weight of the moment settling in.

"I'm at a loss for words," Hope confessed, the heaviness of the negative history with Heather dissipating in an instant. It was as if a reset button had been pressed, clearing the slate for a new chapter in their relationship. Hope embraced Heather, a gesture sealing their newfound understanding. "From now on, we're in this together," she declared.

Heather affirmed with a nod, "Absolutely."

As Hope pulled back from the hug, a swell of gratitude rose within her. "I hate to cut this short, but I've got to get home because I have a lot of baking," she said apologetically.

"Yes, of course. Go." Heather waved her hand in understanding.

Before leaving, Hope extended an unexpected invitation, "How about spending New Year's Eve with us? It's nothing extravagant—just homemade pizzas. The girls would love to have you there."

Heather's eyes glistened with emotion as she agreed. "I'd like that. Thank you." She turned and walked toward the corner of Main Street and waited to cross the street.

"I'll catch up with you later," Hope called out before settling into the driver's seat of her Explorer. She fished her phone from her tote and dialed Claire's number.

"Hey, where are you?" Claire's voice chirped through the phone. "I'm about to head out for some coffee. Can you meet me?"

"Sorry, not now." Hope glanced over her shoulder before pulling out of the parking space. "I'm on my way back home. You won't believe what just happened," she teased.

Claire's cheery tone faltered, replaced by concern. "Are you okay?"

Navigating her Explorer along Main Street, Hope spotted Heather dashing into the hair salon. "Sorry. I didn't mean to alarm you. I just had a conversation with Heather."

Not surprisingly, Claire groaned.

"It's not what you think." Hope quickly recapped the conversation, leaving Claire momentarily speechless—an unusual occurrence for her sister. As Claire finally found her words, Hope's attention was diverted by the sight of Brody locking the door to his antique shop up ahead.

As she approached, she noticed the *Closed* sign hung prominently, an unexpected sight so close to Christmas. Why would he shut down in the middle of the day at this time of the year? Especially since he had opened the shop after both murders. What could have happened now? Parking hastily, she practically catapulted out of her vehicle. Darting around the hood, she sprang onto the sidewalk.

"I have to go," she said to Claire before disconnecting the call. "Brody!"

He turned toward her, his greeting devoid of warmth. "Hope."

"Why are you closed?" she inquired as she closed the distance. "Is it because of what your mom did?"

Brody's jaw clenched. "Not really," he muttered, shoving his keys into his pocket. "Business has dried up ever since Wharton's murder. People are scared to walk in here. Then my mom goes and breaks in? The shop's been in the news so much lately, and not for the right reasons."

Hope hesitated to further discuss Ruth's illegal entry into the shop because she wasn't sure how much Ruth had shared with her son. "You need to talk to her and find out why she did what she did. But are you just going to give up?"

Brody stared down at his shoes, his shoulders slumping. "It's more like accepting the reality of the situation. I don't see a future for the Antique Alcove anymore."

"I'm sorry to hear that." Hope's stomach clenched. This wasn't the Brody she knew. He wouldn't let something like this break him. But what could she say to keep him fighting? "What's the plan now?"

He shrugged, shoving his hands deep into his pockets. "Not sure. Sell everything, maybe. Let the dust settle, then figure things out." His voice lacked its usual spark. "I even called Ralph Lang earlier. I'm going to have the lamp authenticated again. He might have been right about that Higganum."

"That sounds like a good idea." Her gaze lingered on the darkened shopfront. A surge of protectiveness washed over her for Brody and the Antique Alcove. "You may not want to hear this," she continued, her voice softening. "You are grieving. Maybe taking some time away is the best course. Big decisions can wait."

Brody's eyes held a flicker of uncertainty. "You think I'll see things clearer after the holidays?"

"I do," Hope affirmed, offering a reassuring smile. "Take care of yourself, Brody."

Making her way back to her Explorer, Hope's afternoon baking plans with Eliza swirled in her mind. But just as she reached the curb, she was surprised to spot Matt Roydon emerging from the deli across the street with a brown paper bag in hand.

A few extra minutes wouldn't hurt, she reasoned. She'd be fully committed to baking once she got home. So, she altered her course, stepping off the curb and maneuvering through traffic to intercept Matt before he vanished.

"Hey there," she called out to her favorite attorney and Ethan's boss.

When he stopped, his friendly smile grew wider. He was dressed in a neat charcoal gray overcoat, with neatly trimmed sandy blond hair and tiny lines crinkling around his kind eyes.

"Didn't think I'd run into you today, after everything you've been through," he remarked, leaning in to place a friendly kiss on Hope's cheek. "But I'm glad to see you're doing alright."

"Yeah, I'm hanging in there," Hope replied with a nod.

A playful grin tugged at the corners of his mouth. "Leave it to you to keep life exciting, Hope Early. You've got a knack for shaking things up."

If someone had told Hope that defying Matt's warning to steer clear of her sister's murder case would lead to a close friendship, she would have laughed it off. Yet there they were, an unlikely bond forged through the most improbable of circumstances. The twists and turns life took could be utterly unpredictable.

"I like to think of it as keeping everyone on their toes." She chuckled. "So why aren't you at the office today?"

"We closed early. With everyone having so much to do for the holidays and it being a quiet time of the year for us, we decided to take the rest of the day off," Matt explained.

"Hmm, Ethan didn't mention that." In fact, he'd said he had a full day scheduled when he left right after making her breakfast.

"He might be tied up with paperwork. All I know is, I signed some documents and made a swift exit. I'm looking forward to Christmas Eve at your house this year," Matt remarked.

Hope's mind churned over her earlier conversation with Ethan, trying to recall if he had mentioned a half day and she missed it. Nope, he hadn't.

"Hope," Matt's voice interrupted her thoughts.

"Sorry, I should get going. See you Christmas Eve." With a strained smile, she mumbled a goodbye and hurried back to her car, the festive mood dampened by a knot of unease tightening in her stomach.

• • •

Not too long after Hope arrived home, Eliza breezed in with a tin of hot cinnamon tea perfect for any chilly day. Or, to enjoy while baking. As Eliza secured her apron with a flourish, Hope set the kettle on the stove to heat. She then illuminated the room with the soft glow of Christmas tree lights and initiated her holiday music playlist. The lively tunes emanated from a portable speaker, instantly transforming the atmosphere into a festive cocoon for their epic baking venture.

In no time, they slipped into a well-choreographed routine of measuring, mixing, and scooping out batter. Hope's powerful electric mixer hummed with efficiency, blending harmoniously with the bubbling of butter on the stovetop. The enticing aroma of cinnamon, nutmeg, and chocolate swiftly enveloped the kitchen. Eliza hummed along to "We Wish You a Merry Christmas" while deftly cracking dozens of eggs, then Hope swayed to the beat of "Rockin' Around the Christmas Tree," all while Bigelow patiently stationed himself in the work hub, hopeful for any fallen morsels.

Once all the muffins were baked and set out on numerous cooling racks, the duo seamlessly transitioned to crafting brownies. Over a double boiler, Hope melted the chocolate while Eliza fetched more flour from the pantry. While the chocolate cooled, Hope snapped photos of the flour package for a social media post, acknowledging her blog's sponsor, Graham Flour, before diving back into batter mixing and pan preparation.

With the double ovens working overtime, Hope and Eliza skillfully balanced baking and laughter. Next up was making batches of reindeer munch. This simple yet delightful treat, requiring just crunchy cereal, powdered sugar, mini-pretzels, and candy-covered chocolates, spared them from further baking endeavors. They cheerfully mixed the ingredients in Hope's colossal bowl (the one she'd bought on a whim but now couldn't do without) and filled cellophane bags adorned with festive plaid ribbons.

When the timer went off, Eliza sighed and said, "I'm so exhausted, but this is so much fun." She pulled out two pans of brownies from the bottom oven and set them on cooling racks.

"Looks like Bigelow has given up," Hope commented as she rinsed out the mixing bowls. Her furry companion had abandoned his station for a comfy spot on the sofa. "He deserves a treat for his patience. His canister is by the coffee maker. I think he can have two."

Eliza happily obliged, offering Bigelow two little cookies.

"We're almost done," Hope announced as she opened the dishwasher's door and started loading it.

"We need another playlist," Eliza suggested.

Hope wiped her hands with a towel and then tapped on her phone, and a fresh playlist filled the air. The two bakers couldn't resist joining forces in singing "Jingle Bells," filling the final two hours of baking and packaging for the tree lot with a spirited push that carried them through to the sweet finish.

• • •

Hope squinted through bleary eyes, her body protesting every movement as she watched Eliza's car disappear down the driveway. Hosting the marathon baking session might have been an ambitious undertaking, she grudgingly admitted. Even her trusty silicone floor mats couldn't fully shield her from the relentless aches and pains that came with hours of standing on her feet.

She dragged herself back to the kitchen, her phone clutched in hand. She sent a text to Ethan asking about what they were going to do for dinner. Before leaving for work, he'd promised a call later to touch base. Now she was even more curious about his office closing early for the day, yet he hadn't mentioned that to her. While she waited for a reply, dinner options swam in her head. Meatloaf was out of the question, a casualty of her exhaustion. But leftover chicken noodle soup and a batch of homemade rolls beckoned, promising a comforting meal for two.

Though every muscle cried out for rest, she pushed through the fatigue and began cleaning the kitchen. Leaving the cluttered space for the morning would only compound the day's challenges before they even began.

A chime from her phone alerted Hope to Ethan's reply.

Stuck at the office with an errand to run afterward. Don't worry about dinner, I'll grab something.

Stuck at the office? Confusion gnawed at her. She tapped on her phone to call him and waited impatiently for Ethan to pick up.

"Hey, is there something wrong?" he asked.

Yes.

But Hope bit back her immediate reply.

"I thought you'd be home by now since Matt closed the office early today," she replied, trying to keep her voice steady. She wouldn't jump to any conclusions even though he had just lied to her.

Silence lingered on the other end of the line, amplifying Hope's growing unease.

"Why are you the only one working?" she asked.

More silence followed, stretching the tension between them.

"Ethan, what's going on? Are you upset with me about the murder case? That I haven't locked myself in my house to stay safe? What's going on?" Hope's voice trembled with a mix of fear and frustration.

"Nothing. Nothing is going on. Hope, I really don't like being checked on like this. I gotta go. We'll talk tomorrow," Ethan responded abruptly, his words laced with irritation.

The line fell silent for the final time, leaving Hope's heart shattered. The pain of those sharp, fragmented pieces stabbed at her, a sensation she had never experienced in their relationship before.

Chapter Twenty

When Hope was awakened by an intense buzzing the next morning, she had fought the impulse to send her alarm clock flying out the window and burrow deeper into her snug covers until Santa arrived. The marathon baking session, compounded by the lingering effects of the taser incident, had left her muscles in revolt. Even the thought of swinging her legs over the edge of the bed sent shivers down her spine.

As the world slowly came into focus and she stretched out the tension, the events of yesterday flooded back, cascading down on her.

Ethan.

Lying there, she replayed their phone conversation in her head. Why did he get so defensive? Maybe confronting his lie about work wasn't the best move, but then what did it say about their relationship? She'd already had one secret-filled marriage with Tim and she had no intention of repeating history. The hard truth was that no relationship at all was better than one built on silence and deception. *Hold on.* She was getting a little carried away. They were a team. This was just a bump in the road. She wasn't ready to give up on them yet.

Hope fought to redirect her thoughts and reinterpret the previous evening in a more positive light. Being alone last night had allowed her to slip into her comfiest pajamas early, savor a generous bowl of soup, and nestle into the couch for a cozy evening of cheesy holiday movies. It was the perfect remedy for a hectic day.

She nodded to herself. That perspective sounded far better than feeling lonely, sad, and frustrated. And waking up alone.

Though, she wasn't really alone.

Bigelow stretched languidly at the foot of the bed, clearly sharing her desire to remain nestled in the warmth of the covers. Meanwhile, Princess, who had spent the night curled up on the opposite side of the bed, concluded her grooming session, only to catapult her not-so-light body onto Hope with a meow that echoed through the room. The impact of the cat's landing, with four paws digging into Hope's stomach and chest, momentarily stole the air from her lungs.

"Okay, okay," Hope conceded, gently shifting the insistent feline from her body. Princess registered her dissatisfaction with a disgruntled yowl. "I get it. You want breakfast."

Letting out a weary sigh, Hope dragged herself up from the warm comfort of the bed, limbs heavy with fatigue. Princess announced her victory with a smug meow, tail swishing in self-satisfied feline glee. Despite her body's protests, Hope couldn't help but be charmed by the cat's steadfast commitment to ensuring her morning meal arrived on schedule.

In the bathroom, Hope splashed some cool water on her face, the refreshing jolt helping to shake off the last vestiges of sleep. She then quickly dressed in well-worn jeans and a comfy sweatshirt from her walk-in closet, topping it off with a pair of thick boot socks. Now suitably outfitted for morning chores, she made her way downstairs, her furry entourage in tow—Princess purring insistently at her heels, while Bigelow trailed behind, still blinking away drowsiness. Princess stuck close, ensuring Hope remained focused on her path to the kitchen without any unauthorized detours.

Upon arriving in the kitchen, Princess strutted over to her food mat, posture regal and meows insistent—an unmistakable demand for prompt service. Hope obliged, portioning out a generous helping into the feline's bowl. Next, she ventured outside with Bigelow, who could wait until later for his own meal, greeting her feathered friends. A cheerful chorus of clucks and eager pecking from the chickens met her, their welcome a stark contrast to Princess's dramatic flair. Hope couldn't help but smile at the contrasting communication styles between her different animal companions.

Forty minutes later, Hope reentered her kitchen, the warmth a welcome reprieve as the lingering aches slowly dissipated from her body. Despite the physical toll, a sense of pride swelled within her at the sight of the muffin boxes, brownies, and bags of reindeer munch neatly arranged—tempting treats borne of her hard work, ready to delight the tree lot patrons. But first, sustenance was in order for both her and Bigelow, who waited patiently by his bowl.

Her plans were momentarily diverted by a call from Albert. In a reassuring tone, he explained that yesterday had been slower than expected and they had ample baked goods for most of the day, so an immediate delivery wasn't necessary. Instead, he proposed postponing it until evening, ensuring their bakery cases remained well-stocked while allowing his daughter a chance to settle in after traveling and spend time with Julia before taking over the baking duties.

Hope, checking her calendar, saw there was room for a shift in her schedule. She could make the quick trip to the mall for stocking stuffers and then go to the grocery store. Actually, it seemed this change would work out better. She assured Albert that the change was no trouble and promised to drop by after the tree lot closed.

With the call concluded, Hope retreated to her office to draft a new to-do list for the day.

Top on her list was to create social media content for Hearth Life, one of her favorite companies. According to her contract, her deliverable was to be a short video featuring one of the staples in their collection. Then she'd head to the mall and to the butcher shop. With her agenda in hand, Hope returned to the kitchen and set to work.

She swiftly arranged four festive place mats and set out flatware on her table, then maneuvered the box lights from her office, positioning them alongside her camera to shoot the short video. The completion of her studio kitchen out in the barn couldn't come soon enough; it would mean far less hauling things around. With the scene set, she dashed upstairs and changed into a bright red sweater paired with dark jeans. Back downstairs, the white ceramic breadbasket from Hearth Life—they'd sent her a box of products to review and share with her followers—was retrieved from the island and placed on the table.

She had promised them a video before Christmas to coincide with their holiday sale. Setting the timer on her camera, she positioned herself in front of the bank of windows overlooking her snow-covered patio. The light on her camera flashed, and with a practiced smile, she lifted the basket filled with rolls.

"Hope Early here, live from *Hope at Home*!" She beamed into the camera. "Today, I'm thrilled to share this gorgeous ceramic breadbasket from Hearth Life. They generously sent it my way, and let me tell you, it's getting a starring role on my Christmas table this year. Not only is it beautiful, it makes a perfect gift, and if you order ASAP, there's still time to get it under your tree or holiday centerpiece! Don't forget to use my promo code, Hope20, for a twenty-percent discount. Happy Holidays!"

She flashed a smile, held it for a moment and then exhaled, setting the breadbasket down. After a quick dash around the table she stopped the video recording and switched off the lights. Bigelow, sensing his moment, materialized with soulful brown eyes begging for a walk. Happy to oblige, Hope cleared the filming equipment in record time and strapped on Bigelow's harness.

They stepped out into the brisk air. With each passing day, the temperature was dropping, and she was certain they'd be in an arctic freeze by New Year's Eve. Speaking of which, she had to tell Ethan she'd invited his ex-wife to join them for dinner that night, assuming he ever called her back.

Silence from him since their argument was unnerving. She'd left a voicemail explaining her planned errands and the evening delivery to the tree lot, hoping for at least a brief text reply. However, her message had been met with deafening silence.

Reaching the corner, Hope veered right, the familiar path toward the abandoned firehouse a welcome distraction. Bigelow, invigorated by the cool air, trotted beside her. As they walked, her initial irritation toward Ethan softened. She understood his anger, but her resolve held firm. He was the one keeping secrets, and she refused to apologize for wanting honesty.

Hope and Bigelow continued their walk along the side of the road, staying mindful of the cars passing by on the narrow two-lane street. Dwelling on her disagreement with Ethan served no purpose, so she shifted her focus to the murder investigation.

Earlier, over her morning muffin and coffee, she had reviewed her notes. Despite having gathered plenty of information, identifying the killer remained elusive. If only she had caught a glimpse of the person who tased her—that had to be the perpetrator. Try as she might, she couldn't conjure up an image of that individual. She needed to focus on the facts she did have.

The lamp Ralph purchased from Mitty was a counterfeit. Nora had dated both men previously and was aware of their criminal dealings. She probably had connections to Gus Wharton and Denny

Beyer too. But did her ties extend to Denny's wife, Cecilia?

As Hope and Bigelow reached the old firehouse, she told the dog, "Time to head back," though his drooping tail hinted at his reluctance. Hope dove back into the tangled web as they walked back home. The second fake lamp was a dead end, but who supplied the first one to Mitty before he sold it to Ralph?

The murky link between Stan Jr., his family, and Gus Wharton remained a swamp of suspicion. Were they peddling counterfeits? It certainly seemed so. Did Nora and Alena play a role?

Ralph, still the prime suspect in Mitty's murder, was free from police custody. Did he have a motive in Wharton's murder too? As they neared their street, Dorie Baxter zipped by in her car, earning a wave from Hope.

Bigelow woofed—whether eager to continue or head home was unclear—but Hope quickened her pace regardless. She needed to text Drew about a new theory brewing: what if Ralph's motive for killing Mitty wasn't the lamp? Perhaps he wanted Mitty gone to rekindle things with Nora. Or worse, maybe they plotted it together.

But Wharton? How did he factor into this?

As much as she longed to pore over her notes about the murders, unraveling the puzzle pieces that evaded her, Hope had a holiday to prepare for. Friends and family anticipated a stellar celebration from her, and she wouldn't disappoint. So, for now, she would leave the investigating to Sam.

• • •

Her first stop was the mall for two gifts. She was in and out in record time and headed back to Jefferson for her next errand, which was the grocery store. En route, she made a brief detour to Staged with Style to visit Claire.

As Hope entered Claire's home decor shop her sister greeted her warmly as she walked to the design consultation table. Claire, once a successful realtor, had transitioned into this new venture, initially focusing on home staging. The grand opening's triumph had unexpectedly led to an expansion into selling home accessories and offering interior design services—the latter being a delightful surprise that kept Claire busy with a growing clientele. Today, she exuded a professional yet relaxed air in gray trousers and a turquoise sweater. Seated, her legs crossed elegantly, her four-inch stiletto pumps peeked out from beneath her trousers' hem, prompting Hope to wonder how her sister managed to wear such uncomfortable shoes all day long. Hope much preferred her comfy, albeit unstylish, clogs for the long hours she spent in the kitchen.

"Any word from Ethan?" Claire inquired.

Hope shook her head as she settled across from her sister, taking in the shop's tasteful array of knickknacks—perfect for adding that finishing touch to any room. A display of Em Bailey candles, a personal indulgence, tempted her, but she knew one was destined to be a Christmas present from Claire.

"I think he's really upset with me," Hope confessed, nibbling on her lower lip.

"Don't worry, he'll come around," Claire reassured, her nearly twenty-year marriage a testament to its solidity. Reaching across the table, she gently patted Hope's hand. "Remember, it's the holiday season, and despite all the joy, stress can creep in. Toss a murder investigation into the mix, and you almost getting yourself killed, and conflict is bound to arise at some point."

Hope slumped back in her chair. "Since when are you the voice of reason?"

"I've always dished out sage advice. You just never heed it," Claire remarked with a hint of amusement.

Hope's phone buzzed, and she fished it out of her tote. A text from Drew popped up. Finally he was getting back to her about her question regarding the knife that was allegedly used to kill Mitty.

Sorry for the delay. They're keeping the location of the murder weapon quiet.

"Interesting," Hope murmured, eyes glued to the screen.

"What? Is that a text from Ethan?" Claire inquired, gathering swatch books as she rose from her seat.

Hope replied to the text:

Thanks. Dropping off food at the tree lot tonight. Talk later.

Then, looking up, she explained, "No, it's Drew. I should get going.

I have to go to the grocery store. There was a change in the schedule, so I'm dropping off the baked goods to the tree lot later."

"How did the baking session go with Eliza?" Claire walked to the counter, where she deposited the books and propped an elbow on the stack. "I do hope she stays on at the inn. She seems to make Sally and Jane happy."

"I agree," Hope said with a smile, rising to leave. "It was nice having the company while I baked."

Hope lingered a moment longer, casting a final longing glance at the Em Bailey candles before exiting the shop. The drive to her next stop provided the perfect space to ruminate on Drew's message. A reasonable explanation could exist, but caution was needed in her next move. So much for leaving the investigation to Sam and his team.

• • •

After finishing her errands for the day and spending hours proofreading recipes for her upcoming cookbook, Hope almost was late in arriving at the tree lot. Now, with her cargo door open, she plunged into the task at hand—bringing the baked goods into the shop. A frosty bite in the night air spurred her steps on as she shuttled between her vehicle and the closed store. She was eager to wrap her delivery as quickly as possible. The final trip weighed Hope down with the last remnants of boxes of muffins, brownies and trays of reindeer munch bags. With a deft touch, she released the cargo door. Speed was of the essence. Ethan had called, promising to come over for dinner. The sooner she finished this delivery, the sooner they could tackle their problem.

Stepping into the dimly lit shop, Hope set the final boxes down on the worn wooden counter. With her delivery now inside, she removed her hat and scarf, methodically transferring the stacks into the compact kitchen in the back. As she moved between the front and kitchen areas, her mind drifted back to the lingering unease she'd felt since her chance encounter with Dorie and Leila outside the Merrifield Inn.

"D" for Dorie. That made sense.

What didn't make sense was the other necklace she'd seen.

All day, she had grappled with questions surrounding Mitty's murder—the motive, Nora's connection to both victim and suspect, the seemingly out-of-place Gus Wharton, and a passing comment that gnawed at her. Solving these mysteries was the key to unraveling both killings. And to her surprise, Dorie's pendant had triggered an unexpected realization.

"Why wasn't it an *L*?" Hope muttered under her breath, thinking about the necklace she'd seen another woman wearing. She pulled on her hat and wound her scarf around her neck. "Shouldn't she have been wearing the letter *L* instead of *D*?" Before slipping her hands into her gloves, she reached for her tote bag. "And how did she know the knife was found in Ralph's garage? The police never released those details to the public." She pondered that troubling thought for a moment. A leak within the department was possible—it did happen on occasion, she reasoned, rummaging through the depths of her large bag.

Where had she put her key fob?

Chapter Twenty-one

Anxiety gripped her as she hurriedly searched her tote for the missing key fob. With each passing moment, her frustration grew. Mentally, she retraced her steps—from arriving and exiting her car to entering the shop and setting down the first of the boxes.

"I know I put the key fob in here," she said, reaching into the tote. Her hand rummaged through the cavernous interior, searching every nook and cranny. "It has to be somewhere."

After a couple fruitless minutes, she let out a resigned sigh and upended the tote, spilling its contents onto the counter. With a furrowed brow, she meticulously inspected the scattered items. Her heart sank as the thorough examination confirmed her worst fear—the elusive key fob was nowhere to be found.

"Maybe I dropped it?" she wondered aloud, exhaling an exasperated breath. Determination renewed, Hope marched outside to her SUV, scanning the ground for any sign of the elusive key fob. Her search proved fruitless. Expanding the perimeter yielded the same disappointing result, leaving her frustrated and muttering under her breath as she stared at her vehicle. She half-heartedly hoped a mere gaze could somehow summon the key, but no such luck.

A shiver coursed through her as the sky darkened, the chill intensifying. With no other recourse, she begrudgingly accepted the need for help, her thoughts turning to Claire. However, the realization hit her—her phone was in her tote and that was still in the shop. So back she went. As she retraced her steps she battled the biting wind whipping around her, keeping a lookout for the key. Once inside, she shook off the cold, digging through the pile of her tote's contents again on the counter.

Ready to dial for assistance, she was met with an unexpected setback—no signal. How was that possible? Then she remembered her visit to buy her trees, when she couldn't get a signal to post her selfie. Surely there had to be a spot where she could get one. Attempting to push down the panic that was creeping in, she moved around the shop, arm outstretched, trying in vain to catch a bar or two. Even with the door swung open, nothing changed.

"Great. Could it get any worse?" Hope grumbled, dropping the phone back into her tote, along with the rest of her belongings. Suddenly, a realization struck her—there was a landline in the kitchen, a relic from a bygone era. She dashed into the back room, eyeing the avocado green rotary dial with a mix of hope and skepticism. Lifting the receiver to her ear, she anticipated the comforting sound of a dial tone.

No such luck.

"Seriously? No dial tone?" she exclaimed, rapidly pressing the switch, to no avail. The silence mocked her, intensifying the sense of isolation in the dimly lit kitchen. She returned the receiver as a sinking feeling settled in the pit of her stomach.

A sharp gust of wind buffeted the aging structure, prompting Hope to reflexively clutch her coat tighter. The old building seemed to loom around her, enveloping her in an unsettling embrace. Was it merely the biting cold, or the sinister awareness that a killer remained at large, possibly lurking in the shadows? She couldn't dispel the overwhelming sense of isolation, cut off from any means of summoning assistance.

The howling wind amplified the eerie atmosphere, causing the decrepit walls to creak and groan. Hope's heart raced as she strained to detect any ominous movement in the surrounding darkness. Alone and vulnerable, she felt completely at the mercy of the unknown dangers that might be closing in. The oppressive silence was shattered only by the relentless gusts battering the structure. Hope shuddered, both from the chill and the growing dread consuming her.

"Stop. Just stop. I'm not stranded in the middle of nowhere. Plenty of people know where I am," she whispered to herself as she emerged from the dimly lit kitchen. "Besides, my key fob didn't just walk away. It has to be by the car."

With a newfound resolve, Hope navigated her way to the door and stepped out again into the night. The hushed crunch of her footsteps was barely audible. A faint noise made her pause, her senses on high alert. She cast a wary glance over her shoulder, but the darkness revealed nothing. Pushing aside her apprehension, she pressed on, only to hear the sound again.

What was it? The indistinct nature of the noise left her troubled. Perhaps it was a harmless critter scavenging for leftovers from the shop, or maybe it was someone—someone who had possession of her keys.

Refusing to be caught off guard and become a victim once more, Hope dismissed the impulse to identify the source of the noise. Instead, she knew there was a sugar shack on the farm. A spark of hope ignited within her; maybe there was a phone there. With a sense of urgency, she steered her footsteps toward the distant structure.

Her feet propelled her through a silent assembly of towering trees, each one patiently waiting to be chosen and adorned for the holiday. The rhythmic crunch of needles and twigs beneath her boots mirrored the accelerated beat of her heart, and her breaths quickened as she strained to recall the distance to the elusive sugar shack. Crossing a narrow lane, she ventured into another enclave of trees.

And then she heard footsteps echoing behind her, stealthy and disconcerting. Instinct nudged her to glance over her shoulder, but an internal voice urged her to quicken her pace, to reach the refuge of the outbuilding. Her urgency seemed to stoke the pursuit, the rhythmic cadence of her steps now mirrored by the ominous echo of those behind her.

Her heart raced into overdrive, mind swirling with ominous scenarios. If this person meant no harm, why the silent pursuit instead of a friendly call out? The narrow lanes and rows of trees became a maze, and she faced a daunting decision at the crossroads.

She paused, caught between a choice of left or right. Which path led to the shack? A fleeting uncertainty gripped her, but a determined certainty whispered, "Up ahead." She propelled herself forward, now in a frantic run. The footsteps behind her copied her pace, an ominous symphony that quickened her breaths.

Unable to resist, she stole a glance over her shoulder, spying a figure in a bulky coat persistently chasing her down. Just as her focus wavered, an unseen branch tripped her, sending her crashing to the hard ground.

A moan escaped her lips as she reached for her ankle, the pain immediate and searing. Was it broken or just twisted? No time for a self-diagnosis, for the relentless pursuer had closed in. Struggling to stand, she froze at the sight of Lexi emerging into view, wielding a formidable tree limb.

Hope met Lexi's gaze. The friendly church secretary was gone, replaced by a stranger with a terrifying glint in her eyes. The puzzle fragments Hope had been desperately trying to connect slammed into place with horrifying clarity.

"Lexi, we can work this out. I can help you." Hope's voice trembled despite her effort to appear strong. Vulnerability was a danger right now.

Lexi remained silent, her shadow stretching over Hope. The kindness that once softened her features had vanished, replaced by a mask of cold, calculating malice.

Hope didn't need Lexi to say anything. She already knew who Lexi was and why she was there. What she didn't know was how she was going to escape. There was one option but it would be a gamble, a desperate attempt to stall while her mind raced to come up with a plan to get away.

"Bravo," Lexi drawled, punctuating the word with slow, methodical claps. "You've more than lived up to your reputation. I must confess, I'm curious, how did you manage to figure it all out?"

Hope's heart pounded as she weighed her limited options. Stalling for time seemed her best, if precarious, chance. Mustering her resolve, she prepared to engage Lexi, all the while her thoughts frantically searching for a path to safety.

"Your necklace was one of the clues. The initial *D* is for Denny, isn't it? And you're Cecilia, his wife," Hope asserted.

Lexi's hand instinctively sought her neck, but the pendant was concealed beneath the black jacket zipped up to its funnel collar. "I've been wearing the pendant since Denny was murdered in prison. He shouldn't have died there."

"I'm very sorry for your loss," Hope offered, her empathy clashing with the fear consuming her. "From what I've learned, he was a good friend. He never turned Mitty or Gus into the police."

Lexi took a step forward, her eyes filled with sorrow. "And look where it got him. The police offered him a deal. All he had to do was tell them who his partners were. If he had, he would've been out of prison two years ago. He'd still be alive. But no, he was too loyal."

"I had no idea."

"Mitty got to move on with his life and he started a business. No one ever knew he had been a thief. Then there's Gus. He kept stealing and never got caught. And my Denny was killed. How is that fair?" Lexi's voice resonated with bitterness.

Hope, knowing she was in imminent danger, stayed silent, her mind racing for an escape plan.

Lexi, fueled by years of festering rage, pressed on, demanding answers. "Tell me, Hope! You seem to have all the answers for everything. How is it fair?"

"I don't claim to have all the answers," Hope replied, her words measured yet tinged with a sense of urgency. "The fact that all three men weren't punished for their crimes is simply wrong."

Lexi, wielding the tree limb like a menacing scepter, pointed it at Hope. "Oh, but they were punished. I made sure Mitty and Gus got what they deserved."

"You killed them," Hope uttered quietly, her observation met with a sneering smile from Lexi.

"I had no idea how easy it would be," Lexi admitted, her tone sending quivers down Hope's spine. "It took some time, but I tracked down Mitty and moved here shortly after that. I used my dead sister's identity and got a job. He'd never met me, so I wasn't worried about him figuring out who I was. I took my time because I had to make sure no one would figure out that I killed him. I thought I'd have to track down Gus after I finished my business here, but he showed up in Jefferson. It was like a twofer."

A twofer.

The callous comment left a bitter taste in Hope's mouth, the revelation of Lexi's calculated vengeance turning the confrontation into a perilous dance with a killer driven by a vendetta years in the making.

"It was you who attacked me in the parking lot with the taser," Hope declared, her voice now steady despite the lingering sense of vulnerability.

"You were exactly where I wanted you, and then that stupid

detective showed up," Lexi responded with a disdainful shake of her head. "I only needed a few more minutes, and then I would have gotten rid of you and your incessant nosiness. I've been watching you, seeing how you were gathering all the facts. I think the detectives who handled the jewelry store burglary could have used you to find Mitty and Gus. Then I wouldn't have had to kill them and now . . . you."

As Hope scrambled to stand, her ankle still throbbing, she mustered the courage to appeal to Lexi. "You don't have to kill me, Cecilia. There has to be another way."

Lexi, unmoved by the plea, remarked, "Hmm . . . nice touch using my real name to connect with me. Too bad I'm beyond connecting with."

Hope wasn't shocked by the sentiment. The figure standing before her was no longer a mere person; she was a vengeful murderer, driven by a relentless thirst for retribution. Whatever sliver of conscience she'd once harbored had evaporated into the shadows, leaving a hollow shell.

"Now I have to clean up one last loose end. And its name is Hope."

The ominous finality in Lexi's words kicked Hope's instincts into overdrive to find a way out, to outwit the dangerous adversary she faced.

"No, you don't have to deal with any loose ends. You don't need to hurt anyone else," Hope insisted, her arms raised in defense. But the shooting pain from her ankle made her hesitate, unsure of how much she could handle.

"I don't have a choice." Lexi's eyes narrowed and her facial features hardened as she stepped forward again. "I don't intend to go to prison. Not when Mitty and Gus got away with their crimes. You should have stayed out of this, Hope."

Pain shot through Hope's ankle as she dodged Lexi's blow with the tree limb. The makeshift weapon whistled through the air, barely missing her. She lurched back, tripping and tumbling back into the prickly embrace of a spruce tree. The scent of pine needles filled her lungs as she scrambled deeper into the branches, desperately seeking a foothold.

Undeterred, Lexi charged forward, wielding the makeshift weapon with a deranged intensity.

Hope, with no means of defense, relied on the precarious support the tree offered. Without hesitation, she lifted both legs, drawing her knees close to her chest, leveraging the tree to steady herself. Pushing her feet into Lexi's midsection, a surge of power sent Lexi tumbling backward with a yelp, taking Hope with her.

They both landed on the cold ground. Hope wasted no time in trying to grab the tree limb that had fallen from her attacker's grip, but she was blocked by Lexi, who flung her arms wildly as she tried to regain control. Hope retaliated with an elbow to the face, the sickening crunch sending chills down her spine.

She didn't dwell on the possible injuries; she needed to escape.

As Lexi thrashed around in agony, Hope summoned her strength, grabbed the thick tree limb, and pulled herself to her feet, her breaths ragged and her head spinning. Pushing through the physical strain, she fixed her gaze on the twisting figure before her, realizing she had but a fleeting window of opportunity. She had to act swiftly, or risk plunging back into peril. She needed to find a way to get help.

Cautiously approaching the prone Lexi, who cried out in pain, Hope scanned the area for a phone or car keys. If fortune was on her side, one or both might have fallen during their struggle.

There it was!

A key fob—hers!

Her heart hammered against her ribs as she snatched the key and broke into a run, cursing every time her ankle hit the ground because of the pain from her earlier stumble. She urgently retraced her steps but hit a sudden roadblock when another figure emerged from the shadows.

"What on earth is going on?" Drew's voice cut through the darkness, tinged with confusion.

Hope let out a sob of relief, tears blurring her vision. It was Drew!

"Why haven't you returned my texts?" he asked, stepping forward. "Who screamed? Was it you? Why are you out here and not in the shop?"

Before Hope could answer, a guttural snarl ripped through the air. Lexi, her eyes blazing with rage, lunged from the darkness. She tackled

Hope with brutal force, pinning her to the ground and wrapping her fingers around her throat like a vise.

Hope's world narrowed to the suffocating pressure on her throat and the terrifying glint in Lexi's eyes. But then, in a blur of motion, Drew was on top of Lexi, tearing her off Hope and managing to pin her to the ground.

Gasping for breath, Hope scrambled to her feet, her hands going to her throat. She couldn't believe how close she'd come to being strangled. She looked at Drew and was thankful he'd shown up and pulled the crazed killer off her.

"Now would be a good time to tell me what's going on. Why did she just try to strangle you?" Drew asked as he applied pressure to keep Lexi down.

"She's the one who killed Mitty and Gus Wharton," Hope said, rubbing her neck where Lexi's hands had been moments before.

Drew's jaw dropped in disbelief.

"Hold her down while I find some rope," she croaked, her voice strained and hoarse. "And watch out; she's stronger than you'd think." With that, she limped toward the shop, each step a tangible reminder of the peril she had narrowly escaped.

Chapter Twenty-two

The night pulsed with the frenetic glow of emergency vehicle strobe lights, casting an unexpected spectacle against the dark canvas of the sky. Hope couldn't help but yearn for the comforting glimmer of stars instead.

The first responder, a no-nonsense officer with a grim expression, quickly secured Lexi with the authoritative click of handcuffs. The rope Drew had used had been discarded. A call for an ambulance echoed through the night, and within moments, the ambulance's arrival signaled Lexi's impending departure on a gurney bound for the nearby hospital.

With the frigid winds keeping the temperature well below freezing, Hope and Drew faced a choice to either linger by their vehicles or seek refuge in the warmth of the shop while the police processed the scene. They opted for the latter. Still bundled in her coat, Hope scavenged the kitchen for a box of tea bags, set a kettle on the stove, and procured two disposable cups from the hot chocolate station.

Leaning against the sales counter with Drew at her side, she blew on the hot tea, the steam rising like a ghostly veil around her face. Her eyes met his, a flicker of shared shock and disbelief passing between them. They stood in a tense silence, the weight of the night's events settling heavily upon them.

Drew set his cup down, a tremor in his hands belying his outward calm. "Hope," he said softly, his voice raspy, "how are you holding up? Really?"

She offered a nonchalant shrug, unable to articulate the tangled mess of emotions within her. Her stomach knotted, a silent testament to the overwhelming unrest.

Drew's gaze shifted as if drawn to something beyond the glass door. "Looks like the ambulance is departing. Who would've thought the church secretary is a murderous psycho? It's always the quiet ones."

A chuckle escaped Hope, a brief reprieve from the gravity of the situation.

Drew enveloped Hope in his arm. "When did you realize it was her?"

"Not until I got here," Hope admitted, sipping her tea. "I ran into Dorie and Leila at the Merrifield Inn—"

"You went to the Holiday Tea? I heard it was amazing. I hope Eliza does another one before Christmas so I can go."

Hope chuckled, gently steering him back on course. "Focus, Drew."

"Sorry," he said sheepishly. "Go on, please."

Hope nodded. "Dorie was wearing an initial pendant from her niece. *D* for Dorie."

"Makes sense."

"Exactly. What didn't make sense was the initial necklace Lexi wore the day I met her at the Snowflake Holiday Market. It was the letter *D* too. It should have been *L* for Lexi since that was the name she was using, her fake identity."

"But she wore the letter *D* for her dead husband, Denny," Drew said as understanding dawned.

"When I saw the necklace, I started to ask her about it, but she cut me off and then walked away. Then, she let slip the location of where the police found the knife believed to have been used to kill Mitty.

"Ah, I see," Drew said with a nod, comprehension dawning. "That's why you double-checked with me about whether the detail of them finding the knife in the garage had been made public. My apologies for not getting back to you sooner on that. So, when I told you that information hadn't been released, you realized there would have been only one way Lexi could have known where the knife was."

Hope took another sip of her tea, but the warmth did little to penetrate the chill that had settled deep in her bones. A tremor ran through her body, and she shivered involuntarily. "She had to have been the one who planted it, framing Ralph for the murder. Like everyone, she knew how angry he was with Mitty, so he made the perfect patsy."

"It's a good thing I arrived when I did." Drew withdrew his arm from Hope. "You could've been . . ." He trailed off, the unspoken words hanging in the air.

"Yes. Thank you." The words felt inadequate, given that he had just saved her life. Exhausted and sore, finding a grander expression seemed beyond her grasp. "Thank you" would have to suffice for now.

Besides, Drew, being who he was, would never let her forget his heroic intervention. She glanced at him, and her heart squeezed. He was her best friend, and she would be eternally grateful to him. Leaning in, she dotted his cheek with a kiss.

"What's that for?" he asked, smiling.

"For saving my life."

He blushed, then waited for a moment. "I get more than just a kiss on the cheek, right? I'm thinking of something bigger, like maybe dinner once a week for the rest of my life? Or maybe you'll be Trixie's babysitter when I go on vacation? Or maybe . . ."

"Don't press your luck." Her tone may have sounded firm, but she couldn't pull it off any longer. She laughed and he joined in. "Wait . . . why did you come here tonight?"

"Clearly, to save your life."

She swatted at him. "That's what happened. But why did you come to the farm?"

"Oh. I was on my way home and had this incredible craving for brownies. I knew you were here dropping off all the goodies, so I decided to swing by to quench my craving." Drew twisted and picked up a brownie he'd snagged while Hope had prepared their tea, claiming no one would miss one. He bit into the heavenly moist square of chocolate.

"A craving for a brownie brought you here?"

His eyes lit up and he chewed and nodded.

"So, if I hadn't made brownies you wouldn't have come?"

"Focus, Hope, focus on what happened, not the what-ifs." He finished his brownie and then wiped his mouth with a napkin. "That was delicious. So worth wrestling with a killer for."

Hope leaned into Drew, gazing up at him with a smile. "Good thing you had a chocolate craving."

• • •

On Christmas Eve morning, Hope retrieved the first batch of cookies destined for delivery from her Explorer's cargo area. The harrowing night at the tree lot felt like a distant memory. A radiant sunbathed the surroundings in a warm glow, the biting cold had given way to a gentler chill, and an atmosphere of joy permeated not only her heart but the world around her. It was the day before Christmas, and with it came the mission to distribute her delectable creations.

Her first stop? The Jefferson Police Department, as was tradition. Ever since returning to her hometown, delivering her holiday cookies to the officers had become a cherished annual ritual. While it once provided an additional reason to see Ethan, she now anticipated a brief visit with Sam, assuming he was on duty that day.

Hope followed the familiar path to the police station, entering the utilitarian lobby. At the front desk, Chuck, the eager-eyed dispatcher and younger brother of one of her high school classmates, greeted her with a hopeful grin.

"Are those the famous Christmas cookies I've been hearing about all week?" he inquired, his eyes sparkling with anticipation.

"I'm not sure about the famous part, but yes, they are," Hope said.

"You're being too modest. My sister says that you are a big-time blogger, and you're writing a cookbook. How cool is that?" Chuck leaned closer with keen interest. "If you ever need a taste tester, I'm your guy."

Hope's cheeks warmed at Chuck's flattery. She never thought of herself as a "big-time blogger." But it was interesting how others perceived her. Especially her former classmates.

"I appreciate the offer." Hope chuckled. "Now, is Detective Reid working today?"

"He sure is. Let me give him a heads-up," Chuck replied, reaching for the phone as Hope turned away from the counter. She didn't have to wait long.

"Good morning, Hope," Sam Reid greeted with a warm smile as he emerged from the inner offices. For the festive occasion, he had traded his usual tailored blazer for a bright red sweater layered over a crisp, white-collared shirt. "Merry Christmas."

Hope hadn't seen the detective since the night Lexi, aka Cecilia Beyer, attacked her and was rushed to the hospital before facing formal charges, including the murders of Mitty Fitzgerald and Gus Wharton. Despite Hope's twisted ankle, she'd declined medical attention from the paramedics that night, preferring to avoid another visit to the emergency room. Instead, she'd spent a couple hours at the police department, giving Sam her statement. Ethan raced over as soon as she called him and stayed with her as she recounted every detail of her encounter with Lexi. When she was finished, Ethan practically scooped her up and took her home, where he iced her ankle and held her as she fell asleep.

"Merry Christmas," Hope responded. "I wasn't sure if you'd be working today."

"And risk missing your cookies? Not a chance," Sam declared, leaning in for a closer look at the tray. "They look as tempting as always."

Tightly wrapped in cellophane and adorned with a festive plaid ribbon, the tray boasted an array of ten cookie varieties. Planning ahead, she'd prepared the bulk of the necessary cookie dough in early November, freezing it for the holiday rush. This year, with her schedule brimming due to family obligations and a bum ankle, the premade dough was a godsend. Though, as she set out for her deliveries, she found herself walking without a limp—a promising sign for the church service later in the afternoon.

As she handed the tray to Sam, she said, "I hope you and your family enjoy them."

"I assure you, we will. Now, tell me. How are you doing?" Sam's voice took on a more serious tone.

"I'm doing alright. Any updates on Lexi . . . I mean, Cecilia?" Throughout the week, thoughts of the woman lingered in her mind—how she'd deceived everyone, how she'd stalked Mitty and then targeted Hope, and how callously she'd attempted to frame an innocent man.

"She's still in custody and probably will remain so until her trial," Sam replied.

"Good to hear. Did you find out what Nora was doing at the Barlow's shop with Stan Jr.?"

"She claims that she went to talk to him about Alena."

"Really? They all seemed pretty chummy. Do you think she was involved with the fakes?"

"At this time, we have no evidence of that. However, as far as antique fraud goes, it appears that a case could be made. Unfortunately, I can't share any details with you at this time."

"I understand. I should get going. Merry Christmas," she said, bidding farewell before making her exit. Back in her vehicle, Hope set off to her next destination.

• • •

It was like a Christmas miracle when Hope found a parking spot right in front of Brody's antique shop. Ruth's call a few days ago had revealed that Brody had decided to keep the business open, and it would undergo a significant rebranding in the new year. Until then, the shop welcomed Jefferson residents who had shown unwavering support for Brody during the ordeal of losing his father and almost his store. With a tray of cookies in hand, Hope hurried into the shop, where she found Brody behind the counter engaged in conversation with Eliza. A spark crackled between them, and Hope smiled at the budding young love.

"Hope!" Brody exclaimed, his voice carrying across the room. "Great to see you! What brings you by? Are those Christmas cookies?"

"Merry Christmas, Hope," Eliza greeted warmly, pushing herself away from the counter and adjusting her deep blue velvet midi dress, its high collar neatly fastened. A string of pearls were draped elegantly around her neck. "I've been hearing about your famous cookies forever. I thought I'd have to wait until tonight to get a taste."

Eliza, along with her aunts, had been invited to Hope's home for Christmas Eve dinner. As the years passed, the guest list expanded, but rather than feeling overwhelmed, Hope welcomed the added excitement with open arms.

"I wanted to bring Brody a little something," Hope explained, placing the tray on the counter, her gloves still on as she didn't plan to stay long. "Ruth called me about your change of plans, and I'm thrilled you're keeping the shop open."

Brody squared his shoulders. "Dad wouldn't have wanted it closed. He'd want us to fight for what's ours."

"I have every confidence you will," Hope affirmed.

Eliza, arms folded, spoke up. "The whole situation is mind-boggling. The Barlow's selling fakes, their connection to Gus Wharton . . . yet his murder, and Mitty's, had nothing to do with the counterfeit antiques?"

"It appears not," Hope said.

"It's a tangled mess," Eliza said with a sigh. "A web of deceit."

"It most certainly is," Brody said. "The scheme is quite sophisticated, and I have no doubt it will take some serious unraveling not only by the Jefferson police but also the FBI, if they branched out beyond Connecticut."

"And what about the lamp?" Hope asked. "Did you get it authenticated?"

Brody took a deep breath and met her gaze. For a moment he said nothing, as if reluctant to voice the answer aloud. "It's not real," he said finally, his features contorting in a grimace. "Dad was so certain when he bought it at that estate sale. I refunded Ralph's money and he was understanding, thankfully. As for the lamp . . ." He trailed off momentarily, as if still coming to terms with the news himself. "I donated it to a local thrift shop."

"At least the mystery surrounding the lamp is resolved," Hope said with a touch of lightness.

"Thanks to you, Hope," Brody acknowledged.

Eliza cleared her throat, pulling their focus. "Speaking of mysteries," she said, her voice sharp. "Do you think that Alena or Nora knew what the Barlows were doing?"

"That's something for the police to sort out." Hope turned to Brody. "Have you tried reaching out to either of them?"

"I have but my calls are going straight to voicemail." He uttered a hollow laugh, devoid of any real humor. "Somehow I'm not surprised."

"What I can't believe is what Lexi . . . Cecilia, I mean . . . did. How much hurt had she inside of her to murder two people and then try and kill you, Hope?" Eliza asked.

Hope felt a cold dread pool in her stomach.

"Retribution, revenge, call it what you will, it's simply inexcusable," Brody stated, his voice heavy with conviction. "What my father,

Wharton, and Beyer did was undoubtedly wrong. Should Dad have owned up to his crime? Absolutely. But that didn't give anyone the right to take his life."

Eliza's arms uncrossed, and she tentatively placed a comforting hand on Brody's shoulder. "No, it doesn't," she agreed, her tone gentle. "This past month must have been a waking nightmare for you."

"There's no denying that," Hope affirmed, empathy lacing her words. "I should get going. Brody, I hope you and your mom are able to find some peace this Christmas. And Eliza, I'll see you later." With that, she turned and made her way toward the exit.

"Wait, one more thing," Brody called out, causing Hope to pause and pivot back. "I've thoroughly searched every nook and cranny of this place, and there are no hidden jewels or money stashes. So, that's one more mystery solved."

"Good to know." Hope offered a warm smile and a nod of acknowledgment before finally departing the shop.

• • •

The frosted glass doors of Grace Unity Church swung open wide, releasing a cascade of parishioners from the Christmas Eve service into the swirling snow. Tiny diamonds glittered on their upturned faces, reflecting the warm glow of the church's stained-glass windows. Hope, alone in the departing crowd, stepped into the hushed embrace of Christmas Eve night. Ethan's last-minute call an hour before she set off for the service had left her with a sense of disquiet. His vague excuse lingered in her thoughts, but in the flurry of preparing for the evening, she chose not to press for details. The last thing she wanted was a repeat of the conversation they'd had a few days ago and risk ruining the holiday. She'd wait until December twenty-sixth to discuss her feeling that he was becoming distant in their relationship. Before they hung up, he said he'd pick up the girls on his way to her house before abruptly ending the call.

As she made her way through the main door, a baritone voice broke through the wintry hush.

"Merry Christmas, Hope." Matt Roydon came up beside her. A

subtle scent of cinnamon and leather clung to him, a stark contrast to the clean pine aroma of the church.

"Merry Christmas," she replied, tying the belt of her camel-colored coat. Her white trousers, a risky choice for a night spent in the kitchen, gleamed beneath the garnet red sweater she'd chosen for a festive touch. Two murder attempts had taught her to face danger head-on, and white pants paled in comparison.

"Where's Ethan?" Matt asked, pulling out a pair of gloves from his charcoal gray overcoat.

"Seriously?" Hope, walking to the curb with her key fob in hand, shot him a pointed look. "You tell me."

He shrugged, a hint of amusement flickering in his gaze. "Your guess is as good as mine. You know, if I kept him working on Christmas Eve, I'd have to endure your wrath . . . and the potential loss of those legendary Christmas cookies."

Hope glared at him.

"I'm telling you the truth, I have no idea," Matt admitted, raising his palms in surrender. "I promise you I'm not making him work today."

Hope considered his words for a moment before responding. "So where is he? What's going on?"

"I think I'll leave the sleuthing to you . . . for now," Matt replied with a laugh. He glanced at his watch and sighed. "There's a stop I have to make before dinner tonight. See you later." He stepped off the curb and set off across the parking lot, weaving nimbly between the tightly parked cars.

"I am a sleuth," she muttered to herself. "I will find out what's going on."

Just as she was left pondering Ethan's mysterious absence, another familiar voice called out. "Hope!" Amy Phelan, wearing a technicolor explosion of a puffer coat and pom-pom hat, barreled toward her, her breath puffing out in white clouds.

"Merry Christmas, Amy." Hope adjusted the strap of her purse on her shoulder, catching a glance at her watch. Time was ticking away. She needed to get home to get the roast in the oven for her guests. She had a simple menu planned for the evening, roast beef with roasted potatoes, green beans served with Parker House rolls and a salad. Her mouth watered thinking about the meal.

"The service was lovely, wasn't it? My mom loves it every year. I'm sorry we haven't had a chance to catch up since Lexi's attempts on your life. Especially the last one at the tree lot. Wow! It's still mind-boggling. She seemed so sweet," Amy remarked, her smile faltering. "But then again, don't they all?"

Hope blinked, her friend's words striking a little too close to home. Hadn't she questioned relationships herself, come to learn even those closest could keep secrets? For a moment, her thoughts flickered to Ethan before she shut them down firmly and refocused on Amy.

"Listen to me. I sound so cynical. I blame the podcast. Mom thinks I should call it quits," Amy said, scanning the departing crowd. "I thought she was right behind me."

"What do you think?"

"The podcast? I'm not giving up. I've got my first sponsor, and I've hired a consultant to help rebrand it. The name will probably change too." A glint of excitement sparked in Amy's eyes. "You know, I think this recent case is perfect material."

"Mitty's and Gus Wharton's murders?"

"This whole saga is podcast gold because it goes way beyond just the murders," Amy explained. "Sure, Mitty's and Gus Wharton's killings are captivating storylines, but I'm even more intrigued by the antique fraud angle. Can you imagine being one of those collectors, utterly deceived by those slick con artists? I've never had much interest in antiques myself, but my great-aunt Eloisa was obsessed. If she'd been duped by someone she trusted as a reputable dealer, it would have devastated her. Then you've got the whole drama surrounding Alena and her romance with one of the Barlow men. It's like we're all living in the middle of a soap opera plotline! At this rate, I wouldn't even be surprised if someone's long-lost twin sister showed up next week." She let out an amused chuckle.

Hope's blood ran cold. The thought of a hidden twin lurking in the shadows sent a jolt of unease through her. "Let's hope not," she murmured.

"Amy! Come on, we don't want to be late," a melodic voice cut through the air. A gracefully dressed gray-haired woman waved from a short distance away.

"There's my mom. Gotta run. Merry Christmas, Hope." With that, Amy swiftly turned and joined her mother, leaving Hope with the buzz of holiday anticipation in the air.

Hope continued her trek to her Explorer, gracefully stepping off the curb and navigating the parking lot. She burrowed deeper into her coat, relishing the small snowflakes cascading around her. The enchanting dance of little white flakes created a magical ambiance that kindled warmth within her.

As she aimed her key fob at her vehicle, a voice interrupted the moment. Turning, she spotted the Langs approaching. Their progress was deliberate, with Julia cautiously maneuvering along the snowy pavement using crutches, guided by Albert and Ralph on either side.

"We couldn't let you slip away without wishing you a Merry Christmas," Julia said, slightly breathless upon reaching Hope.

"How are you holding up?" Hope inquired, giving a careful hug to the older woman. "You seem to be managing well on those crutches."

Albert snorted, earning a sharp glare from his wife. "Ignore him," Julia said. "These darn things are so cumbersome, but it's the only way I can get around."

"You'll be off them soon," Hope reassured her.

"Not soon enough," Julia said, shaking her head. "I'm lucky it's just a broken leg. Mitty and that other man are dead. And you . . . it makes my heart sick that you were almost killed at our tree lot."

"We're so sorry that happened. I should have never asked you to help with the baking," Albert said.

"No. What happened wasn't your fault. Lexi would have found another opportunity to confront me," Hope assured them, patting Albert's arm. "Actually, being there saved my life."

"How so?" Ralph asked. Donning a black overcoat with a coordinating fedora, he looked very dapper.

"Because Drew was on his way home and decided to stop at the tree lot for a brownie. So, you see, you have nothing to feel bad about," Hope explained.

The Langs exchanged glances, still appearing unconvinced.

However, when their gazes returned to Hope, a sense of relief had replaced the guilt.

"Hope, I want you to know how grateful I am that you believed in my innocence from the beginning," Ralph expressed.

"And for everything you've done," Albert declared, his voice gruff but sincere. "You'll have a free tree from our farm every Christmas. A small token of our immense gratitude."

"That's not necessary," Hope protested. The incident at the tree lot, Julia's injury and the shadow of Mitty's and Gus Wharton's murders all weighed heavily on the Langs. Yet, their concern for her, their gratitude for her unwavering belief in Ralph's innocence, warmed her like a sip of hot cocoa on a frosty day.

"Perhaps not, but we want to do it," Julia insisted. "So, there's no arguing. I'm sorry, but I need to get into the car and sit. Standing on these things is killing me." She glanced at the crutches.

"Of course. Have a wonderful Christmas." Hope bid farewell as the Langs walked away. She continued toward her car. Sliding into the driver's seat, she started the Explorer, activating the windshield wipers to clear the light layer of snow. Leaning forward, she gazed upward at the sky as the snowflakes descended like tiny sparkles of light.

Chapter Twenty-three

A wave of warmth embraced Hope as she slipped through her back door. After shedding her coat, she entered the kitchen and reached for an apron. Bigelow, his nose twitching at the promise of a feast, watched with eager anticipation. Before heading out to church, Hope had meticulously set the stage for an unforgettable Christmas celebration. The buffet table gleamed with plates and utensils, but that was just the beginning. She'd spent extra time arranging tiered pedestals, antique platters and pops of greenery. The dessert table, draped in a flowing cloth, was strategically positioned in front of the windows overlooking the patio. Now, the falling snow outside added a touch of whimsical magic to the scene.

The familiar strains of "White Christmas" filled the kitchen, propelling Hope's focused energy. The seasoned roast nestled into the oven, she swiftly wiped down the island before turning her attention to the dessert table's crowning glory—the annual croquembouche. With practiced ease, she sculpted the cream-filled puffs into a tapering tower. Rich caramel, soon to be drizzled over the puffs for a spun golden effect, was prepped next. Under the warm kitchen lights, the croquembouche glistened. As if on cue, fat snowflakes began drifting past the windows, blanketing the world in a pristine winter wonderland.

With careful precision, she moved the masterpiece to its designated spot, flanked by platters of freshly baked cookies. At the far end stood the hot cocoa station, creating an irresistible tableau of holiday indulgence. The table resembled a banquet fit for Santa himself.

The buzz of the timer signaled it was time to check the roast and attend to the potatoes in the bottom oven.

Suddenly, a burst of lively chatter filled the room as Claire swept in, her family trailing behind like a joyful procession, their laughter reverberating throughout the house. Dressed elegantly in green velvet with gleaming earrings, Claire greeted her sister with an affectionate kiss.

"Andy will be here in a little while," Claire announced. "He had to swing by the long-term care facility to visit his grandmother."

Hot on Claire's heels were the Merrifields. Jane, a vision in a red wrap dress, balanced a platter of assorted cheeses and crackers. She placed it on the buffet table and hurried back to Hope's side.

"The roast smells heavenly, Hope," Jane complimented, her eyes taking in the festive decorations. "And your house looks like a Christmas wonderland! You truly outdid yourself this year, dear. It must be such a relief to have all that murder business behind you."

"Outdid herself almost getting killed, you mean," Sally interjected sharply, entering the kitchen with her companion, Jeffrey Dodd, the local mail carrier. "From the way Drew tells it, this was a close one, Hope."

"Now, now," Jeffrey boomed, his voice cutting through the tension. "Hope is a resourceful young woman. We were all worried sick, of course, but tonight, let's focus on the festivities! It is Christmas Eve, after all."

"Have you not met my sister-in-law?" Sally's gaze flicked to Jane. "It's impossible for her not to talk about murder."

"I think we should try," Hope suggested. "Sally, would you mind taking these stuffed mushrooms to the buffet?" She gestured toward a platter.

Jeffrey stepped forward, a bottle of cabernet sauvignon in hand. "Since it's a roast, I thought this might be a good pairing."

"Quite the wine connoisseur, isn't he?" Sally remarked with a playful nudge before whisking the mushrooms away.

"Thank you, Jeffrey. It's a perfect choice." Hope placed the bottle on the counter, then ushered Jeffrey and Jane toward the Christmas tree.

"Speaking of gifts," Jane interjected, "we have something for the girls in the car. Also, for Bigelow and Princess. We'll bring them in later."

"You really didn't need to buy them gifts," Hope said. "Thank you."

The kitchen door swung open as Eliza entered in a ball of energy, her eyes sparkling with delight. "Hope, it all looks simply marvelous!" she exclaimed. Reaching into the tote slung over her shoulder, she retrieved a finely crafted wooden tea box. "I brought a little something for you as well." With a warm smile, she extended the gift, revealing an assortment of aromatic loose-leaf teas nestled inside.

"Thank you, Eliza, this is lovely. We'll set it out for dessert. Now, go mingle and enjoy some food!"

Eliza beamed and strode toward the buffet table, joining Sally.

Claire returned to the kitchen and reached for a bottle opener near the wine. "This cabernet looks delicious," she announced.

"Jeffrey brought it," Hope explained as the back door swung open.

Matt entered, holding a small gift bag. He greeted Claire and then offered the bag to Hope.

"Just a small token for our incredible hostess, who seems to have a knack for solving crimes," he said with a grin.

Hope peeked into the gift bag. "Matt, you really shouldn't have!"

"I hope you like it. It's a hand-blown glass olive oil pourer. One of a kind," he announced proudly.

"I absolutely love it." She embraced him warmly before carefully setting the gift aside for safekeeping. "Please, help yourself to the appetizers. There's more on the way."

"Wonderful. I'm famished." He wasted no time moving toward the buffet table, where he exchanged greetings with Jeffrey.

Claire, now holding a newly opened bottle of white wine, quirked an eyebrow at Hope. "Any word on Ethan's arrival time?"

"Not a clue," Hope said. "Something's definitely going on, but trust me, there will be a serious talk after the holidays."

Claire offered a knowing smile before heading into the family room, the bottle of wine in hand. Sally, Jeffrey, and Matt were already settled, creating a small pocket of predinner conversation.

Hope glanced at the oven where the roast bubbled away and then down at Bigelow, who sat patiently beside it. "You're a smart dog," she said, heading toward the refrigerator for a platter of shrimp.

The back door creaked open and Drew ambled in, cradling Trixie, who was decked out in a festive red and white sweater matching her owner's holiday attire. "Merry Christmas, everyone!" Drew announced with a warm smile, stepping into the inviting scene.

"Matching outfits! How precious you both look," Hope declared.

"Is Princess around?" Drew asked.

"No, she skedaddled a while back. It's just Bigelow." Hope wiped her hands with a towel before moving to the refrigerator and pulling out a platter.

"Great. I have no clue how this one will react to a cat," Drew remarked, planting a kiss on Hope's cheek. "Seems you've got a full house already. Ooh . . . Appetizers . . ." His voice trailed off as he spotted the buffet.

"Go ahead and help yourself," Hope offered, unwrapping the shrimp platter just as a knock sounded. Answering the back door, she welcomed Maretta and Alfred Kingston with warm hugs. "Glad you could join us this year!"

Despite the tension that existed between Hope and Maretta, Hope wouldn't dream of excluding the couple from her holiday celebrations. She had known Maretta since childhood, and despite their strained relationship, she believed holidays and life's milestones were meant to be shared with all those who mattered—loved ones, and in Maretta's case, even the not-so-lovable people in one's life.

"We left our coats in the mudroom, is that alright?" Alfred asked with a big smile. He owned the real estate agency where Claire used to work. Both she and Hope adored the man, who was also beloved by the community. Some praised him for being a saint for putting up with Maretta all these years.

"Of course it is," Hope said and smiled.

"This is for you," Maretta said, handing over a gift bag. "Claire mentioned your love for those candles."

"An Em Bailey candle? You shouldn't have but thank you!" Her voice softened as she pulled Maretta into a grateful hug. "This is so thoughtful," she whispered.

Maretta stiffly patted Hope's back in return. "Just a little wax and a wick."

"Why, Hope, your home is an absolute picture-perfect vision of an old-fashioned Christmas," he exclaimed, his eyes alight with wonder as he surveyed the gathering room. "We're always so grateful when your invitation arrives." Alfred's genuine warmth and kindness filled the room, drawing smiles from all present.

"Help yourselves to food and drinks," Hope directed, setting out the shrimp with the other appetizers. She retrieved the Parker House rolls, nestled in two tea towel–lined baskets, from the warming drawer. "Dinner will be ready shortly."

Claire flitted around the island with a filled wineglass in hand. "The kids are engrossed in a movie, and Andy just texted—running late. Seems his grandma trumps Christmas Eve dinner."

"Perfectly understandable," Hope assured her. "There will be plenty of leftovers, so you can make a plate for him to enjoy later." She pulled the fragrant roast from the oven, Bigelow on her heels.

"Still no sign of Ethan?" Claire's voice held a hint of worry. "And we never did find out why he missed the church service."

Hope felt a flicker of irritation rise within her. Her sister knew she was upset, yet she was still harping on the touchy subject. With a sigh, Hope covered the roast beef with a foil tent. "No. You know it's not like him to keep things from me."

As if on cue, the back door flew open. Becca and Molly, a whirlwind of giggles and Christmas spirit, barreled into the kitchen, their arms wrapping tightly around Hope.

"Merry Christmas!" they exclaimed in unison.

"Took Daddy forever to get here," Becca grumbled playfully.

"Yeah," Molly chimed in. "He's always complaining about how long we take. But today it was him."

"But we weren't upset with him," Becca added with a wink directed at Hope.

Becca's unexpected gesture caught Hope off guard.

The girls turned to each other and giggled at their inside joke, but they were interrupted by a ball of fur racing their way. "A puppy!" they squealed in unison, eyes lighting up as they took chase. Nothing else seemed to matter in that moment but the puppy darting around the room.

"She's not your gift!" Ethan called out as he entered the room and closed the door behind him.

"Uh-oh," Hope murmured under her breath.

"About time you showed up," Claire commented, walking away from the counter.

"Good evening to you, too," Ethan replied as Claire brushed past him. "Babe," he continued, extending his hand to Hope. "We need to talk in private."

"Now?" Hope glanced around the family room filled with guests. "Can't it wait?"

"No." Ethan gently tugged on Hope's hand, leading her out of the kitchen and through the hallway into the living room.

Nervously biting her lower lip, Hope shuffled her feet across the hardwood floor of the living room. What was Ethan about to say? She let out an impatient huff as they came to a stop before the second Christmas tree. Shorter than the towering centerpiece in the family room, this one held deep sentimental value. It was adorned with beloved ornaments passed down from her grandparents and topped with an angel that had belonged to her great-grandmother. Its twinkling lights cast a soft, inviting glow.

"Please, can we discuss this, whatever this is, later?" Hope pleaded. "We have guests, and dinner is ready to be served."

"They can wait a few more minutes," Ethan reassured her, clasping her hands in his. "Do you remember our talk the other day about Christmas after I hung the wreath on the barn?"

She nodded. "I do. You were right. We need to focus on the good things around us."

"And accept that life changes," he said softly.

"I'm no longer afraid of change," she declared. She was prepared to face anything he was about to reveal. After all, she had confronted danger head-on and emerged stronger. Hope realized she was capable of weathering any storm.

He smiled. "That's good to hear because another change is on the horizon. Or at least, I hope so. Remember when I told you I was working, but you discovered that Matt had closed the office? I was actually in New Jersey."

"New Jersey? Why? Is it another job opportunity?" Hope asked cautiously, unsure if she could embrace that change. She loved living in Jefferson and couldn't see herself uprooting the life she had built in her hometown. Nor could she envision a long-distance relationship. Those never seemed to work out.

"No, it's nothing like that. I went to visit my aunt because she had something for me."

Hope tilted her head. "My Christmas gift?" As soon as the question left her lips, she glimpsed the truth in his eyes, and a flutter of anticipation danced in her stomach. His visit to his aunt held a significance beyond a mere Christmas gift.

Reaching into his jacket pocket, Ethan retrieved a small ring box and dropped down onto one knee before Hope.

Her breath caught in her throat as he opened the box, revealing a dazzling solitaire diamond ring that seemed to sparkle with its own radiant light.

"Hope Early," Ethan began, his voice thick with emotion, "I love you, and I cannot envision a life without you by my side. I want us to spend the rest of our days together. Will you marry me?"

A rush of excitement and disbelief swept over Hope, causing her body to tremble. He was proposing! "Yes!" she exclaimed fervently. "Yes, I will! Yes!" Her left hand extended instinctively, and she watched, awash with joy, as Ethan slipped the ring onto her finger. "I love you."

"She said yes!" Claire's voice rang out from the doorway, followed by applause as everyone rushed in. They encircled the jubilant couple, cheering and celebrating.

"This is the best Christmas ever," Hope proclaimed, sealing her words with another kiss.

• • •

A sense of peace washed over everyone after a delicious dinner and a decadent dessert spread. The Kingstons savored mugs of hot chocolate while the Merrifields were absorbed in a card game, Bigelow snoring softly in the background. In the kitchen, Ethan, Matt, and Jeffery discussed sports, their voices a lively counterpoint to the children's laughter as they were captivated by a movie. The soft glow of holiday lights cast a warm ambiance over the room. As her guests relaxed, Hope sat on the sofa beside Claire in the family room, her gaze fixed on her new sparkling engagement ring.

"You knew about the ring and that he was going to propose the whole time, didn't you? That's why you had that look on your face when I mentioned Ethan and I were going to have a serious talk," Hope said.

"Absolutely," Claire replied, a wide smile spreading across her face. "What amazed me was that the girls managed to keep the secret when they entered the room."

"That explains Becca's wink." Hope chuckled. "He told them when he picked them up from Heather. He wanted them to know so they wouldn't be caught off guard. But he was worried they would accidentally let it slip when they arrived."

"It is a beautiful ring. Ethan told me that his aunt was so happy to know he was giving it to you." Claire dropped her head against the back of the sofa.

"It was his grandmother's ring." Hope held her hand out, her eyes welled with tears as she admired the simple yet elegant ring gracing her finger. She couldn't believe she was engaged. Engaged to the man who had long since stolen her heart. All those years of hoping and praying that one day he would see her not just as a friend, but as someone to spend his life with. And here they were, making all her dreams come true, on Christmas Eve, no less.

A sharp meow pierced through the tranquility, shifting Hope's attention from her engagement ring to a blur of fur racing by. Princess darted through the kitchen, followed closely by the exuberant Trixie in hot pursuit.

"The rescue place clearly misled me," Drew exclaimed, chasing after his energetic puppy. "They claimed she was one hundred percent Jack Russell terrier, but it feels more like seventy-five percent hurricane! You should see the mess in my house! Where's her off button?"

Hope's stomach sank at the thought of the mess the puppy was about to make in her house.

"What on earth is going on?" Claire demanded as she twisted in her seat to keep an eye on the puppy. "She's chasing the cat!"

Princess gracefully leaped onto the buffet, dashing across the table and causing the decorative runner that Hope had acquired at a flea market to flutter in her wake, skillfully avoiding the dishes.

"No! No! No!" Drew called out in frustration, his voice echoing through the room.

Trixie, determined to catch up with the cat, attempted to follow Princess's lead and jump onto the table, but instead her mouth caught the corner of the runner.

"Stop! Come here, Trixie, now," Drew commanded, his tone firm.

Hope sprang from her seat, silently hoping the dog wouldn't heed her owner's call.

Trixie bounded toward Drew, still clutching the runner in her mouth, just as Princess elegantly leaped off the table, resulting in a symphony of crashing plates and silverware as they met the floor.

The room fell into stunned silence as everyone froze, taken aback by the sudden outbreak of chaos.

Claire leapt up from her seat. "That dog is an absolute menace!"

"Hope, I am so incredibly sorry," Drew began, his apology dripping with remorse. "She didn't mean to do this."

The silence stretched between them as she surveyed the shattered platters and scattered trays littering the floor. Shaking her head in dismay, she stood and walked to Drew and Trixie.

Desperate to lighten the mood, he added lightly, "Well, at least we know how Trixie reacts with a cat."

With a gentle touch, Hope tugged the runner from Trixie's mouth and gave her furry head an affectionate scratch. Trixie responded with a playful bark.

"You know what? This is truly the best Christmas ever," Hope affirmed with a smile gracing her face. Some Christmases were merry, others were messy, but what truly mattered was that love filled her home. "Merry Christmas."

How to Set Up a Hot Chocolate Bar at Home

Blog post from *Hope at Home*

Winter is here, and what better way to warm up and indulge in some delicious treats than with a hot chocolate bar right in the comfort of your own home? Whether you're hosting a gathering or simply craving a cozy night in, creating a hot chocolate bar is a delightful way to spread warmth and cheer. Here's how to set one up that will have everyone reaching for seconds.

1. Choose Your Hot Chocolate Base

Start by selecting a variety of hot chocolate bases to cater to different tastes. Offer classic milk chocolate, rich dark chocolate, and perhaps even a white chocolate option for those who prefer something a little sweeter. Don't forget to include a dairy-free alternative like almond or oat milk for guests with dietary restrictions.

2. Gather Toppings Galore

The fun part of a hot chocolate bar is decking it out with an array of mouthwatering toppings! Set out bowls filled with mini marshmallows, whipped cream, chocolate shavings, crushed candy canes, cinnamon sticks, and caramel sauce. Get creative and add some unconventional toppings like sprinkles, coconut flakes, or even a pinch of sea salt for a gourmet twist.

3. Provide Flavor Enhancers

Enhance the flavor of your hot chocolate with a selection of flavorings and mix-ins. Offer options such as vanilla extract, peppermint extract, ground cinnamon, nutmeg, or even a splash of flavored liqueurs like peppermint schnapps or Irish cream for the adults to enjoy.

4. Offer Warm Accompaniments

Complement your hot chocolate bar with a variety of warm treats. Freshly baked cookies, biscotti, or even mini doughnuts make perfect dunking companions. For a healthier option, consider serving fruit skewers or a platter of sliced bananas, strawberries, and oranges for dipping.

5. Set Up a Cozy Atmosphere

Enhance the ambiance of your hot chocolate bar with some cozy decor. Light a few candles, string up some fairy lights, and lay out plush blankets and cushions for guests to snuggle up with. Play some soft holiday tunes in the background to complete the inviting atmosphere.

6. Don't Forget the Mugs!

Finally, don't overlook the importance of the vessel! Set out an assortment of mugs in different sizes and designs to suit everyone's preference. Consider providing some festive mugs or personalized cups to add a special touch to the experience.

With these tips, you're all set to host a memorable hot chocolate bar that will warm hearts and satisfy sweet cravings alike. So, gather your loved ones, cozy up by the fire, and indulge in the ultimate winter treat!

Who's ready for a cup of cocoa?

Recipes

Bigelow's Just for Pups Pumpkin Donuts

by Hope Early

Nothing makes Bigelow perk up more than hearing the lid of his treat jar being taken off. It's as if he has supernatural powers because he suddenly appears out of nowhere. That's how fast he moves to get a snack. And one of his favorites is this simple pumpkin donut recipe. Not only does Bigelow enjoy these, but so does his best friend, Buddy.

1 cup oat flour
1 teaspoon baking soda
1 cup pumpkin puree
¾ cup oat milk
1 egg
Topping: (optional) peanut butter for dogs*

Combine all ingredients in a large bowl. Use coconut oil to grease mini-donut pans, then fill with mixture. You can use a piping bag, a zipped plastic bag with a corner cut off, or a spoon and spatula.

Bake at 350 degrees for 20–25 minutes.

Cool donuts on a rack, then drizzle with peanut butter.

*You'll want to use peanut butter especially made for dogs, which can be found at pet supply stores or online.

Eggnog Scones

by Hope Early

Calling all eggnog lovers! And even those of you who aren't, because this scone recipe is going to become your new favorite. I promise. These light and flaky scones have a hint of eggnog flavor in the pastry and in the glaze with a subtle hint of cinnamon. These are perfect for a quick breakfast or with a cup of tea for an afternoon snack. They would also make a delicious Christmas morning treat.

For scones

2 cups all-purpose flour
½ cup granulated sugar
2 teaspoons baking powder
½ teaspoon baking soda
½ teaspoon salt
¼ teaspoon cinnamon
⅛ teaspoon nutmeg
¼ cup butter
2 teaspoon vanilla
¾ cup eggnog, plus extra for brushing scones before going into the oven

For glaze

1 cup sifted powdered sugar
2½ tablespoons eggnog
½ teaspoon vanilla
¼ teaspoon cinnamon
⅛ teaspoon nutmeg

Preheat oven to 400 degrees.

Whisk together flour, granulated sugar, baking powder, baking soda, salt, cinnamon and nutmeg.

Cut in cold butter.

Mix in vanilla and eggnog with a spoon, then knead with your hands to incorporate all the dry ingredients. Be careful not to overwork the dough.

Form dough into an 8-inch circle. Cut into 8 wedges. Place each wedge on a baking sheet lined with either a silicone mat or parchment paper or use a baking stone, spacing them a half inch apart. Brush with eggnog.

Bake for 18–20 minutes.

Cool on a baking rack.

Glaze

Mix the powdered sugar with the eggnog and vanilla, add in the cinnamon and nutmeg.

Drizzle glaze over cooled scones.

Enjoy!

Note: I use a baking stone for my scones.

Reindeer Munch Mix

by Hope Early

Need a quick foodie gift? Or a snack to whip up on a wintery afternoon for kids (big and small)? Then look no further than this Reindeer Munch recipe. Either in a big bowl or divided into festive cellophane bags, this mixture of cereal coated in melted chocolate with M&Ms and pretzels will satisfy both sweet and crunchy cravings.

4 cups Chex cereal mix
½ cup semi-sweet chocolate chips
2 teaspoons vegetable oil
1 cup powdered sugar
3 cups mini-pretzels
2 cups red and green M&M candies

Place cereal in a big mixing bowl.

Melt chocolate with oil in the microwave for 30 seconds at a time, and stir after each warming.
Pour chocolate over the cereal and toss gently to coat.

Place the cereal in a resealable bag and add ¼ cup of powdered sugar. Close and shake. Add in remaining powdered sugar by ¼ cups until all the cereal is coated.

Place cereal in a serving bowl. Add pretzels M&Ms.

Serve.

Christmas Button Cookies

These are one of my favorite cookies to bake at Christmas. They are sooo good. They're soft cookies packed with a lot of flavor. While they are a staple at Christmas, I love baking them for Easter and I just change up the color of sprinkles I use. They got their name because when Claire and I were little, we told our grandmother when she was baking them that they looked like buttons. And the name has stuck.

3 cups all-purpose flour
1 tablespoon baking powder
½ teaspoon salt
3 eggs
½ cup sugar
½ cup cooking oil
1 teaspoon vanilla
Almond icing

In a medium bowl combine flour, baking powder and salt. In a large bowl with an electric mixer beat eggs, sugar, oil and vanilla until combined. With the mixer, beat in as much of the flour mixture as you can. With a wooden spoon stir in the remaining flour mixture.

Drop dough by rounded teaspoons two inches apart on an ungreased cookie sheet. Bake at 350 degree for about 15 minutes or until golden. Cool on wire rack. Spread or drizzle almond icing on cookies. Shake a few colored sprinkles on each cookie.

Almond icing

1 cup sifted powdered sugar
½ teaspoon almond extract
1–2 tablespoons milk (enough to make desired consistency)

In a medium mixing bowl combine powdered sugar, almond extract and milk, stirring until desired consistency.

Makes about 60 cookies.

Acknowledgments

Writing this cozy mystery has been a delightful journey, and I am deeply grateful to everyone who contributed to its creation and success.

First and foremost, a heartfelt thank-you to the Recipe Review Crew: Tammy Barker, Maria Reyes Doktor, Chelsea Hatfield, Shannon Malloy, Donna Page, Debra Derbyshire, Kathleen Kendler and Marijo Yates. Your enthusiasm, meticulous testing, and invaluable feedback have ensured that every recipe included in this book is perfect for my readers to enjoy. Your dedication has been extraordinary, and I couldn't have done this without you.

To my dear author friends, Jenny Kales, Linda Reilly and Lena Gregory, your encouragement and unwavering support have been my pillars of strength. Whether it was through insightful advice or shared experiences, your friendship has meant the world to me.

A special thank you Lt. Michael Confield for answering my procedural questions with patience and clarity. I am deeply grateful for your help.

To my editor, Bill Harris, and the wonderful team at Beyond the Page, your expertise, patience, and hard work have shaped this book into something I am truly proud of. Your guidance and vision have been instrumental in bringing this story to life.

Lastly, and most importantly, to my readers—thank you. Your love for cozy mysteries and your enthusiasm for my stories inspire me every day. Your support is the reason I write, and I am endlessly grateful for your loyalty and encouragement.

About the Author

Debra Sennefelder lives and writes in Connecticut, where she shares her home with her family and slightly spoiled Shih Tzu. An avid reader across a range of genres, mystery fiction is her obsession. Her interest in people and relationships is channeled into her novels against a backdrop of crime and mystery. She's the author of the Food Blogger Mystery series, the Resale Boutique Mystery series, and the Cookie Shop Mystery series. When she's not writing, she's either baking or reading. To learn more, visit her on the web at debrasennefelder.com.

Made in the USA
Coppell, TX
12 November 2024